the haunting of MADDIE PRUE

Alfred Silver

GREAT PLAINS FICTION

Great Plains Fiction
An imprint of Great Plains Publications
3–161 Stafford Street
Winnipeg, MB
R3M 2X9
www.greatplains.mb.ca

Great Plains Publications gratefully acknowledges the financial support
provided for its publishing program by the Government of Canada through
the Book Publishing Industry Development Program (BPIDP); the Canada
Council for the Arts; the Manitoba Department of Culture, Heritage and
Citizenship; and the Manitoba Arts Council.

Design & Typography by Taylor George Design

Title font designed by Cari Buziak

Printed in Canada by Friesens

CANADIAN CATALOGUING IN PUBLICATION DATA

Silver, Alfred
The haunting of Maddie Prue

ISBN 1-894283-10-4
I. Title.

PS8587.I27	H38	2000	C813'.54	C00-920006-1
PR9199.3.S51765	H38	2000		

Here's looking at you, Jane.

Prologue

THERE WERE FOURTEEN in the circle that night, standing naked around a bonfire holding hands. Maddie had a man's fingers gripped in her right hand and in her left the larger, gnarled fingers of the old woman who was the leader of The Circle. The voices that were new to the ceremony grew more confident as Celina led the repetitions of the chant, alternating between English and Sanskrit, like stringing two different colors of beads along a chain:

> Lady of barley,
> Lady of bread,
> Lady of beer,
> Lady of abundance.

At unpredictable intervals among the repetitions, Celina's voice led them to string on a third-colored bead:

> Isis, Ishtar, Esther, Astarte,
> Isis, Ishtar, Esther, Astarte...

Maddie could feel that the chant and the drugs and the dancing flames were beginning to do their work, but there was something holding her back. She realized that from where she was standing she could see the lighted windows at the back of the house, locking her in the present. She shifted and shuffled to her right, wheeling the circle a quarter-turn around the hub of the fire.

When the windows and the house were out of her line of vision, she stopped and stood still again. She looked up and saw the three stars of Orion's belt as The Hunter climbed over the trees.

The choral chant kept on as though they were all equal parts of The Circle, but Maddie could feel the others' eyes on her, with that expectant look she'd known since before she had breasts. It was the same look her younger brothers and sisters had turned on her when their mother shrieked Dad wouldn't be coming home; the same look that everyone else on stage turned on her when the show started coming apart at the scenes. The look said: "What are you going to do, Maddie?"

What she did was what she'd learned long ago was the only thing to do: put a wall between her and the eyes from the sidelines and focus on what was in front of her. What was in front of her this time, as it had been many times before, was the fire doing its dance of the seven veils, flickering hypnotically from yellow to red to orange to searing white to incandescent blue. Finally she felt the old numbing, tingling wave washing through her and washing her out to sea. The chanting faded into a seashell roar and the hands she was holding melted away.

She was still standing in front of a fire, but it was a different fire, crackling so high and hot she had to stand five paces away. She was standing alone but there were many other people behind her, singing and beating on hand drums and blowing wooden flutes. Beyond the fire were the half-lit shapes of low, round huts like time-browned skulls.

She was wearing a raw linen dress that was sleeveless and shapeless, except for the shape cinched into it by the braided leather thong belted around her waist. Fixed to the back of the thong was a sheathed, bronze-bladed knife. She could feel its weight resting against the ticklish skin where her buttocks met.

Out of the forest and into the smoke drifting from the fire came a semi-human figure: a naked man with antlers on his head. The smoke made him a blurred silhouette, but she could picture him clearly in every detail from the way he walked. Those were the arms that had held her every night for a year now and made her feel that it was safe to sleep. Those were the legs she'd wrapped her legs around when his body made her forget who she was.

When he came out of the smoke and into the firelight, she saw that his eyes were glazed black with pupils swollen like autumn moons. The deerskin harness holding the antlers on his head was slipping slightly.

Her heart was battering against her ribs. The singing and drumming had grown too loud for thought. When he stopped in front of her, he planted his legs wide as though the ground was moving under his feet. His eyelids were drooping and he seemed to be finding it hard to hold his head up under the weight of the antlers.

She tightened her face into a stone mask and reached both hands behind her back—one to hold the sheath, the other to draw the knife. She swung the knife up swiftly and punched it down into his chest. It was supposed to go straight into his heart, but it caught on a rib and swerved. She felt the heel of her fist around the knife handle slap his skin, but he didn't fall. He screamed, threw his arms up and staggered back, tearing the knife out of her hand.

For an instant he hung there in the firelight howling, with the bone handle of her knife sticking out of his chest and blood pouring out around it. Before he could fall, the crowd of drummers and singers leaped forward and were tearing at him with knives and sickles and bare hands. Their roar drowned out his howls. Slick white strings showed through the ripped muscles of his arms. A stone hammer broke his head open like a walnut so that hands could pry the shell apart. A woman had torn off one of his fingers and was trying to crack the knuckles. Another was unraveling the long tangled rope of his guts. They were tearing him into ever-smaller pieces as his blood and brains and marrow soaked down into the earth that fed them.

Maddie screamed and fell backward out of the circle, yanking her hands free from the hands that held them. The others were all around her in an instant, holding her head up and forcing a sip of brandy between her lips. She could hear them and feel them, but they wouldn't focus. Everything was blurred and whirling. Her stomach was trying to force its way out up her throat and the only way she could get air in was frantic, shallow panting.

Finally, Celina's seamed, silver-haloed face swam into focus—close and expectant. She said: "Did you go further back?"

"Uh-huh." The panting had grown less frantic, but it was still hard to get words out. "Not... not back to the beginning, but far enough to know... to know why."

"Why?" The question gushed out of Celina with such eagerness and hunger that Maddie wanted to grab a fistful of gray hair with her left hand and drive her right fist into the wise woman's mouth until it couldn't ask any more questions. Practically salivating, Celina barked: "Tell me why!"

Maddie told herself her sudden loathing for Celina and the others was just the drugs and exhaustion. After all, Celina had spent half her life looking for the answer to that question, small wonder she should get a little grabby when it came in reach. Maddie said: "I don't... I don't know how to say it... yet. But

I do know why now." A belt seemed to tighten around her throat, squeezing tears out of her eyes. "And I know who."

"Who?" Celina looked perplexed. "Well that hardly matters, does it? The question is why."

Maddie suddenly flailed her arms and legs out to push the others away from her. She rolled over, levered herself up onto her hands and knees and started crawling away from the fire, into the dark. Her bare breasts slapped from side to side against her arms, and the rough ground was grinding her knees. She shouted through choking sobs: "Damn your bloody eyes, don't you fucking understand what you've done? She's in me now!"

1

J OHN LENNON'S In My Life *wafted out of the CD player. She lit a black candle, slipped the cassette tape in a bubblepack and reached for the Scotch tape. It was tricky keeping the adhesive side of the tape from sticking to her surgical gloves instead of the envelope. She looked one more time at the dummy package she'd mailed to herself last week. Just like it had the last time she looked, the cancellation stamp gave away nothing but New York NY 04/12/95 and the digits of a post office that processed thousands of packages a day. She rolled a label sheet into her printer, selected the most anonymous-looking font on her menu and keyed in:*

Cpl. H. J. Ryon, RCMP
Wahpeston
Manitoba
R0C 6B9
Canada

Corporal Ryon climbed out of the RCMP detachment's 4×4 and leaned over to check his mailbox. Through the gaps in the pine windbreak he could see there were lights on in the house, so Lisette had shown up to do the weekly sluice-out. The fresh-faced constable who'd driven Ryon home rolled down his window and said: "You want a lift into town again tomorrow?"

"I'll call if the truck don't start."

"It won't start. You should put a bullet through its head and buy a new vehicle. God knows you must have enough socked away, you never spend it on anything."

"She'll start, as soon as the rain finishes evaporating. She hates humidity— good prairie truck. Well, should be a quiet night for you."

"Oh, maybe not." The constable winked and grinned. "I think I've finally got a line on old Norbert."

Ryon shifted his mail into his left hand and leaned his right arm on the vehicle. "What kind of a line?"

"He's been bootlegging."

"Who says?"

"Come on, Corporal. I know he's a bootlegger. You know he's a bootlegger."

"I have no definite information as to that possibility at the present time."

The constable rolled his eyes as Ryon drummed his fingers on the metal. "Constable, when they stood you up in your brand new red serge at Depot Division, you swore to 'Maintain the Right'. Right?"

"Right."

"What they didn't tell you is that maintaining it's the easy part—figuring it out is what they pay us the big bucks for. The only thing that matters a damn in this world is kindness. Norbert's seventy-eight years old and trying to get by on barebones pension. Whatever he's been doing to scratch up cigarette money, he's been doing it for a long time without causing any trouble to anybody.

"Another year or so you'll be gone to another posting, and I'll still be here trying to convince the people who live here that we got better things to do than chase down an old man who maybe picks up twenty bucks on a Sunday night selling a case of beer. Understood?"

"Understood, Corporal."

"Have a nice night." Ryon patted the vehicle to send it on its way and headed up his muddy excuse for a driveway. He highly doubted that the constable really understood, but he had not a smidgen of a doubt that he would follow orders. There was a certain weight advantage to being just about the oldest serving corporal in the history of the Force. And in a one-horse detachment like this, the corporal was God.

Ryon fully expected to reach retirement age without another promotion. He was amazed that he'd even made corporal, given that niggling little pimple on his service record. No big deal—he'd just happened to disappear for a year as soon as he graduated from the Depot.

He was dead sure the only reason the Force had even let him back in the door was that they'd already invested so much time and money in his training. Well, that and that he'd had an aunt who was acquainted with the Justice Minister of the day. And the fact that he'd conveniently resurfaced in a psychiatric hospital, so the Force could just file his record-setting AWOL under "nervous breakdown". Sometimes he thought the only truly crazy thing he'd ever done was ask the Force to take him back.

As he slogged through the frosted gumbo to his back door, Ryon tried to suss-out what his mail was by the light of the moon. There were two letters with the bright-logoed envelopes of junk mail, and a padded package that felt like a cassette tape. He didn't remember ordering any tapes lately. He'd canceled his audio club membership when they'd gone over entirely to CD's remastered by computer engineers who thought the point of the exercise was to separate everything so cleanly that Don and Phil Everly sounded like they were singing in different counties—like "band" was a four-letter word.

The cats were waiting on the back step. Ryon let them into the mud room with him and stopped to take off his coat and hat. Lisette shouted from inside: "Ryon, if you let them cats put muddy paws on my clean floors I'll skin them! And the same goes for you!"

He considered shouting back that they weren't really her clean floors, but decided to just take his boots off instead. Drunken lumberjacks with baseball bats were all in a night's work, but five-foot-five-ish, twenty-five-ish, French-Cree cleaning women were a little out of his league. He negotiated his way through the inner door fending the cats off with his sock feet. He knew that if they were shut up in the mud room for a few minutes they would come clean. He didn't know why cats preferred to have mud on their tongues instead of on their feet, he was just grateful that they did.

Ryon tossed his mail on the kitchen table and hung his Sam Browne belt on the hook by the door. No need to lock away his sidearm when he and Lisette would be the only people on the premises. He could hear Lisette rattling away in the laundry room. Bob The Dog looked up from her bed by the fridge and wagged her tail, which was about as close as she could come these days to leaping up and trying to lick his face off. Emmet The Skunk poked his nose out of the cupboard where he'd been hiding while the vacuum monster was on the prowl.

Ryon opened the fridge and popped a beer, sloshed a slug into Bob's dinner dish and plopped down to look at his mail. The package was postmarked from the center of the world—New York City—but had no return address. As he was prying it open, Lisette came into the kitchen grumbling the old song: "If you have to live out of town why couldn't you get yourself a nice place instead of this old dust trap?"

"Then how would you earn your walking-around money?"

"Oh… by walking around."

"This place has character." It was one of the last old farmhouses left from the days when people still could make a life out of a few acres of gravel and scrub brush. Nowadays the only sense in farming was if you leased three sections of prime topsoil from some agri-business corporation. It crossed Ryon's mind that if he'd lived a hundred years ago he might've been a happy hermit homesteader, instead of spending his days filling out arrest reports in triplicate. Then again, he was a farmer in a way, or a gardener, pulling out the weeds and spreading fertilizer…

He gave up on the "Easy-open, Patent Pending" package and just took a knife to it. The cassette inside the bubblepack looked like a home dub, but with the title and song list computer-printed in the same generic typeface as the address label. The album and band both had the same name: 'The Doudes'.

Ryon said: "Weird."

Lisette said: "What's weird?"

"I don't have a clue in hell who'd send me this. I sort of vaguely knew the people on the tape, Fergus and Audrey Doude, way back in that year when everything was vague. But there's no way in hell they'd remember me."

"Who were they?"

Ryon laughed: "Were? That's the question old rock stars love to hear: Didn't you used to be whatsisname? Well, they weren't exactly stars when I knew them. They were part of a band called Anemone. Back in the days when Kermit the Frog was your favorite singer —"

"He still is."

"—there was the Celtic Revival, or Celtic Rock or whatever you want to call it. They used Celtic harps and flutes and things, but they sounded about as much like this cutesy New Age shit as Chuck Berry sounds like the Partridge Family. Most of the bands were Brits or Bretons, but Anemone was an American band built around a singer who grew up in Scotland. There was some kind of law that you couldn't have a Celtic band without a chick singer.

"But Maddie Prue was a lot more than a singer. She played piano and guitar for them, and, you know how on album credits when a band does some old folk song it'll say: Traditional, Arranged by…? That's so the leader of the band can get royalties even though it's Public Domain. Well, on Anemone albums it was: Traditional, Arranged Prue. She was one uppity broad."

Ryon pursed his lips. "Anemone was just getting to be a big deal, getting right up there with Pentangle and Allan Stivell and all, when Maddie Prue quit to go solo. Without her the band was just a bunch of decent musicians, and there's eighty million decent musicians kicking around. And as for Maddie Prue, she had a stupid accident, slipped on a footpath behind her house in Carmel and fell a hundred feet into the ocean. Went solo with a vengeance."

"You knew her, too?"

"Not really. I wouldn't bet she even knew my name. I was just this crazy kid who was on the run from something-or-other and could carry an amplifier if someone pointed me at it."

Ryon took another chug of his beer and said: "Well, no, I guess there was one moment she noticed I was there, 'cause I made her laugh. She did love to laugh. It was in some green-room or other, and some guy was going on and on about this great new piece of equipment that could make your solid-state bass amp sound just like an old Fender tube amp and only cost two thousand bucks. I finally got fed up and said: 'Why not just go down to the nearest pawn shop and shell out fifty bucks for an old Fender tube amp?' Maddie laughed so hard she fell in my lap."

Lisette opened a beer of her own and blinked her enigma-eyes like he'd left out the punchline. He shrugged, "Crazy, isn't it? Half the time I couldn't even tell you what city I was in that year, and yet a little thing like that sticks in my mind."

"Maybe not so crazy."

Ryon picked up the tape and said: "Well, I'll go change into something human—"

"Fat chance."

"I meant clothes—and then slap this on the stereo and see if the bozo that sent it put a message on to explain. Probably it's 'Congratulations, you have been selected to join our new bootleg audio club, your Mastercard has automatically been billed three hundred dollars...'"

"I'll make us some supper before you drive me home."

"Good deal."

Out of his knife-creased uniform trousers and into old jeans and a sweatshirt, Ryon came down to the living room, injected the cassette and glanced again at the home-printed credits. Given the album title and the date of the initial release, 1981, he figured it for the Doudes' first after Anemone. He'd never heard it, though, or any of their other albums. He'd known that the Doudes had been the only members of Anemone to stay relatively hot after Maddie Prue stepped away, building themselves a following in Art Rock circles. But as far as Ryon was concerned, the minute some picklenosed magazine writer started attaching the word "art" to rock and roll, it was the same kiss of death as when jazz musicians started putting music stands on stage.

Ryon was perfectly willing to admit that maybe he was just like those constipated assholes who crapped on Van Gogh a hundred years ago. But it wasn't exactly going to be a pivotal point in human evolution if H.J. Ryon of Whatsitsname, Manitoba didn't get it up for the cutting edge of twentieth century pop music.

There was no message at the start of The Doudes' tape, just straight into the first cut. It sounded even weirder than "art", no bottom end at all. Then Ryon remembered he'd left the equalizer set up to damp out bass frequencies, so he could thump along on the old Hagstrom and pretend he could do a better job than Bill Wyman, or Willie Dixon, or—fat chance—Duck Dunn.

He re-jigged the equalizer and sat back down, sipping Canadian imitation Coors and listening for some clue as to why someone in New York City thought some backwater prairie boy had to hear this. He found it more than a little eerie how much Audrey Doude's voice sounded like Maddie Prue's, although without the effortless surges of power. But then, no one this side of Edith Piaf had the same power as Maddie Prue when she leaned back and kicked it into overdrive.

He reminded himself that he shouldn't have been surprised that Audrey Doude's voice echoed Maddie's. Audrey and Maddie had sung a few duets on Anemone's last albums, after Audrey Something-or-other married Fergus Doude and became an Anemone auxiliary. In the first duet Maddie and Audrey had recorded, Audrey Doude's voice was just a pale background shading. But in the later ones you had to listen carefully to tell who was taking which verse, as Audrey Doude's voice took on the coloring of Maddie's like a chameleon on a bright leaf.

As the third cut on the Doudes' album started to unfold, Ryon found himself leaning back into his chair and cradling his beer. It was Audrey Doude singing a mournful melody about a young woman who had been and was no more, a woman with "a silver throat and golden hair." It had to be Maddie Prue. The song wasn't too blindly sentimental to be touching; it made it quite clear that the fallen angel wasn't always an angel.

Then the chorus ripped out of the speakers and Ryon froze. It wasn't the transmission-grinding musical gearshift that froze him, it was the words: *But when push came to shove he put her down.*

The song shifted back to its softer, verse form, and this time slipped-in something about: *he gave her back to the sea.* The songs Maddie Prue wrote had been filled with sea images and mermaids stranded on land. And, he remembered, her corpse had been found in a tidepool below the Carmel cliffs.

The song ended. Ryon sat not hearing the next one. Then he jolted up to his feet and went into the kitchen. Lisette said: "You want cheese on your burger?"

"I'm not hungry. Stick it in the fridge and I'll nuke it later." He snagged a shotglass and the bottle of Jameson's to go with the beer and headed back to the tape machine. He hardly ever drank hard liquor anymore, and then only at home. Some metabolic quirk made his body react to whisky like other people's did to cocaine. A cranked-up Ryon was not a sight for public consumption.

He rewound the tape and listened to the song again. It seemed impossible that not one of the thousands of people who must've heard that song over the years had taken it as a kickstart to get curious about Maddie Prue's "accident". Maybe everyone had assumed it was just another sensitive art song, and that "when push came to shove he put her down" meant some wiseass made a snarky comment at a record launch. Maybe that was all it did mean.

Ryon said to himself: "Straighten out, smartboy, you know what happens when you start hearing things no one else does." But he kept on rewinding the song and hearing it again.

He looked again at the date of the album's original release. Two years after Maddie Prue went off the cliff. That was just about exactly how long it would take to assimilate a severely mind-fucking event into a song, record an album and work through all the details of packaging and distribution and all.

When he'd listened to it enough times that he could rewind it in his mind faster than the machine could, Ryon switched over to the turntable and took out the Maddie Prue boxed album set that some obscure label had put out on the tenth anniversary of her death. He'd only ever listened to it once; some of the songs put him back in places it wasn't healthy to go. But this time he wasn't listening for the sake of the music. He was listening for her recorded life to tell him there'd been nothing sinister in it, just his imagination running away with him.

He put the first side on, training his ears on the music while his eyes occupied themselves with the glossy booklet of photographs, lyrics and recording credits. The first cut was from the very first Anemone album. There was an electric fiddle intro and then Ryon's eyes went unfocused as that voice came out of the speakers—kind of a cross between Janis Joplin and Vera Lynn.

Even given that there was that voice and all its dynamics—not *gymnastics*, just singing every shading without bending the song out of shape—Ryon still found himself amazed that there'd actually been an era when hundreds of thousands of people would happily sit and listen for twelve minutes while a haunting singer and her band spun out the story of the housecarpenter's wife and the demon lover. Well, when you're too stoned to get up and do anything else...

He reminded his sarcastic self that he'd been just as much in lala-land as the rest of them, living by candlelight and papering his walls with posters of the paintings Anemone used for their album covers. The covers were all images from Burne-Jones and William Morris and all that Pre-Raphaelite crew, those dead Victorian goofballs who figured that Raphael had done the same thing to painting as the Bee Gees did to rock and roll. Get back, Loretta.

As the song spun on, Ryon refocused on the photographs in the boxed-set booklet and started turning pages. Some of the pictures were airbrushed glam shots, some were live-on-stage, some were home Polaroids, but all of them were in black and white—someone who hadn't seen her live wouldn't know that her hair was red-blonde, but would be able to tell that it was thick and long and usually cut with hedge-trimmers, except in the solo-album-covers' glam shots. There were enough group shots that any stranger could see by comparison that she was built more like a fireplug than a willow, and some of the home Polaroids proved she wasn't joking when she'd said she could look at a plate of french fries and put on weight. But she always took it off pretty fast when the band was steady-gigging and she was spending five nights a week sweating and roaring and piano-pounding under klieg lights.

As he looked through the pictures, Ryon kept having to wipe the mist out of his eyes and wash the knot out of his throat. Here was a twenty-year-old Maddie in blue jeans and velvet; there was Maddie making closed-eyed-love through a Shure 57 while the rest of the band pumped on around her; there was Maddie in a recording studio trying to fit a fiddle under her chin while laughing her guts out; there was Maddie alone at a grand piano in the last concert she would ever play...

The personnel in the Anemone photos changed. Sometimes even elfin Fergus Doude—a Tolkien elf, not a Disney pixie—would be gone one year and back the next. But Maddie Prue was always in the picture.

There was one thing the pictures did make clear, now that Ryon looked at them closely. For all Maddie's kamikaze leaps wherever the music wanted to take her, off-duty she was a terminally domestic woman. Whether in band PR shots by the seashore, or amateur flashbulbs in someone's rec room, she was always snuggled up for security against her boyfriend of the moment, or he had his arm around her protectively.

From the pictures, she must've gone through at least half-a-dozen of those cosy arrangements during Anemone's lifetime. Good bet that had something to do with the changing faces in the band. But what the hell, the pictures did cover ten years, and she'd been in her twisted twenties. Nobody even begins to figure out what they want—or who—until they hit thirty.

Ryon surprised himself by not feeling all that jealous of the string of guys who had their arms around Maddie Prue. If anything, he felt sorry for them. He didn't want to imagine what it felt like to get dumped by a woman like that—as if there were any other women like that. She seemed to like them rangy and sinewy. One of the guys was very tall and thin with a clean-cut face and surfer sun-bleached hair; another was very tall and thin with a Fu Manchu mustache and dark ringlets; another was very tall and thin with a long, thin nose and pencil-line beard…

Ryon got a funny little twinge and flicked back through the pictures again. They were all the same guy. It was just that the shape of his face seemed to change with his hairstyles, hats and facial hair. But one thing that didn't change was the possessive way he always had a hand on Maddie Prue, even when they weren't touching. It put Ryon in mind of a white Ike Turner.

Ryon read down the list of musicians, but none of the names helped him. When he called up memories of Anemone on stage, all he could see was Maddie Prue, or occasionally Fergus Doude when Maddie stepped aside to play back-up. The tall guy must've been around in all those green-rooms and acid jams, but Ryon knew that a lot of files from that year had been deleted. Not just blacked-out by psychedelics and psychosis, but by his instinct for self-preservation.

Whoever the guy in the pictures was, he'd obviously been a full-term member of Anemone. His laid-back, cocksure poses made it just as obvious that he considered himself at least as responsible for Anemone hitting the big time as

Maddie Prue was. Must've come as a hell of a shock to his system when Maddie went solo and the world found out different...

"Ryon!" Ryon was so far away that the voice cutting in made him half-drop his beer, but he caught it and only sloshed a bit of foam on his jeans. It was Lisette in the living room doorway shouting over the music: "Guess I'll have to stay over."

Ryon got up and turned the stereo down, saying: "No, it's all right, I'll give you a lift home."

"You can't be driving tonight."

"I haven't had that much. Anyway, who's going to pull me over for a breathalyzer?"

"You can't drive anyways. The truck won't start."

"Sure it will. You just have to jiggle the key."

"I jiggled it. It won't start. You can drop me off tomorrow when they come to pick you up. You should have something to eat."

"I will later."

Lisette chewed on her lower lip like she was deciding whether or not to say something. She said: "It's not good for you to drink without eating. Everybody thinks you're so calm and cool, but don't forget I know about your Sick Days."

Ryon's face tightened. "It only happened the once. I don't make a habit of it."

One morning a few months ago he'd woken up shivering and shaking and feeling like if anybody looked him in the face he was going to start crying. So he'd called the Detachment and told them he had some kind of flu bug, "probably be over it by tomorrow—just have to sweat it out." But he'd forgotten it was Lisette's cleaning day. She'd walked in and found him curled up in a corner hugging a whisky bottle and wearing a blanket. If it had been anyone but Lisette, it would've been all over town in half an hour.

Lisette looked like she was thinking of saying something more, but settled for: "Well, good-night," and headed up the stairs toward the spare bedroom. It wasn't the first night Ryon had watched Lisette's dapper, little blue-jeaned butt twitch up that stairwell. More than once he'd had a powerful urge to follow her, but he'd always come to his senses. He wouldn't go so far as to say that women were nothing but trouble, or that he was, but the two of them together definitely were.

Lisette paused on the landing to look out the stained glass window, cocking her head from side to side. Ryon could tell by the glow through the time-waved, colored-glass rectangles—amber gold and fresh-blood red—that she'd turned on the yard light he'd installed when poor old Bob The Dog started sleeping too soundly to raise a ruckus if anyone but him or Lisette stepped on the property at night.

Lisette said without looking back from the window: "Funny, depending on what pane you stare through, that old pine tree looks different. Same tree, but you see different parts of it…"

Time's only prisms,
  One era or next

Just facets the vision,
Cons caved or vexed.
Con text
Reflects.
But blood still tastes the same.

—Maddie Prue

11

THE COAL GRATE *in the parlor had ceased emanating heat, but she was too rapt to feel the chill. By the flicker of a black candle she wrapped the book in butcher's paper and tied it tight with string. A sudden flare of light in the dark window in front of her made her jump and nick her finger with the knife. She laughed at herself: it was only the lamplighter doing his rounds late as usual. She stuck her finger in her mouth and looked for the hundredth time at the dummy package she'd mailed to herself yesterday. It hadn't changed; the postmark still revealed no information beyond London SW, Apr. 1895. She dipped her pen in the inkwell, turned the wrapped book around and painstakingly printed upside-down:*

H. J. Ryon, Esq.
Wahpeston P.O.
Province of Manitoba
Dominion of Canada

Henry Ryon whoaed the horses pulling the cultivator, tugged off his hat and mopped his sleeve across the sooty sweat seeping over the dams of his eyebrows. Taking his hat off allowed the wind to ruffle some air into his damp-matted hair—and allowed the full blaze of the sun to sear his unshaded eyes. Forty-four years old and still too dumb to come in out of the sun. Or was it forty-five…? Well, he wasn't about to rack his baked brains with arithmetic that would make no difference to anybody; and memory wasn't an organ he cared to exercise. *Exorcize*, perhaps, if somebody presented him with the right bell, book and candle.

The wind was hot, blowing west off the prairie rather than east off the lake. The lake was the reason he'd chosen to pick a piece of land up here, instead of down south where the topsoil was deeper and less filled with rocks. That and the splendid scarcity of neighbors.

Ryon twisted around to squint back past the cultivator blades at the new-turned furrows invading the black crust of burnt-off meadow. He said: "At this rate, cleverlad, you'll have the new field ready for sowing by the Twentieth Century."

It was at moments like these he got the niggling feeling that the other remittance men of his acquaintance were dead right to make mock of him for playing at homesteader instead of living on his income. He'd tried it their way for the first few years, but soon grew disenchanted with a future that consisted of four extravagant spending sprees a year interspersed with months of borrowing and scrounging until the next remittance check arrived.

He'd been handed the same bargain as every other remittance man scattered throughout the colonies: his august family would furnish him with a modest allowance for the rest of his days, on the condition that he never again set foot in the Mother Country.

His final straw with the other "jolly chaps" had been when one of them got the bright idea that they could ride to hounds here like they did back home. It wasn't pleasant what happened to the dogs when they cornered a timber wolf. Too bad it couldn't have been their masters.

Ryon stood up off the cultivator seat and shaded his eyes. A horseman was coming in off the road, shimmering in the heat waves. Ryon didn't like strangers crossing his property line any more than he liked crossing other people's property lines.

As the horseman drew closer, Ryon saw that he wore a faded red tunic and a slouch hat, and rode with the spring-spined ease of someone who spends much of his life in the saddle. Riding behind him with her hands on his shoulders was a copper-skinned young woman with long, black hair blowing free in the breeze.

Ryon climbed down off the cultivator, stretched his back, and took the bits out of Esther and Edgar's mouths so they could chew on the grass at the end of the furrows while he was chewing the obligatory fat with Constable Ducharme. The constable reined in and said: "Good morning, Mr. Ryon," while the young woman raised her right leg high to arc it around the red-coated back and slide down off his horse.

Ryon glanced at the sun, replied: "Good afternoon, Constable," then turned to the young woman. "And to you, Lisette."

Lisette said: "I know I did say I would be here for morning, but my brother he borrow my pony without tell me. I was walk along the road when Constable Ducharme he come along. Summer your laundry don't take me long anyways."

Ryon said: "No fear, Lisette. You always get done what needs to get done, regardless when you start."

Lisette shrugged: "Indian time."

Constable Ducharme said: "I had to pass by this way anyway, and they told me at the post office this came in for you a week ago…" He reached inside his tunic. "Thought you'd want it sooner rather'n later." He leaned down and handed Ryon his quarterly remittance check.

"Thank you."

"And there was this, too." The constable squirmed around in the saddle to rummage in his saddlebag, and came out with a package wrapped in waxed brown paper. Ryon turned the package in his hands, looking in vain for a return address. There was nothing but a postmark identifying that it had come from someone in the center of the known world: London. He broke open the wrapping. Inside was a leather bound book embossed with the sort of pseudo-medieval design favored by the Pre-Raphaelites and the Arts and Crafts Movement. The cover read: *Windflowers Gathered by The Doudes.* There was no note enclosed and no inscription on the flyleaf.

Ryon muttered: "Damned odd."

Constable Ducharme said: "Something from home?"

"Well, from England by the postmark, but certainly not from any of my family. I knew the people who wrote the book—Fergus and Audrey Doude—but only vaguely. No earthly reason they should send it to me."

Constable Ducharme said: "You knew people who wrote a book?"

Lisette said: "He knew *many* people who wrote books."

Ryon shrugged: "Writing books was an infection in some of the circles I traveled in. I might've succumbed myself if I'd stayed in England much longer. All it takes to write a book is time on your hands and enough spare cash to hire a printer. To write a book that anyone wants to *read* is a different proposition."

Ryon riffled the gilt-edged pages distractedly. He was more than a little annoyed at whatever anonymous idiot had sent it to him. It put him in mind of things he hadn't thought about for a long time. In particular, it put him in mind of someone he'd worked long and hard not to think about. He was sufficiently disjointed that Constable Ducharme's: "Well, I'd best be getting along," took a moment to register.

"Hm? Oh, you won't stop in for a cup of coffee?"

"More'n glad to, but word has it the sergeant wants my boots in front of his desk in jig-time. Something about a whisky-trader caught with two dozen bottles and only one dozen presented as evidence. You should get into town more often, 'stead of spending all your days out here alone."

Ryon just said: *"Alone?"* It was too bizarre that anyone could think he lived alone.

As Constable Ducharme rode on his way, Ryon tucked the book inside his shirt to free his hands, and Lisette helped him unhitch Edgar and Esther to take them into some shade for the heat of the day. When the procession neared the barn, Bell and her pups rose up panting and fell in as escorts, to give the impression they were earning their living. The barn cats peered down from the loft suspiciously and the crow he'd found with a broken wing last fall swooped in to make catcalls from the rafters.

In the cool of the house, Ryon shooed the raccoon off the table, muttering: "Alone indeed," then flopped onto his chair and tossed the book down on the space the raccoon had vacated. The gilt flowers on its cover stared back at him, taunting him with dusty images of opium dreams, candlelit salons, and a crazed young man standing in the fountain in Trafalgar Square bellowing William Blake at three o'clock in the morning.

Lisette said: "Who has step on your grave, Ryon?"

"Hm?"

"You have go far away. You almost did put Esther in Edgar's stall."

"Oh, too much sun, I expect. I should've come inside an hour ago."

"I think not just sun. I have see you work all day in sun like this. Who were these people you know who did write this book?"

"Probably *are.* I haven't seen or heard of them in fifteen years, but I expect they're still alive. Fergus Doude and his wife Audrey were part of a..." He groped for some way to explain it to someone whose universe consisted of earthier concerns than whether William Morris's Guinevere rang truer than Tennyson's. He found it difficult enough explaining even to himself that there'd been a time when he'd found a painting of a wheatfield more real than the one he was making with his cultivator. "...part of a group of people called the Anemone Group. They put on performances that weren't exactly music concerts and weren't exactly plays."

He realized he was speaking to someone who'd never seen a concert or a play. "There was a…well, there was a…magic to them. It's hard to believe without seeing, but big-bearded men with names a lot more famous than Anemone would find themselves weeping and laughing at the same time. Well, we all wept and laughed a lot more easily in those days. But there was undeniably something about them, something ancient and new, something of the sky and the earth…" He was starting to embarrass himself.

Lisette said: "Like to hear a wolf howl while the priest is singing midnight mass."

"That says it a hell of a lot better than I did. Well, no one outside Anemone knew exactly who in the group did what. When they published a book or presented a performance, the author was just 'Anemone'. But despite that, one of them stood out. She wasn't fashionably beautiful, and she dressed carelessly—huh, *carelessly*—but painters fought each other to do her portrait. Not that any of them captured her. And she wasn't a trained singer or elocutionist, but there was a quality in her voice…

"Madeline Prue. Mad Maddie Prue." Feeling that nickname in his mouth after all those years made Ryon chuckle and shake his head, but he could feel buds of tears in the corners of his eyes.

He blinked them away, told himself he was turning into an old woman, and went on more matter-of-factly. "Well, not long before I left England, Maddie Prue left Anemone to go on her own. A year or so after that—I got the news much later, back in the days when I was still bothering to order newspapers from home… There was a small item in a corner of a page…

"You see, when she wasn't in London, Maddie Prue lived in a cottage on the coast of Cornwall. One evening she was out walking along the cliffs, and she lost her footing. She wasn't yet thirty years old."

He shrugged stiffly at Lisette. "Ridiculous, isn't it? We thought we were at the center of the cosmos, that the artists and philosophers we rubbed shoulders with were immortals who were re-making the world. And then it turns out that someone so full of promise, someone who amazed the people who amazed the rest of us, could be wiped out in an instant by a patch of mud on a footpath. I doubt more than a handful of people in England even remember her name."

Lisette said: "You and this Maddie Prue, then, you were… *amoureux?*"

Ryon laughed. "Not hardly. We chatted a few times, but I was just a face in the crowd. And there was always a crowd around Mad Maddie Prue."

"But, so then why do these Dow-oods...?"

"Doudes."

"Why do they sent you this book?"

"It couldn't've been them. I can't think of *anybody* with any bloody reason to send me this damned book."

"Hm. Have you eat since breakfast?"

"Oh, I was going to get around to it..."

"I make us some coffee and something to eat before we work."

"Good thought. Thank you. There's a cold chop in the pantry, and some fresh eggs."

While Lisette busied herself ferrying foodstuffs and cookery gear out to the summer kitchen awninged against the side of the cabin, Ryon glared at the book and then picked it up and opened it. The publication date was more than ten years old, a few years after Maddie Prue fell off the cliff, but the spine had never been cracked. Ryon suspected there hadn't been a second printing.

He began to leaf through it, looking for some clue as to what might've possessed someone in the old country to send it to him. The flowery lyricism seemed like a foreign language; it had been years since he'd read anything but penny dreadfuls and *Bateman's Home Veterinary*. There were poems and short stories and some pieces that weren't exactly one or the other. But none of them seemed in any way even remotely addressed to Henry Jalesford Ryon of the Fourth Section Road outside Wahpeston, Manitoba.

He turned another page and came across a poem in dialect. He hated dialect poems; or he had back in the days when he used to read poetry. They were nothing but mangled gibberish, unless the hapless reader were lucky enough to guess whether the narrator was speaking in a South Yorkshire dialect or Cockney or East Hebridean... He was about to skip over the poem when a phrase caught his eye: "...bright copper mane, blunt nose..." That sounded like someone trying to describe Maddie Prue. He turned back the page.

> Her tooke what time she needed,
> Her tooke no time to lie,
> Her 'ad a voice must-heeded,
> Her 'ad a rovin' eye...

Although the poem wasn't long enough for extensive details, and never named its subject, there was too much coincidence for "her" to be anyone but Maddie Prue. Who else had "a child's charm" that she could "wield like surgeon's knife" on occasion? What other woman of the Doudes' acquaintance was both a devilish good piano player and a "surefoot dancer"?

Each verse ended with a rather eerie refrain:

> D'ja think her fell?
> Then believe it true,
> As all fools did and all fools do.

It didn't take much strain of the imagination to notice that if there'd been one more line to the refrain, a logical rhyme would be "Prue." But Ryon had to strain disused poetical muscles to translate the lines that were there in black and white. Taken out of the dialect, the refrain would say: "Did you think her fell?" And "fell," in one of its ancient usages, meant fierce and ruthless, with more than a soupçon of the supernatural. Like fairies before Victorian schoolmarms turned them into pretty little confections with butterfly wings.

It came as no great surprise to Ryon that someone might've described Maddie Prue as "fell". That had been part of her attraction, like moths to a flame. The only surprise was that the bloody Doudes couldn't've just come out and said it straight, instead of couching it in some precious bloody dialect that made a simple prairie farmer wrench his brains to wrest out that "tooke" was supposed to stand for "took", and that "her" meant "she"—

He suddenly shivered upright in his chair. He looked at the page again. If "her" meant "she", then what the Doudes were saying was: "Did you think she fell? Then believe it true, as all fools did and all fools do." *Did you think this surefoot dancer slipped on a path she'd walked a hundred times before?*

Ryon found himself laboring to breathe. He went to the cupboard and took down the bottle of doubleberry wine, so-called because the barrel of fermented saskatoon berry juice was stood in the snow to freeze and then the alcohol drained off. He sat back down at the table, rolled himself a cigarette and read the poem again. It still said what he'd thought it said. In fact, he now could hardly believe that anyone might think it said anything but.

Lisette came in with two plates of scrambled eggs and a pot of coffee and started cutting slices off the chop. She paused with the knife in her hand and said: "You seen a ghost or something?"

"Yes. Yes, I have. There's a… poem in this book that says… that says Maddie Prue's death was no accident."

Lisette furled her forehead, chewed her cheeks, looked down at the chop and started sawing at it again. She said: "How would those Doudes to know that?"

"They knew her better than anyone. They would know things about her private life no one else did."

"If they think someone did kill her, why did they leave it be said to be accident?"

"I don't know. Maybe they were afraid. Or maybe they had suspicions but couldn't prove it. So they put it in a poem and hoped that someone would understand and start asking questions. But no one did. Or at least no one pursued it enough to get any answers."

"But all that was long years ago, you did say. Why now?"

"I don't know. Maybe something new's come to the surface. Or maybe someone else who had their own suspicions only came across the poem recently."

"I think maybe you should think about whether you do see what you think you see. It make no sense. Why would someone want for *you* to get this message, so far away and long ago?"

"Well, that's the one thing that does make sense, of a sort. You see, the reason those artistic people tolerated me hanging about on the periphery was that I could be useful. When I had enough liquor or other things in me—and in those days I always had a skinful of something-or-other—I was a bit of a bulldog and too bone-stupid to think twice about jumping in at the drop of a hat. It was always: 'Ryon, there's a drunk at the front door who won't go away,' or 'Ryon, Rossetti's been locked-up swilling chloral for three weeks and his sister thinks it's time someone dragged him out in the fresh air.'"

Calling up those days made Ryon feel again Maddie Prue's small, warm hand on his shoulder after he'd knocked down the lout who'd thought that a flowered gauze costume signified her breasts were free for the grabbing. There'd been a wry twinkle in her: "'Twas Lancelot at good need." His cronies had called him *Sir* Harry for weeks afterward.

Ryon shrugged at Lisette: "I know it's hard to believe now, but that's who I was in those days."

"No. Not so hard to believe."

"But that was a long time ago, and whoever sent me this was a fool to think otherwise. The Wild Ryon is as dead and buried as Maddie Prue."

"You should eat something before the egg and coffee do get cold."

He managed to swallow a couple of mouthfuls, but drank no coffee. Then he re-filled his cup with doubleberry wine, rolled another cigarette and sat staring out the window at the pine windbreak he'd planted when he'd decided where to build the cabin. He had an urge to dig out his old books and search through them for some clue as to why the Doudes might think Maddie Prue hadn't died accidentally. But he'd sold off his Anemone books long ago, in a job-lot with all the other first editions inscribed by Morris or Swinburne or Christina Rossetti or all the others. They were probably being used to level someone's table legs today.

But even without the books he could remember. All he had to do was call up an echo of Maddie's voice and all the words came back to him. Anyone who'd heard that voice once and couldn't recall it was only using his ears to hold his hat up. Whether speaking or singing, she never made any attempt to disguise her peat-mossy North Country accent, while everyone else who hadn't been born with West End London up their noses was doing their damnedest to pretend. Although she was true-pitched and could glide from hushed to rafter-shaking like a gull riding the wind, there was always a trace of a rasp in her voice, like a caress from a scarred hand.

Ryon was vaguely aware of Lisette clearing the table and taking the scraps out to throw to the pups or the chickens, depending on whether Bell or the rooster were feeling the fiercer. He thought of getting up and going back to the cultivator, but it would wait. He could hear Lisette outside building a fire and wrestling the rending pot over it to stew his clothes. He changed into his dressing gown so Lisette could wash what he'd been wearing, then sat back down, rolled another cigarette, re-filled his cup and listened in his mind's ear to Maddie Prue singing one of the ancient ballads that Anemone had been famous for resurrecting:

> Come back, come back, with the wild geese,
> Come back, I am waiting for you...

He couldn't remember it all. For the first time since he'd rid himself of his Anemone books, it seemed a pity that he didn't have them to hand. But it seemed even more of a pity that the people who *did* have them—and many of the people who'd bought new copies in bookstores—had never heard her voice; they could only read the bald words. He rubbed his hand down his face and reached for the—

III

—headphone jack to kill the speakers as Lisette's sneakered ankles disappeared past the top bars of the stair cage. Then he snagged another beer, clapped on the headphones and sat listening to Maddie Prue sing about moonlight on Stonehenge, silver daggers and Beltane fires across the hilltops. It was a pity she had such a magical voice—a lot of people got so spellbound by the voice they never heard the words.

Some of the songs were by Maddie Prue or Fergus Doude, some by prolific old A. Nonny Mouse—1570's songs with 1970's musical treatments, the same but different, the past reflecting onto the present's funhouse mirror and vice versa. Maybe if you stood two funhouse mirrors face-to-face and looked back and forth between them, their convexities and complexities would show you a truer picture than a straight mirror. Maybe there was no such damn thing as a straight mirror.

Not all the songs Maddie Prue was singing to him were mystic and misty—after all, the point of the Celtic Revival had been to put bagpipes and Fender Stratocasters together and see what happens. But even when she sang about bumping into an old lover at the duck pond in Central Park, there was a whiff of ancient mysteries lurking. And whatever she sang, there was always that central conundrum about Maddie Prue no one had ever been able to explain: how the hell could any human being come across as so ethereal and so down-home at the same time?

But no matter how hard he listened to her voice and lyrics, Ryon couldn't hear any evidence that Maddie Prue had felt like an endangered species. Outside of the general fact that she'd been into some pretty strange stuff, but everybody was in those days.

By the time Ryon put on the second last side of the boxed set, he'd gone through half the bottle of Jameson's and six or seven beers. The first cut was a long song written hundreds of years before Maddie Prue was born—*The Great Selkie of Sule Skerrie*—so he didn't have to listen carefully to see if there were any clues in her lyrics. He leaned back and drifted with the music...

He was walking along a concrete corridor backstage at a real concert hall—not the kind of rat-traps Anemone was playing in when he first met them. Well, maybe "walking" was an exaggeration—he was maintaining a brisk forward momentum so he wouldn't stumble sideways. But he felt lean and springy and his knees didn't have that creak in them that came on after he turned forty. The walls had a glowing pattern that kept changing from purple leopardskin to neon zebra. The only sounds were his own turbo-charged breathing and the 2/4, echoing bass drum of his footsteps, so the show must be over and the audience all clapped out.

He rounded a corner and found what he knew he was bound to stumble across eventually—the entrance to the green-room and dressing rooms. Standing in the doorway were a rent-a-cop and a guy who looked like more serious hired security—black leather sports coat sausage-skinned across linebacker's biceps. Ryon stopped in front of them and said: "I wanna see Maddie," except that his mouth seemed to be filled with cotton candy.

The bearded linebacker said: "*Everyone* wants Maddie tonight. You had two hours of her on stage, that's all you get."

Ryon tried to push between them, but they pushed him back. He took a swing at the linebacker and missed cleanly—everything was too fuzzy to get a bead on. But the large fist that walloped into his solar plexus wasn't fuzzy.

His body jack-knifed, gasping for breath. But they straightened him up and pushed him back against the wall to finish the job.

"Leave him alone!" The voice was a slightly burred, husky alto that had been known to blow out speakers if the sound man set up for a voice the size of her body. The concrete corridor made a nice echo chamber. "I said leave him alone!"

The pinning arms let go of him and he slid down onto his knees and doubled over. He thought it would be a good idea to stay there for a while. A pair of suede boots and the hem of a long skirt appeared in front of him. He smelled marijuana and roses.

A small hand with callused fingertips came down softly on the back of his neck. She said: "What the hell have you been doing to yourself?" Even if he'd got his breath back yet, he wouldn't've been able to answer her. "You'd better come with me…"

In his La-Z-Boy chair, Ryon's body shook itself like Bob The Dog escaping from a pond that was deeper than she'd figured. That was as far as the memory went—or the recovered hallucination. The only sound coming through the headphones was the repeating hiss-click of the end of the record. He'd jammed the auto-return with a toothpick months ago, when it kept returning halfway through a side and he'd discovered that getting a turntable fixed these days cost as much as getting new parts for a '52 Studebaker.

He got up and turned the record over to the last side of the boxed set. As soon as the side started up, he remembered why he'd only ever played it once. It was the saddest part of all, because there were no sad songs. It was bits and pieces of the things she'd recorded between the time she left Anemone and the night she fell. Some cuts were fully-produced songs, some homemade demos with no other musicians, some just snippets of fooling around while the tape happened to be rolling.

There was a goofy lightheartedness to all of them. In one of the studio sound-check snippets, she was riffling along the piano and singing breezily:

Birds druid, bees druid,
Singers who audition on their knees druid…

Even when it came to one of her patented, sweeping, love songs with full strings and back-up singers, the undercurrent was playful:

But it doesn't seem right and it doesn't seem fair
That I should wake up in the morning and find you there,
After all the crimes of passion I've indulged in.
If this weird world ran halfway right
I'd be waking up alone in the cold moonlight,
But if you can live with such injustice, I guess that I can find a way…

Ryon told himself the beer was making him weepy. Maddie Prue's posthumous releases were just following a law of nature. It seemed to be a general ordinance that great singer-songwriters who died suddenly had to've just finished recording something that made you feel like Rod Serling was writing the script. Sam Cooke got shot to death eight days before his record company released *A Change Is Gonna Come*. The last song Hank Williams put on vinyl was *I'll Never Get Out of This World Alive*.

Ryon informed himself that this wasn't the same syndrome at all. What he got out of Maddie Prue's last songs was that she'd just hit that point that happens somewhere around thirty, if you're lucky—when you've kicked around long enough that Heartbreak Hotel no longer seems like a romantic place to live or invite other people to visit. She had just started getting comfortable with being human. And then some sonofabitch had pushed her off a cliff.

IV

ALTHOUGH THERE WAS a distant boom of prairie thunder, and the cultivator still sitting in the field naked to the elements, Ryon stayed sitting at the kitchen table in his dressing gown—hand-rolling cigarettes and smoking them down to his fingers, periodically refilling his cup of doubleberry wine when he noticed it was empty, listening to his memories of Maddie Prue's performance voice and watching the pictures that it painted. The rhythm of Lisette washboarding his laundry out in the sun carried him to a dark salon where Maddie Prue was dancing with a tambourine and singing *John Barleycorn Must Die*. That led his wandering fancy into another song, and then an epic poem he could only remember the half of, and then another ballad...

The next thing he knew, the window had turned dark red and Lisette was telling him: "I did milk Melinda, and your clothes is all done, but too late to walk home. Okay I sleep here?"

Ryon nodded. It wouldn't be the first time Lisette had spread out blankets on the kitchen floor while he bedded down in the only other room in the house. On several of those occasions he'd come within an ace of making a fool of himself by suggesting she'd be more comfortable in his bed. Even though he was twice her age, the halfbreed girls of western Canada were no more averse to older men with incomes than their titled English sisters.

But when it came down to it he'd always reminded himself that sex was for the young and heartless, and he wasn't young and Lisette wasn't heartless. If his body were desperate for release it would find it in his dreams, where the experience was usually more salubrious and there were no recriminations.

On this particular occasion he didn't even have to argue with himself, since he and Lisette might as well have been on two different planets tonight. But when he climbed into bed, with Bell and her pups pushing and shoving to see if they could all fit on, he didn't immediately sink into sleep as he had every other night since he first started breaking sod on his little corner of scrub prairie. He told himself that's what he got for dazing away the afternoon instead of working himself into healthy exhaustion.

He snuck back into the kitchen and poured himself another cup, feeling his way in the dark. From Lisette's slow, steady breathing he hadn't waked her, or maybe she was just pretending. He climbed back into bed and rolled another cigarette—Bell would wake him up if he fell asleep with it still burning.

Some while later he found himself walking into a room that had a meadow for a floor and muraled walls. There were men in velvet jackets, and women in silk gowns printed with William Morris patterns. Out of one of the murals stepped Mad Maddie Prue. Ryon could clearly see her moving through the fair, even though she was shorter than most others in the crowd—broad in the shoulders and hips, a charwoman's daughter among the sylphs. She wore her hair the same as always: rough-cut, schoolgirl's bangs between cascading curtains of the red-blonde tinge called Saxon Gold. The Saxon Gold curtains framed a moon-face with heavy cheekbones, somewhat like a pale-skinned, blue-eyed Eskimo.

Maddie took up a position in a corner and raised a long, cherrywood, tenor recorder. She licked her lips and moved them up and down the mouthpiece to moisten it, cocking an eyebrow at the audience. That was one of the myriad inexplicable facts about Maddie Prue: what might seem whorish in any other woman was just Maddie's mischief. And her giggling mischief could segue in an instant into a melody of Medea taking her revenge.

But before Maddie could start playing her recorder, her fingers turned into gnarled, tangled pine roots sprouting out of her sleeves. It didn't seem to bother her; she just opened her mouth to sing instead. But no sound came out, at least no sound Ryon could hear over the nattering of the crowd. He started grabbing people's shoulders and telling them to shut up and listen. They just looked at him offendedly.

He saw Maddie Prue turn and walk through the wall. He hurried after her. It was night outside. He blundered around looking for her. He heard the sound of surf breaking against rocks, and a woman grunting and gasping. She was dangling from the lip of a cliff, and a boot was coming down on her hands.

Ryon jolted awake. There was light coming in through the window. Bell and her pups were gone, and in their place were a fresh-laundered shirt and trousers. He put them on and stepped into the kitchen. Lisette was slicing bread beside a platter of bacon and fried potatoes. She said: "Good morning."

"That's the World's Champion oxymoron."

"What kind of moron?"

"Damn good question."

She set down the bread knife and pushed the butter dish beside his plate. "Another minute and I would to wake you up. You did sleep loud last night."

"Snoring?"

"No. Shouting. Sit down and I bring in the coffee."

After breakfast, Ryon hitched up the wagon to drive Lisette home, then shifted Edgar and Esther from their wagon traces to the cultivator. But his mind wasn't where it should be; he kept tilling over furrows he'd already broken, or discovering that he'd left a lane of unbroken ground between his last pass and the next one. He said to himself: "If you had any near neighbors, cleverlad, they'd say you're getting 'spooked'. They'd be righter than they think."

His disquiet grew worse as the summer wore on. He was doing things by rote, and losing his temper when the cow or the dogs or the potato patch didn't respond mechanically. Sometimes Maddie Prue asked him what the hell he was doing breaking his back to build a farm that would die when he got too old to work it. He had no answer.

He grew afraid of the sunset: afraid that he wouldn't be able to sleep, and equally afraid of what was waiting for him if he fell asleep. He slept later and longer; sometimes the sun was over the barn by the time he opened his eyes.

There came a night he didn't sleep at all, just lay listening to the songs of the wild geese flying across the moon. In the morning, he threw a saddle on Edgar and rode over to the little patch of hardpan that was all Lisette's father and mother had been allowed to keep of the measureless country their fathers and mothers used to roam at will. He told Lisette: "If you and your family will take care of my place, you can have the harvest. I'm going back."

Lisette studied him with those night-black eyes that seemed much older than the skin around them. She said: "She won't let you be, will she?"

"No, she won't let me be."

"Ryon, you did tell to me long ago that the only reason your family do send you the money to buy harness and plough, and keep build your farm, is if you never go back."

"There's no shortage of crowds in England to lose myself in. They'll never know."

"Ryon, whoever did kill that woman would think it no sin to kill you."

"I'm going back."

"You think you can go back in time?"

"No. I know I'm sixteen years too late. But I'm going back."

v

ON THE CONNECTING FLIGHT from Toronto to Newark, Ryon floated travel-parched eyes across his complimentary *Globe and Mail*. Time zones could change, but it was still fourteen hours since he'd headed south from Wahpeston for the Winnipeg airport. A filler article said that, depending how you counted, the end of the millennium could just as easily be the end of the nineteenth century as the twentieth—like that the last day before your twentieth birthday was actually the last day of the twentieth year since you popped out of Mom.

It put him in mind of the first time he'd met Lisette, through the grill between the front and back seats of a patrol car. When he'd asked her age, she'd said: "Could be nineteen or twenty, depends how you conjurate it." Once he'd figured out that conjurate meant conjugate, he was still stumped. She'd enlightened him with: "In French I could say 'I have nineteen years,' or 'I've had twenty years.'" Turned out she wasn't exactly telling the truth, but it wasn't indictable.

He folded the newspaper away, leaned his head against the vibrating plastic wall of the plane, closed his eyes and dive-bombed into a dream he'd thought he'd stopped having years ago. He was an invisible movie camera in a prairie farmyard on a summer night. Down the driveway, a corporal of the Royal Canadian Mounted Police was in a huddle with two rookie constables, male and female. The corporal kept pointing at the licence plate of a mud-spattered, white Lincoln Continental snugged in close to the windbreak.

The huddle broke and the three of them came marching toward the farm-house, the female constable drawing her sidearm and the other two officers unflapping their holsters. The female constable had dull brown, brillo-pad hair and a lumpy nose too big for her eyes—eyes bright with adrenaline.

The male constable proceeded around the back of the house. The female constable followed the corporal's point to a spot about fifteen feet and forty-five degrees from the house door, and assumed the two-handed aim stance drilled into her at Depot Division. She was planted out in the open like a duck in a shooting gallery, in the full glare of the yard light, pointing her service revolver at the door.

Ryon tried to scream at her that the corporal wasn't God, but cameras don't have voices.

The corporal walked slowly to the door, squared his shoulders and knocked. The door opened a crack and a conversation ensued, with a low voice inviting the corporal to come in and the corporal inviting the citizen to come out.

There was a picture window up to one side of the door. The female constable suddenly shifted her eyes and her aim in that direction. Ryon's camera lens angled with her. There was a large, shadowy figure moving in the dimness behind the glass, with its arms hanging slackly by its sides. The shadow had a long, narrow object in its hands—longer than the shadow was wide—but kept its arms down by its sides.

The corporal suddenly shouted: "He's got a gun!" and jumped for cover like any sensible human being would. The female constable had nowhere to jump to. She held her ground and her aim, staring across her gunsight into the eyes of the shadow who was staring out at her. And then the picture window exploded outward in a blaze of smoke and sparks and flying glass that movie critics would've given five stars.

Ryon's dream-camera switched to the point of view of the shotgun pellets moving in super slo-mo toward the sitting duck in the farmyard. Someone had played a Special Effects trick. The potato-faced constable with her kinky hair pushed up under her cap had turned into wild-haired, wide-cheekboned, sea-blue-eyed Maddie Prue.

As the buckshot tore into Maddie's face and breasts, sending little geysers of red and pink out of the puffed-front, olive-brown shirt, Ryon flailed awake. The business-suited woman in the seat between him and the aisle seat was pretending she hadn't been staring at him nervously. He pretended not to notice, put his walkman headphones on and reached into his jacket pocket to press the play button. But before he could press it and escape into the land of: *I can't hear you over the headphones, so I'm not here,* she looked straight at him and said: "It's about time."

He looked at her. Her skirt-suit wasn't off-the-rack and her blouse looked like real silk. She was traveling with a boy about five years old and she'd brought along a canvas carry-on filled with pop-up books and games and gizmos to get him through the flight. Maybe she was a very expensive nanny. At the moment she was holding up an airline glass filled with water and keeping the kid amused with the trick done with baking soda, where a raisin or something will move up and down in the water like it's swimming and diving.

Ryon said: "Uh, what's about time?"

"This." She smiled at Ryon and indicated the glass of water. It was the same smile she used on the kid. "What this is about, is time. Time is a liquid. The raisin moves up and down in the water, from one time to the next, but the raisin doesn't change."

She didn't *look* like a nut, but they came in all shapes and sizes these days. Ryon said politely: "You mean like, uh, reincarnation and that…?"

She laughed. "No. We can't *all* have been Cleopatra in another life. Besides, the Cleopatras and the Abraham Lincolns and such are locked in time—by making themselves into signposts of one era, they become rooted there. Only us little folk have the anonymity to slip in and out.

"See? the raisin doesn't just move in one direction; it flows up and down with the currents. Back and forth. Or forth and back, I should say, because it's a mistake to suggest that human history is constant evolution toward some kind of perfect clarity. Every era has its own distortions."

"Um, you mean sort of like, say… looking at the same tree through two different colors of stained glass. The same but different."

"Exactly!" She tapped his knee as though she would've stuck a gold star on his forehead if she'd had one to hand. "There are windows of time that intersect—where different-tinted panes can fit in the same frame. Or you could describe it as a conversation carried on while shuttling between two rooms—say the billiard room and the library…"

Ryon thought: *Colonel mustard with the candlestick,* but didn't say it.

"…the story of the conversation doesn't change from room to room, but the windows and ambience light up different parts of it. We're not *aware* of the altering—we can only be in one room at a time—but it happens to us."

"So, like, you could wake up tomorrow morning as Mary Poppins."

She was not amused. Her frosted pink fingernail tapped against the glass and she said: "No. I would still be the same raisin, in the same glass of water—

just of *that* era, part of *that* level in the glass. I would know things I don't know now, and not know things I do know now. But just cosmetic changes. Like putting on a different costume for the same play. It's a documented phenomenon, called 'timeslip'. Well, documented anecdotally…"

"I'm as fond of a good anecdote as the next guy."

"Einstein said time folds back on itself—"

"I thought that was space." A space cadet should know that. "Well, I guess he said a lot of things. Anyway, um, sure was interesting talking to you." He turned to look out the window, took the Walkman out of his pocket so she could see he was booking off, and pressed the play button. Nanny took the subtle hint.

Before he'd left home he'd dubbed the Maddie Prue boxed set onto cassettes, along with all his old Anemone albums. Into his ears and the space in between flooded Maddie Prue and the band singing *John Barleycorn:*

> *There are three men come from the west,*
> *Three men both great and high,*
> *And they have sworn a solemn oath*
> *John Barleycorn must die…*

He could see Maddie prowling around the stage, or the studio, one fist pumping the air and the other clamping the mike to her mouth, lost in the song. Listening to her fiercely reeling off how they "took a weapon long and sharp and cut him by the knee," and "crushed him between two stones," Ryon stumbled across lost scraps of his own fixated digging into the ancient myth of the Corn King, back in that lost year. He couldn't for the life of him say now why he'd been so hooked on sifting through the endless variations on the king who has to die so the barley can grow again—or the grapes, or the mangoes or whatever crop was the big deal in that part of the world. But whatever his so-called reason might've been, he'd waded through *The Golden Bough* and *The White Goddess*, Joseph Campbell's *The Masks of God*, heaps of Carl Jung and God knows what else.

It wasn't healthy stuff to remember. Smartboys who lost themselves in it found themselves waking up in the happy-times ward pumped full of enough valium to make Genghis Kahn take up knitting. Ryon didn't know for certain what'd been cause and what effect, but he knew he didn't want to walk his fingers along that map again.

He did have to admit, though, that there was a pleasant feeling attached to the memories of reading Jung, even if Krazy Kraut Karl was tough slogging. How could you not have a good time hanging around with someone who lays out a fifty-page, head-twisting theory on the wiring between the collective unconscious and the individual subconscious, and then declares at the end: *"Vell, dat's de vay it seems like to me today—tomorrow, who knows?"*

When the uniformed woman in the Immigration cubicle asked Ryon his name and citizenship, he didn't answer her. He just handed her his ID card and said: "This'll save you going through the whole routine."

"Not if you're coming down here for an extradition, Corporal. Please tell me you're not."

"No, just a holiday. Even Mounties get leave from time to time."

"Thank God. You got any idea how many forms I gotta fill out for an extradition? Well, enjoy your stay. Say hello to Dudley Do-Right for me."

"Will do. Give my regards to Dirty Harry."

VI

A S THE MANTLE CLOCK CHIMED *the third hour of darkness, she turned down the gas jets in the parlor lamps and lit two green candles standing on either side of a pan of salted water. She wound a bowstring around two stalks of wheat—a bowstring for the hunter. Then she floated the bound wheat stalks in the pan and breathed on them softly, blowing from the west.*

McNulty's Tailors of Montreal was a packrat's nest of celluloid collars and bolt-ends of Harris tweed, but the price was right. Ryon emerged with a promise that two serviceable suits of clothes and an Ulster coat would be ready before his ship sailed—the last England-bound ship before the St. Lawrence River grew too dangerous with ice. The Canadian Pacific Railway had carried him across the country, Canadian Pacific Steamship Lines would carry him across the ocean, and in between he was staying in a Canadian Pacific hotel. Monopolies did have aspects of convenience.

Canadian Pacific couldn't conjure him new duds, though, and until McNulty fulfilled his promise Ryon was resigned to the blocky, bunchy, mail-order suit he'd bought for Lisette's grandfather's funeral. The trunkful of exquisitely-tailored clothes he'd brought with him when he emigrated had all been given away years ago, when they no longer came close to fitting him across the back and shoulders.

He made his way along the winding, snow-dusted, cobbled streets of what passed for an old city in the New World, studying the directions the hotel clerk had written down for him. He was aware that his tattered buffalo coat made him the object of second glances. And he had to keep reminding him-self that in civilization he oughtn't to spit whenever his throat felt a bit of a tickle, and that loud bodily noises were to be held-in until he was closeted alone. It amazed him that he'd managed to get through the first twenty-five years of his life without expiring of clogged lungs or exploded bowels.

The rare bookstore the desk clerk had directed him toward turned out to be below street level in a slanting cul-de-sac. Ryon was hoping that the books he was looking for would turn out to be "rare" only in the sense of unusual, not in the sense of expensive. He had a bank draft for the totality of his autumn remittance check, plus the money he'd been squirreling away to buy a new reaping machine, and what he'd got from selling a few acres with a creek running through which his nearest neighbor had been coveting for years. But he didn't want to spend it all on this mad odyssey—*odd-*yssey indeed—if he could help it.

Three stone steps in an iron-railed cage brought him down to the bookstore door. A bell jingled as he pushed the door open. Inside were ranks of tables with cribbed sides, like sardine tins of books, and beyond them rows of laden bookshelves. The comforting musk of aging bindings filled the air. Ryon said to the man behind the counter: "*Bonjour, monsieur.*"

The bookseller frowned. "No French here."

"Ah. Perhaps you could help me in English, then. I'm looking for some old books."

The man cocked his eyebrows up over his spectacles, and dryly surveyed the crammed tables and shelves fading into the distance.

"Some *particular* old books," Ryon specified. "Published in England in the 'seventies and early 'eighties. Some are poetry, some are—"

"Angelique!" the bookseller cut him off with a bellow, then explained: "Poetry's my wife's bailiwick."

A bright-blue-eyed woman in a faded blue dress emerged from the stacks and said to Ryon: "Might I be of some manner of assistance to you, sir?" She'd obviously labored long and hard to eradicate the fact that she'd grown up speaking French—and probably would've succeeded if she hadn't made her English more than proper.

Ryon said to her: "It's a bit of a long shot, actually. I wouldn't be surprised if you never heard of the books I'm looking for. They were published under the name of a group who styled themselves Anemone—"

"No!" the bookseller pronounced emphatically. "Nothing of that ilk here."

Ryon looked from the bookseller to his wife, who was supposedly the keeper of the keys to the poetry selection. She had adopted an expression blander than bread pudding. Her husband had gone red-faced and huffy.

Ryon said: "Oh. Well, I suppose I'd best look elsewhere, then. Sorry to trouble—"

"Oh dear, George," the bookseller's wife interjected, "I have neglected to keep a watchful eye upon your schedule. It is past time you should be upstairs to take your luncheon."

"It's not gone noon yet. Only quarter to."

"Oh. Well in fifteen minutes, then, and I shall watch the store alone for a half an hour." The bright blue eyes blinked like a heliograph as they transited across Ryon to the rows of bookshelves.

Ryon said: "Well… Good day, then," and took his leave. Back up on the street, he glanced at his pocket watch and proceeded to walk a circuit of the neighborhood. He wasn't sure if he were imagining things, but the signals from the bookseller's wife seemed pretty obvious. What she wanted him to come back for, though, was another question.

She was certainly not an unattractive woman. The twin, bright-blue, arresting orbs were no more arresting than the larger, softer, corseted blue ones farther down. Ryon hardly considered himself deathly magnetic to women. His skin was baked Indian from the prairie sun, and there was more gray in his hair than brown. Someone had once told him he had handsome, dark eyes; someone else had once told him that his nose was far too wide. He was only of medium height, and his hands looked leathered like a pair of old boots. But there was no accounting for taste. And the bookseller seemed the type whom a lively woman might describe as "leaving something to be desired."

Whoever had sent Ryon the Doudes' book had also brought back to him the days when things went on behind shop counters and on kitchen tables that didn't figure in *Mrs. Beeton's Household Management*. And the bookseller's wife, unlike Lisette, was past the age of taking things too seriously.

Ryon told himself he was being ridiculous. Nonetheless, he continued ambling the general vicinity until heading back down the bookstore steps at five minutes past the hour.

The bookseller's wife was alone behind the counter. She smiled at him, cupped her hands and lifted up a pair of rosebudded, leather bound, slim volumes. He recognized the faux-medieval rosebuds as the design Anemone had chosen for the covers of all their collections. It had been intended that another rose branch would be added on each succeeding volume, but there'd only been two.

Ryon said: "Oh."

"You are no scholar, are you?"

"Why do you say that?"

"Anemone is not a name which scholars use in polite company, not since long years now. My husband instructed me to throw these into the rubbish receptacle, but I thought that there might come a time when someone might wish to purchase them. You must forgive my husband his volatility upon the subject. It is because of his uncle, who was the great hope of the family: accepted into Oxford, and all the family clubbed their finances together to make it possible for him to attend. He prospered at Oxford, until the Anemone scandal."

"Scandal?"

"It was rather like the Ossian scandal, I suppose, or the suicide Chatterton. Anemone you see, re-discovered a number of long-lost, ancient, epic ballads and brought them into the light…"

"Yes, I know."

"Well, several very promising young literary scholars made a *cause célèbre* of those ballads, writing papers upon what these ballads revealed of the Dark Ages, and making disputations of each others' theories."

Ryon noticed in passing that she had even managed to train herself to pronounce *cause célèbre* like an English-speaker attempting a foreign phrase. Whatever else might be said about the bookseller's Angelique, she was certainly diligent. Lisette could be that determined when the spirit moved her, but the reasons compelling Angelique's particular diligence would've moved Lisette's spirit to reach for her father's shotgun.

While Ryon smiled about Lisette, he continued listening to Angelique. "This scholarly activity pertaining to those ballads not only contributed to the reputation of Anemone, but made the scholars' reputations as well—by their thoroughness of research and reasoning, and their knowledge of ancient lore. And then it came out that the ballads were not ancient at all. They had been written by someone no more ancient than the scholars themselves, and a woman at that."

Ryon laughed. "Maddie Prue."

"You may laugh if you like—many people did at the time—but it was not so very funny to those scholars. University colleges do not like to be associated with laughingstocks. My husband's uncle was by no means the only one.

There must be at least a half-dozen men in Britain today who'd seemed well on their way to a chair at Oxford or Cambridge or Edinburgh, and instead are drudging away their lives teaching ABCs in backwater charity schools."

"Yes, I see. Not particularly funny to them."

"Not particularly funny at all." But Ryon still found it hard not to laugh. There was something he'd always found appealing about experts hoist upon their own expertise. "What was that name you mentioned—a woman's name?"

"Maddie Prue. Madeline Prue."

"Ah, I thought so. Would it inconvenience you greatly to wait here for just a moment, please?"

Ryon said it wouldn't. Angelique disappeared into the labyrinth of bookshelves, leaving Ryon to wonder whether even a literary scholar might not summon up the wherewithal to push someone off a cliff, if that someone had ruined his life.

The bookseller's wife came back with another slim volume clutched against her right breast, distractingly demonstrating that there was a give to them even encased in dress and corset. The book had a plain black cover with no print on it. When Ryon opened it to the title page, he found: *A Posthumous Collection of the Hitherto-unpublished Poems and Stories of Madeline Prue, issued through a Subscription of Bereaved Friends, and by the Kind Assistance of an Anonymous Donor.*

On the steamer across the Atlantic, Ryon had more than enough time to practically memorize all three books. Although for the first few days he didn't get much reading done, what with his stomach going queasy whenever he focused his eyes at one quadrant for more than a minute at a time.

Once he was able to take things in again, he discovered a thread running through Anemone's works that he hadn't noticed before. In their early days, Anemone had been fascinated with the story of Arthur and Guinevere, as every other writer or painter in London at the time had been. Small wonder, given that the *Morte d'Arthur* was the cord of myth that bound all Britons together, even if most of them had never read Thomas Mallory. But Anemone had carried it further back, to somehow connect Arthur and Guinevere to Venus and Adonis: the Queen of Love and the hunter whose death she mourns forever after he was gored to death by a wild boar. And back from

Venus and Adonis to Ishtar, the great mother goddess of Babylon, and to Astarte, her counterpart among the Scythians and Phoenicians. For six months of every year, Ishtar, or Astarte, lost her lover—the beautiful hunter Tammuz—to the Queen of the Dead. For that half of the year, while the goddess of fertility was in mourning, wombs and orchards stayed barren.

Anemone had somehow connected those stories with the Greek legend of the Bacchantes, women who left their families to run riot through the woods with Dionysus, the god of wine. The Bacchantes grew wilder and wilder with wine and orgies until finally "some of them did take hold of their beloved Dionysus by his right arm, and some by his left—gripping so fiercely that their nails sunk into his skin and his blood did flow like wine. Howling and laughing, the women twisted and pulled against each other until his arms were ripped from his shoulders and his blood fountained over them. With their teeth and fingers, they tore his living body into scraps of flesh and scattered the pieces across the fields." Dionysus would rise again at the next grape harvest, but not so a certain king who tried to stop the bacchanals. The king was torn to pieces by the women of his own household when Dionysus made them see him as a wild boar—like the boar that gored Adonis.

Ryon couldn't exactly grasp the supposed connections, but it seemed as though Maddie Prue and Anemone had been gradually peeling the layers of civilization off something buried with the bones of Eve. One of their printed performance pieces intermittently repeated, like a chant, "Ishtar, Astarte, Esther, Isis." Ryon couldn't fathom any reason why the Old Testament Esther was included—except that her name sounded euphonious in the list and she was a seductive queen who wasn't averse to a few thousand people being hacked to death. But Isis seemed a logical fit with the other two, being as how she was the Egyptian fertility goddess who'd roamed the banks of the Nile looking for the scattered pieces of her brother and husband's dismembered body. A long Anemone poem titled "Isis" had a refrain that felt like a rough translation of something a lot more ancient than medieval ballads:

> Lady of Barley,
> Lady of Bread,
> Lady of Beer,
> Lady of Abundance...

There wasn't much of that kind of thing in Maddie Prue's own book, though —almost as though she'd had some premonition and was determined to spend what time she had left attending to the here and now. As Ryon read and re-read her poems and stories about seals sporting on the rocks below her cottage in Cornwall, or the old flower-seller in the village, she grew more real to him. Her appearances in his dreams had been growing steadily less elusive ever since he'd started on the long road back—although still a good deal too elusive to suit him.

He woke in his cabin one morning to find Maddie standing by the stove pushing bangers and mash around a skillet. The cabin seemed to be half his shipboard cabin and half his homestead cabin. She smiled at him and chirped: "Good morning," in that voice like a scratchy-throated child's. Her hair was tousled and windblown, hanging in wisps across her sea-gray eyes and awning cheekbones, and she was wearing a cotton nightgown so carelessly unbuttoned that it kept sliding off her shoulder.

Ryon said: "Um, good morning." He couldn't think what else to say. She put down her spatula, came and perched on the side of the bed and raised her hand to his cheek. He tentatively put one hand on her bared shoulder. His fingers sank in: down into the pulpy, bloated flesh of a corpse that had been fished out of the ocean. He yanked his hand back. The ruin of Maddie Prue said to him tearfully: "I thought you wanted to know me," then melted away.

VII

THE NEW YORK HOTEL the travel agent had booked Ryon into was on 44th Street off Times Square. The times he'd spent in New York City before, he hadn't stayed in hotels. Except for a few nights in the bubbling madhouse of the Chelsea. Or maybe it'd been a few weeks.

This hotel wasn't exactly the Royal York, but even the fanciest places in Manhattan had a casually run-down aura in the corners. And Ryon was pleased to discover that one of this place's unadvertised features was a very large, blue-blazered black man at a monitoring station in front of the elevators, who politely asked to see his room key before allowing him to proceed further.

In his room, Ryon dropped his bag on the bed and pulled the window curtain open so he could see where he was. South-east corner of the building—through the grimy glass he could just make out a corner of Times Square down the block. Funny, though, it seemed to him there used to be an ice cream store on that corner. He remembered, and started to laugh.

On a New Year's Eve twenty years ago, he'd gone into that ice cream store with Maddie Prue and a half-dozen other Anemone types, to load up on cones on the way down to Times Square. Maddie had got the idea she wanted to do the tourist thing and watch the big, brass ball come down at midnight. As usual, Ryon was just hanging around the edges, trying to keep his mouth shut except for sticking ice cream into it.

When they'd come back out of the store, licking each other's flavors, two cops in semi-riot gear—helmets, black leather jackets, long batons—were standing on the corner waiting for the traffic light. When the light turned green, one of the cops started to step off the curb, but his partner grabbed his arm and said: "Where do you think you're going?" The younger cop pointed his chin ahead towards Times Square and their assignment. The older one shook his head and said: "I ain't going down there. We can see just fine from here."

The rest of the ice cream crew had taken that as a sign to find another place to see the new year in. But Maddie just laughed and kept on going. Ryon stood on the corner watching her go, chewing his lower lip instead of his Blueberry Swirl. He made up his hash-soaked mind and followed her, close enough to keep her in sight, just in case.

Times Square had been jammed and rowdy, but didn't seem all that dangerous, given the number of families from the 'burbs with kids in tow. Ryon had to bob and weave to keep his eye on Maddie as she moved through the fair smiling stonedly and taking in the people. Hard to keep good surveillance on even a red-gold head at shoulder height to most of the mob.

Maddie hadn't been the only one moving through the crowd. Four or five baseball-capped guys went running by, whacking heads and grabbing asses. None of the whacked or grabbed had whacked back, even though none of the tough guys looked more than fifteen years old. The Morlocks and the Eloi.

One of the Morlocks swerved in Maddie's direction. Ryon whispered at the running, shouting baseball cap, and to himself: "Don't do it. Please don't do it." Maybe the tough kids were only fifteen years old, but there were at least four of five of them, and none of the Eloi would raise a hand to help. But it was Maddie.

Ryon threw his ice cream cone down and jumped ahead to intercept. Just before his trajectory intersected with the Morlock's, the kid swerved again, away from Maddie, knocked the fedora off the tourist behind her and kept on going. Maddie didn't turn around.

Ryon dropped back further into the crowd and kept on following her from a distance, saying to himself: "What—you were going to get yourself into a gang fight with no gang, just because some kid was going to grab her ass or slap her head? You gotta lay off the ice cream."

As soon as the big, lit-up ball had slid down, and Auld Lang Syne been bellowed, the suburban families had begun to clear out fast. Ryon was glad when Maddie seemed to decide she'd seen enough and headed back toward her hotel. He followed her, keeping about half a block back. At the entrance to her hotel, she turned and called down the street: "Good-night, Lochinvar."

Ryon pulled the curtain shut on his hotel room window and wiped his eyes. Was it memory or just Memorex? He was sweating, and the scar on his chest was suddenly itching like crazy—you'd think the damn thing would heal after twenty years, or whatever it was. He went into the bathroom and sluiced cold water over his face and hands. He dried himself off and saluted himself in the mirror. "Stop thinking and get to work, Corporal."

Before heading out into the street to get on the case, he unpacked his bag and stood his flashlight on the bedside table. When he'd wrapped it up in his sweater in Wahpeston, he'd been aware of the fact that he could probably find somewhere to buy a flashlight in the commodities capital of the world. But not like this one. At least not without a lot of looking around.

It had a two-foot long handle made out of extremely sturdy metal. The official line was that standard-issue RCMP flashlights were built that heavy-duty to protect the row of batteries inside, but part of the subduing-and-self-defense courses at Depot Division had been Flashlight Techniques. Ryon had expanded on those basic techniques considerably through experience. During his first while of being backwatered at Wahpeston, he'd gone through two or three flashlights a year. Now, even the most belligerent solvent-sniffer could usually remember that it was better to get into the van when the nice police-man said to get into the van.

At the bottom of Ryon's suitcase was the picture book from Maddie Prue's boxed set, already getting a little dog-eared. He slipped it into the drawer beside the Gideon Bible. As he slid the drawer shut, his eyes caught on the design on the back of the booklet—all the paintings Anemone had used for their album covers laid out in miniature, making a mosaic of Victorian medieval fantasies. Ryon shook his head at the kind of pretentious expropria-tions everyone had got up to in the 'sixties and 'seventies. He didn't know much about William Morris and Sir Edward Burne-Jones and all, but he did know they were serious artists who had to work at it, not a bunch of stoned kids into sex, drugs and Celtic rock and roll...

VIII

THE SEEMINGLY-INCESSANT clatter of iron-shod hooves and wheels on the Brixton Road kept Ryon awake through most of his first night in London. What aggravated his aggravation was that he knew he could have had at least a few hours of relative quiet on Craven Street, where short-term visitors to the greatest city in the greatest power in the modern world could always find a tidy hotel or lodging-house.

But Craven Street was far too close to The Strand and Pall Mall and the haunts of fashionable society. All he needed was for some old school chum to recognize him and mention it in the wrong quarters, and Ryon's older brother would happily put a stop to the checks that kept a scrub-land farm on the shores of Lake Manitoba from going under. Ryon knew that twenty years in the colonies had given him a natural disguise, but some people were too sharp-eyed for other people's good. So here he was in a run-down little inn on The Brixton Road, where farm wagons rumbled north to market during the hours when cabs and carriages had decently made themselves scarce.

At breakfast he asked the waiter if there were a cabstand nearby.

"Not so near, guv. But what destination was you thinking of going, if you don't mind my asking?"

"Hammersmith."

"Then why not take the Underground? There's a stop just down the road, and it'll get you there a lot quicker for a lot less lolly."

"And give me black-lung into the bargain."

"Oh it must be a time since you been in London, sir. The Underground's all gone electric-motored, or most of it. No more busted eardrums or sooty gobs. Take my advice, guv. You won't regret it."

Ryon didn't regret it, except that the lack of booming coal-engines meant he couldn't mutter aloud without attracting attention. So he rehearsed silently, preparing his prevarications and oiling the extremely rusty springs of civilized cadences. He wasn't planning on a conversation of more than a few minutes, but it would be more words than he spoke to other human beings in the average month back on the farm. And it had been a very long time since he'd had to tell even the whitest of lies.

In jigtime and for only a few pennies, the Underground spat him up onto the Hammersmith High Road. He kicked his boots along through the gray sludge Londoners called snow, until he came to the Upper Mall and turned toward the river. The ends of his gloved fingers were tingling, and not with cold. He'd been under the impression that he'd been fully awake since his first pot of tea, but now he could feel a last layer of sleepless bleariness sloughing away as he finally approached some possible living link to Maddie Prue.

After the clamor of the highroad, Ryon was pleased to find himself walking along an elm-shaded towpath, with the wide Thames on his left and tall houses standing shoulder-to-shoulder on his right. But none of the houses looked particularly like they might be the home of the man who had revolutionized the appearance of English homes.

In front of one of the gates, a woman with the steamed cheeks of a cook was dickering with a fishmonger. They paused when Ryon stopped beside them. Ryon said: "Excuse me, might you be able to direct me to the house of Mr. William Morris?"

The cook said: "You ain't one of them Socialists, are you?"

"Nope—that is, certainly not." All that the term meant to Ryon was vague memories of dotty clerics handing out tracts on Christian Socialism, whatever that was supposed to mean. Maybe Morris and his cronies had gone and made a fashion of it, as they had so many other things.

"Mr. Morris's house is five houses down. Five or six…."

The fishmonger said: "Seven."

"No, I'm sure it's six."

A voice from behind Ryon said: "Anything I can help you with?"

Ryon turned around and found a policeman standing behind him. "They're trying to get me sorted out, constable. I'm looking for the home of William Morris."

"I'm walking that way myself, sir, I'd be glad to point it out to you."

As they stepped along, the constable said: "Not a Londoner are you, sir?"

"No, I'm here on a visit from the colonies—from Canada."

"Ah, *Our Lady of the Snows*, as Mr. Kipling would have it. Here you go, sir, that's Mr. Morris's house there."

"Obliged. That is—thank you very much."

"No trouble at all, sir. I could tell by the cut of your jib you was a gentleman, not one of them Socialists. Enjoy your stay in London, sir."

The house looked unremarkable: flat-faced three storeys of red brick. It was certainly larger than the old place at Turnham Green—where Ryon had watched Maddie Prue delight Jane Morris with one of her husband's medievallish poems set to music—but not a patch on the Morrises' country place. There was barely enough room for a few shrubs between the front steps and the low, iron fence. Knowing Morris, Ryon assumed there had to be a long swath of gardens behind the house.

On his way up the walk, Ryon tugged out of his waistcoat pocket one of the calling cards he'd had printed-up in Montreal:

> *Henry J. Ryon*
> Winnipeg Gazette
> *Manitoba*
> *Dominion of Canada*

"Ryon," or "Ryan," was a common enough name that no one was likely to connect it with the Ryon-Chiltons of Chilton County and Grosvenor Square.

The maid who opened the door had fluttery hands that looked raw from the scullery. Ryon told her he had no appointment, but only required a moment of Mr. Morris's time if he could spare it. She carried his card away up the staircase, leaving Ryon to contemplate the wallpaper in the foyer. It was typically Morris: entwining flowers that looked almost carnivorous, in the hand-mixed colors that somehow managed to be startlingly bright and soothingly liquid at the same time. Odd way of thinking, Ryon thought, to carve wood-blocks that were the obverse of the pattern one wanted to be seen.

Ryon was just beginning to envision Morris envisioning the mirror-image dye-blocks which only became a fullness when overlaid, when the maid came back partway down the stairs and said: "Mr. Morris will see you." Ryon followed her up, passing by several mounted sketches by Dante Gabriel Rossetti of the lady of the house. The sketches weren't all Rossetti had mounted.

Ryon was ushered into a cloud-blue drawing room as long as two barns, lit by a wide expanse of windows fronting the river. There were blue-patterned hangings on the walls, and flowerbed carpets broken by only a few monumental pieces of Morris & Co. furniture. One of the pieces of furniture—a cowl-backed, pew-like settle snugged by the fire—was one Ryon had seen before. The same two men had been sitting on it then.

An icicle slid down Ryon's back. *Didn't think of that, did you, cleverlad?*

One of the men on the settle was short and blocky, wearing a spattered, blue smock and soft, round hat. Twenty years hadn't altered Morris's taste in work clothes, but his thicket of hair and beard had gone dead white.

The other man was long and spare, with a frayed horsetail beard and a thinning forehead that still bore the scar Ryon knew the cause of. Sir Edward Burne-Jones. Ryon called himself several kinds of idiot for not expecting to find Topsy and Ned settled on the settle nattering together as always. But it was too late to back out the doorway now.

The icicle down Ryon's back was that Burne-Jones had a good deal more reason to remember him than ever Morris had. Twenty-some years ago, Burne-Jones had become more than professionally entangled with one of the Mediterranean lovelies the Pre-Raphaelites used as models when Jane Morris was too ill or bored to sit. The Greek woman had decided that she and Burne-Jones had formed a suicide pact, and when that failed to pan out she'd decided to drown herself in The Grand Union Canal in front of Robert Browning's house in Paddington. What Browning had to do with it, if anything, was more than Ryon ever knew. But as usual, whenever there was something messy in the wind, someone-or-other had got word to Ryon to see if he couldn't go help with the sweeping-up.

Ryon had arrived to find Burne-Jones wrestling with the Grecian beauty on the edge of the canal, and several bobbies trying to interfere with what they took to be an assault on a lady's virtue. Ryon had to admit that it probably hadn't been entirely necessary to toss that constable into the canal, but he'd been young and impulsive.

Even though a quarter century had passed, it was the kind of intense period in Burne-Jones's life that was likely to stick in his mind. So intense, in fact, that when Burne-Jones had come upon someone introducing The Greek to his wife, he'd fainted dead away and gashed his forehead on the mantlepiece. Some said that the entire unpleasant affair had given Morris and Lady Burne-Jones even more reason to be simpatico.

Morris swung his stubby legs down off the settle, holding Ryon's card in his left hand and extending his right. Then he noticed that his hand was emerald green and lowered it, shrugging apologetically: "Blocking wallpaper." His voice was still as booming with over-enthusiasms as always. "Don't do much wall-paper these days, mostly designing books."

There was a third man by the fireplace, poised on one of the rush-seated, straight-backed wooden chairs that Morris enthusiasts swooned over and that a working sod would consider a damned silly alternative to an overstuffed monstrosity. He was a younger man, long and angular, with a rust-colored beard, jug ears and pointy, pale eyes. He seemed to be doing his damnedest to look Mephisthophelean, but he rather put Ryon in mind of an Irish Wire-haired Terrier, if there were such a breed.

Morris carried on with the introductions: "Mr. Henry Ryon, Sir Edward Burne-Jones, Mr. George Bernard Shaw."

"How do you do?"

"How do you do?"

"How do you do?"

No one, of course, answered the question. Ryon said: "It's a great privilege to meet you all," guessing that Mr. Bernard Shaw also considered himself famous for something or other. The point of the remark was to reinforce the notion that he'd never clapped eyes on any of them before. "I was hoping, Mr. Morris, that you might assist me with a favor, one that will only take a moment of your time.

"My editor, you see, has long been an admirer of the Pre-Raphaelite Brotherhood and The Arts and Crafts Movement. When he heard I had to travel to England on family business, he commissioned me to write a series of articles on some past elements of your circle that might be obscure to the general public. For instance, Anemone."

Morris blushed and huffed like a chuffed schoolboy. "Your editor certainly knows his stuff, I must say. All the way out in The Wild West, who'd've thought...? Not that I wasn't pleased with it at the time, but it was twenty years ago and early days. And it was an honest attempt to put fine design within the reach of the working class."

Ryon said: "Um, forgive me, sir, I don't quite follow you."

"The 'Anemone'—my first design for a machine-woven fabric."

"I was, um, referring to the Anemone *Group*, sir."

The roots of Morris's beard went pink. Mr. Bernard Shaw said lightly: "Vanity will out."

Morris guffawed, clapped his hands together and bellowed: "Did you engi-neer this, Shaw?"

Burne-Jones said softly, as he said all things, "Madeline Prue." His eyes were fixed on Ryon in a disconcerting manner.

Ryon said as blandly as possible: "I don't believe that's one of the names my editor gave me."

"He wouldn't. She's dead. She had an accident."

Burne-Jones's eyes stayed focused on Ryon, and Ryon could almost feel the portraitist's memory at work behind them. He could also feel his remittance income slipping down the drain. If he were recognized, he could try explaining the situation and plead with them to keep the secret. A secret would appeal to Morris's and Burne-Jones's sense of drama, but they were also hopelessly addicted to gossip. As for Mr. George Bernard Shaw, he looked about as trustworthy as the average medicine show doctor.

Burne-Jones's gaze held on Ryon an instant longer, and then gratifyingly slid away to take in the other two. He said: "Before *your* time, Shaw. But you must remember Mad Maddie Prue, Top. She was a stunner. Somehow a combination of peasant wench and pagan priestess. Tried to paint her once, but some types of female beauty don't translate in repose, at least in my hands.

"Despite all the Anemone performances I'd seen, it was only when I started the life sketches that I realized her head was too big for her body—but that hardly mattered. Even a Critic like you, Shaw, might've felt a little guilty after an Anemone performance. She always put her heart in it and then some."

"Why would that make me feel guilty?"

"I said it *might*. Because after an Anemone performance, one always felt like one were leaving with a stolen piece of Maddie Prue's soul in one's back pocket."

Ryon said quickly to Morris, before Burne-Jones's memory could dwell too long, "You see, sir, my editor wants me to try to trace down some of the people who once were figures in the movement but have since disappeared from the public eye. I thought perhaps your secretary's address book might point me the way to one or two of them, if you don't consider it an intrusion."

"Not at all. My secretary's working in my study this morning, it'll be on your right just before the front door. Tell him I said to furnish you any assistance you require."

"You're very kind. Well—"

"Not at all; fair trade for keeping the tale of my little Anemone faux pas to yourself. Not that Shaw won't have it bandied from here to Bloomsbury before sundown. If you're still in London on Sunday, Mr. Ryon, perhaps you'd care to come around to our regular evening meeting. I've converted the coach house to a lecture hall, and there's always a free supper for all comers."

"Served *after* the lecture," Bernard Shaw put in, "to ensure an audience."

"Not always," Burne-Jones drawled. "As I recall, Shaw, when the program was your piano duets we ate first, to ensure no one's appetite was spoilt."

Morris ignored the asides. "Your editor might find the subject of our meetings very interesting, as all men should. Shaw and I may not agree on how best to bring it about, but there's no disputing the basic principle of Socialism— that all citizens should share equally in the wealth of the nation."

Ryon refrained from asking how many citizens had shared equally in William Morris's wealth lately, or how much his house servants appreciated cooking and cleaning-up a free supper for all comers once a week. There was no point trying to talk reality to someone who'd come into eight hundred pounds a year the day he turned twenty-one. It would've been just as pointless to ask such questions of Harry Ryon-Chilton, back in the days when the only work he ever expected to have to do was finding ways to keep himself amused.

"I sometimes wonder," Morris went on in a voice that suddenly sounded almost drained of enthusiasm, "if I might not have done more good devoting my life to promoting socialism, and left art alone. The Firm was intended to brighten the lives of the poor and the middle classes, but so much of our work was done for the rich. I sometimes think our most lasting legacy will be Tiffany's of New York."

"Remember, Top," Burne-Jones said gently, "you did say long ago that since labor is so despised, happiness is only possible to artists and thieves."

"Did he, now?" said Bernard Shaw. "That's bordering on epigrammatic."

Ryon said: "Well, good of you to invite me to your meeting. Now I'd best be—"

But before Ryon could make his adieus, Burne-Jones interjected: "Are you sure, Mr. Ryon, we've never met before?"

"Quite sure, sir. I was only a child when my parents decided to emigrate."

Mr. Bernard Shaw put on an exaggerated brogue, "Faith, the English are so inbred they are constantly mistaking each other for each other."

Ryon silently and fervently blessed Mr. Bernard Shaw and his penchant for epigrams. But Burne-Jones wasn't thrown off the track. "When you were but a child…? I never would've thought. You have the manners of a gentleman about you...."

"There are gentlemen in North America, sir." All three of them laughed appreciatively, Burne-Jones the heartiest of all, and Ryon got out while the getting was good.

As Ryon started down the staircase, a woman started up it: a tall, stately woman with silvered, crinkly hair. Her ivory tower of a neck had grown a little wattled, and it seemed an effort to her to climb the stairs. But her long, thick eyebrows were still blue-black, her draughtsman's-dream of a jawline was still firm, and she was still the languorous Gypsy Queen who'd made every man from Henry James to Algernon Charles Swinburne grow a little short of breath when she entered the room.

Ryon shifted aside to let her have the bannister. Jane Morris nodded kindly at the stranger passing by and murmured: "Good morning." Ryon could only nod mutely in reply; he'd suddenly found it necessary to vice his teeth to hold back laughter.

Seeing Jane Morris had dredged up one of the few moments when Ryon could swear that Maddie Prue had been aware of him as more than an anonymous hanger-on, because she'd laughed so hard she had to be helped into a chair. She had chanced to overhear him remarking to one of the other young bucks: "If Morris spent less time blocking wallpaper and more time putting the blocks to Jane, he wouldn't have to worry about Rossetti."

As the echoes of Maddie Prue's full-throated laughter faded in his memory's ear, Ryon felt a little ashamed of himself and of her. Rossetti had long since drugged himself into an early death, and the Morrises and Burne-Joneses were growing old and frail. What business was it of anybody else's that Morris thought marrying Jane Burden meant he could frame her on the wall and forget about her, or that Rossetti was such an overbearing swine that everyone wondered whether his young wife's tragic overdose had been an accident? In the end, they had all put more beauty into the world than Henry J. Ryon was ever likely to. And they had made a revolution with their heresy that artists still had something to learn from life and nature, instead of only studying the classical techniques perfected by Raphael.

Ryon muttered apologetically to the passing wallpaper, "We were young," and then had second thoughts about the apology. Maddie wouldn't have found it funny if he'd just been making mock of some poor sod whose wife was boffing another man. What had made her laugh was that the people involved professed to be rarefied souls who were only moved by artistic passions or noble romance. If anyone had tried to paint that kind of pose on Maddie Prue, he would have found his brush stuck in an uncomfortable receptacle.

Ryon turned through the doorway into Morris's book-crammed study—bookcases even hanging from the ceiling. Morris's secretary seemed more than happy to pull his nose out of some dusty medieval manuscript and open a thick ledger of an address book. There was really only one address Ryon was looking for: Fergus and Audrey Doude.

"I'm afraid I can't give you any such address, sir. Mr. and Mrs. Doude, you see, have been living separately for some while now. It's proved rather an embarrassment to her in more ways than one. Mr. and Mrs. Doude, you see, always published as 'The Doudes,' so it was assumed they shared equally in the work. But after Mr. Doude removed himself to wherever he's removed himself to, her solo efforts made it abundantly clear that she'd rarely contributed much beyond the occasional snippets of decoration. I believe she still resides at their old address in Cambridge, and has turned the place into a boarding house. Sorry I couldn't be of more help, sir."

"It's more help than I've had from anyone in a long time."

As he left William Morris's home behind him, Ryon thought of the poem that had made Morris's literary reputation—*The Defense of Guinevere*, one of the recitations Maddie Prue used to stand and deliver. The poem went on through many verses of Guinevere presenting her defense to the court trying her for betraying the king. Just when it becomes clear that nothing she can say will prevent them from burning her at the stake, there is a distant bugle. The members of the court turn nervously to look out the windows toward the sound of approaching hoofbeats heralding the imminent arrival of the *real* defense of Guinevere—'Lancelot at good need.'

Ryon knew he was no Lancelot, and certainly too late to be of any good need to Maddie Prue. But at least he could find out the truth for her.

On his way back to The Brixton Road, Ryon bought an up-to-date *Bradshaw's Guide*. It took him awhile to reacquaint himself with the cramped columns of rail stations and arrival times, and Mr. Bradshaw's cabalistic system of asterisks, daggers and arrows. But it appeared that tomorrow's morning train for Cambridge left Paddington Station at 7:32.

Mr. Bradshaw's system wasn't all he had to adjust himself to. Without noticing the transformation, in the twenty years away he'd become a colonial, a Canadian—whatever that might be. He felt like a kind of younger foster brother of Imperial Britain; someone vestigially attached to the society he was traveling through but not really part of it. The difference was simple but insurmountable: unlike the people all around him, he did not carry the inborn conviction that he was, at the very least, a piece of solder in The Crown of Creation. Well, given the shape of the world at the end of this nineteenth century, who was to say that any true Englishman's inborn conviction wasn't entirely correct? "Cruel Britannia, Britannia waves the rules..."

IX

Forty-Fourth Street through the hotel's plexiglass door looked like a country boy's worst nightmare. Ryon paused before taking the plunge, and muttered a little nervously: "Hello New York; if I can fake it here I'll fake it anywhere." Then he pushed open the door and headed toward Times Square—the beating heart of the heart of the American Empire. As if half-a-continent's-worth of people crammed into one city wasn't enough to confuse him, there was the added fact of being a Canuck in Yankeeland. To the other people on this street, the country he came from was foreign but not foreign; the goofy kid brother of the Imperial U.S. of A. But one thing was definitely foreign. Everybody around him, even goggle-eyed tourists from darkest Ohio, carried in their DNA the certainty that the American Constitution was the most important thing that had ever happened anywhere, and they constituted part of it. And who could blame them, these days? He was the cop of Wahpeston, Manitoba; they were The Cops of The World.

Ryon found he had to make a conscious effort not to pay more than navigating attention to the hordes of other people on the sidewalk, or he'd get dizzy. It wasn't just New York; nowadays it took him a while to adjust when he went into any city.

Schubert Alley was constipated with theater-goers crowding in for the evening show. The better-heeled tourists were pouring out of Sardi's with their tickets in their hands and their wallets a few pounds lighter. Ryon was glad to see the Star Lite Deli was still in operation, where a man could get a custom-built sandwich and a few cans of beer to take back to his room at the end of the night.

In Times Square they were boarding up the Tkts Booth; the day-time hustlers were folding up their suitcases and the night-time hustlers were trotting out their wares. The ambient aroma of warm bagels and roasting chestnuts hadn't changed in twenty years. Maybe some of the bagels hadn't, either. Neither had the fact that ambling lackadaisically along the sidewalk could get you trampled from behind. But Ryon couldn't see any of the streetlamp signs he used to find so cheeringly unbureaucratic: "LITTERING IS UGLY AND STUPID SO DON'T DO IT!" And the kid break-dancing for quarters had his ghetto-blaster turned down low, looked clean-cut enough to be a Huxtable and was probably licenced by the city. All of Times Square seemed shinier and brighter than Ryon remembered, more polite. It was disappointing.

Something else that had changed was fashions, and Ryon laughed out loud when he realized how that was going to help him. Twenty years ago, the hair-cut he was sporting now would've pegged him a mile away as a cop or military. Today, he looked like a middle-aged man trying to appear hip.

The cop in his head reminded him that he wasn't walking through Times Square to take in the ambience, he was looking for something in particular. He got down to 42nd Street without finding it. On the corner of 42nd Street he stopped dead and gawked, then quickly pasted his back against a lamp post to keep his stunned self from getting ground-under by the perpetual stampede.

The all-night peep shows and clip joints had all been covered over with bright-colored construction hoarding, except for a lit-up, sandblasted wedding cake of a theater that used to be a sooty porn house. A five-foot Minnie Mouse was skipping along the sidewalk without any apparent worries about pimps and purse-snatchers. For a minute he thought he was Ryon In Wonderland. Then he remembered reading somewhere that Disney Corp. had bought the rights to develop 42nd Street.

Ryon's heart went out to the pickpockets, street-jivers and porn-hawkers. He felt their pain, or their embarrassment. Every officer of the Royal Canadian Mounted Police was in the same boat as they were. Ever since the Force signed the rights to licence its image over to Disney, you never knew what kind of wiseass comments you would have to endure from the guy you just pulled over for speeding.

Ryon caught something out of the corner of his eye, adjusted his focus and saw what he'd been looking for. There were two leather-jacketed police officers ambling along the sidewalk. Ryon moved to intercept them, calling: "Good evening, gentlemen," and reached his right hand inside his jacket.

One of the officers swung his nightstick up, the other quick-drew his sidearm, and both of them shouted: "Freeze!"

Ryon froze. He squeezed some saliva into his freeze-dried throat and said in the most unthreatening voice he could manage without squeaking: "I just want to show you something. May I take my hand out very slowly?"

The one pointing the gun at him squinted, then nodded, but didn't lower his revolver. It was no standard-issue, service sidearm—more like a .357 Magnum. American policemen got to carry their own choice of sidearms if they wanted to lay out the money for something with more punch than what came with the uniform. Ryon couldn't say for certain, since he'd never seen a .357 Magnum up close. At least not from this angle.

Ryon brought his hand out very slowly and held out his ID. The one with the nightstick took it, looked at it twice and then laughed: "He's a goddamn Mountie!"

The other one frowned, then gradually lowered his gun and holstered it. Pedestrians who'd flattened themselves on the sidewalk or ducked behind parked cars got up and went on about their business.

The officer who'd taken Ryon's ID handed it to his partner and said to Ryon: "Don't they teach you fucking anything in Mountie school? You coulda got your head blown off."

"Sorry. Where I come from, civilians don't carry handguns."

"Must be nice."

"Not *so* nice; means we can't shoot 'em. I'm just passing through on holiday and wondered if there was a bar around here where I could shoot the shit with some fellow officers."

"You almost got more than shit shot. Let's see… Probably your best bet around here is O'Halloran's, on Ninth and Forty-Fourth."

His partner said: "Hookers on Eighth, cops on Ninth. Handy."

Ryon said: "I think I'll settle for cops tonight. But first I'll have to go back to the hotel and change my shorts."

They laughed and ambled off along their rounds. Ryon called after them: "Officers…? Could I have my ID back, please?"

"Shit. Almost got away with it."

Ryon *did* have to back to his hotel, but not to change his shorts, just to pass by it on the shortest route to Fourty-fourth and Ninth. If he'd turned right instead of left when he'd stepped out of his hotel's front door, he would have stumbled across O'Halloran's within a block. But then he would have missed the free Adventureland land of staring down the barrel of a .357 Magnum, or whatever the hell it was.

He could see the O'Halloran's sign when he turned the corner, but he hesitated, leaning against a wall chewing his lip and staring at the sign. *You don't wanna try this, smartboy.* It had seemed like such a cakewalk plan when he'd thought it up while waiting for his leave to come through.

Into his mind's eye crept one of the black-and-white candid shots of Maddie, day-dreamy and twining a finger in her hair. It was a habit of hers. He could see her in color at a party, where she'd got so zoned-out she'd wound a strand so tight and tangled around a finger with a knobby ring on it that she was canvassing the room with her hand stuck to the side of her head, gigglingly begging if anyone happened to have a pair of scissors. When scissors finally came at her, she'd shrieked like a Monty Python victim: "No, the hair, the hair!"

Ryon wasn't sure if he was remembering or imagining, but it seemed to him it would've been just like her. He pushed off from the wall and started forward.

O'Halloran's turned out to be one of those down-home, New York taverns with a beautiful, oak bar that'd been propping up elbows since before Prohibition, and probably during. Ryon stood at the bar sussing the place out and drinking real Miller, brewed to be light and thin, not the watered-down Canadian beer they put in Miller cans back home. He knew he had to get enough alcohol in him to feel relaxed in a room with so many people in it, but not so much that he turned manic.

When he judged his level was about flotational, he waited for a lull in the noise of conversation and the juke box, then thumped his hand down on the bar a few times and called out: "Gentlemen and ladies—The Royal Canadian Mounted Police would like to buy a round for anyone in this establishment carrying a badge."

Within a very few minutes, Ryon was ensconced at a table with a dozen callous-knuckled New York cops who were happily singing along with what he swore to them was the RCMP marching song:

> *He's a lumberjack and he's okay,*
> *He sleeps all night and he works all day...*

Ryon raised his glass and said: "Might I propose a toast to the finest police force in the world: The Royal Canadian Mounted Police."

"I heard they'd turned into a Mickey Mouse outfit."

"That's Mickey *Moose*," Ryon corrected him. "But we still got tradition and pride. In fact it was a Mountie, Sir Sam Steele, founded the South African Police Force. That's something to be proud of."

The ranking officer at the table was a tall black woman named Lieutenant Sumter. Ryon amused the hell out of her by calling her *Lef*tenant. Once the general introductory bullshitting was out of the way, he got down to business. Although he made his speech to the general crew, he was really directing it to Lieutenant Sumter, at the far end of the table.

"I'm not just down here on a holiday. I'm looking into a case. But it's personal, not official, not yet. A woman I was acquainted with, American citizen, got killed in an accident sixteen years ago. A few months ago, someone in New York City sent me an anonymous tip that it wasn't an accident. It was only a hint, not enough to launch a formal investigation."

Ryon sipped his beer and tried to sound casual. "I know of a couple of people down here who might be able to tell me more about it, if I could find them. But I can't exactly march into the IRS or the Social Security Registry and ask them to track down an address for me. And by the time I've looked through every phone book in the New York Public Library, my leave'll be up. The people I'm trying to hunt up wouldn't have any criminal records, so far as I know, but there'd be parking tickets, driver's licence records…"

Ryon trailed off, since it was obvious he didn't have to spell out what he was asking for. A cone of silence had descended on the table, and everyone except Lieutenant Sumter had found something else to look at than their friendly foreign visitor. Ryon couldn't blame them for being pissed off that all this jolly buying of rounds and singing silly songs had just been a con to try to get something out of them, and something a long way from strictly legal. RCMP ID or not, without an official investigation he was just a private citizen asking these nice folks to smuggle him restricted information.

Lieutenant Sumter was looking at him like he'd just crapped on the table. She said suspiciously: "'Corporal…' They must have a different ranking system up in Canada. We don't have police corporals, but in our army a corporal'd be just one step up from a grunt."

"Same in the Force. We got different grades of constables, but yeah, a corporal's basically just one step up from a grunt cop."

"You pretty old to be just one step up from a grunt cop, ain't you?"

"That's for damned sure."

"You keep getting your ass into trouble or something?"

"Not really. Just the once that was worth noticing. As soon as they gave me my badge, I went AWOL for a year."

There was a quarter note rest, and then the entire table cracked up. Some of them were slapping their chair arms, some were struggling to breathe between guffaws, some were bellowing: "A *year?*" And the Crazy Canuck was their buddy again.

When the laughter died down, everybody was looking at Ryon like the M.C. had just waved him to the mike. He said to himself: *Didn't think of that, did you, smartboy? Now they want you to tell them what happened.*

He said: "Well, uh… Around the time I was graduating from the Depot, a friend of mine got killed in the line of duty. Myrna Melnick. We didn't go to the same High School together. Skipping classes didn't make much difference to Myrna—she could get straight A's standing on her head—but me… The plan was we were going to go into the Force together, but I got held back to boost up my academics."

A stubby detective with a mustache chortled: "Too bad. That would've been cosy—you and your girlfriend bunking in barracks." Ryon was sure the stubby guy was a detective, because he was wearing a rumpled suit and tie while most of the others at the table were in the sweatshirts and jeans you changed into out of uniform.

Ryon's fingers gripped the rim of the table while he decided how he was going to respond to what had come out from under the mustache. His first impulse was to turn the table over on top of the guy and stomp on it, but he thought maybe he should think about it for a second. While Ryon was considering his options, Lieutenant Sumter said to the detective: "You don't have to work so hard to be an asshole, Wilson, you were born that way."

Ryon said to the tabletop: "I said a *friend* of mine," then leaned back and tried to figure out how he was going to explain why he went over the wall all those years ago. He'd never tried to explain it to a tableful of strangers before. Hell, he'd never tried to explain it to anybody, except Lisette one night when he was too drunk to consider that she had better things to do than listen to him babble. He didn't want to try to explain it now—except now that they'd asked, his only other option was to tell them it was none of their fucking business and walk out.

He said: "So… Myrna got engaged before I did," then laughed. "That's what we call it when the Force accepts your application—you get engaged. Up until then, and the reason we skipped so much school, we played in a band together. Wasn't much of a band, except for Myrna's brother.

"We used to call him The Mystic Moron—'cause he could barely tie his own shoelaces but he could play a guitar like Elmore James on acid. Well, he could when he wasn't getting plugged into the wall socket at the local psychiatric institution. You see, he had this habit of every now and then he'd go a little catatonic and just sit for days staring at the TV getting messages from Venus. Made people nervous, so they'd call Emergency to come and take him away in handcuffs.

"One of those times, when they'd finished the shock treatments he had to teach himself to play guitar again. They'd accidentally burned out that part of his memory while they were at it. Shotgun therapy."

Ryon washed the sour taste out of his mouth, and then chortled. "But they couldn't burn out his sense of humor. The Mystic Moron, you see, was incapable of being responsible—except he was too responsible in one way. He hated the idea of unwanted kids, so even back in the 60's he always used safes—and The Mystic Moron got laid a lot. Then in the course of some sort of medical tests they found out he was sterile. He thought it was the funniest damn thing, all that money he'd spent on safes...

"Anyway, that was more or less the band—The Mystic Moron being a genius and me being barely competent and Myrna... Myrna just stood in the background and played bass. To this day I don't know if she really got off on the band, or just tagged along to look after her brother. That was Myrna—always in her brother's shadow, but also her brother's keeper. There'd always been just the two of them, living with their mother in a ratty little apartment.

"Well, I guess none of that matters, I just wanted to give you the general idea of, um... So anyway, Myrna had only been in the Force about a year, when she was out on night patrol and spotted a suspicious vehicle in a farmyard—white Lincoln Continental with out-of-province plates—looked like the vehicle described in a Canada-wide APB. She called for back-up and her corporal and a male constable responded and the corporal took charge..."

He told them the basic set-up, up to the point where Myrna was left alone like a spotlit sitting duck pointing her revolver at the shadow in the window. One of the New York cops bit out: "Pull the fucking trigger!"

"Well," Ryon shrugged, "it's The Policeman's Dilemma, eh? What if it's only a broomstick and you blow the guy away? Who knows what she was thinking—if she was thinking anything—might've been only a quarter of a second. Maybe she figured the suspect was smart enough to see that if he started raising a gun she'd blow his fucking head off. It takes a lot of years in uniform to learn that the guy on the other side of that door might not be just crazy but stupid."

Ryon swallowed some beer to moisten his throat and said: "Anyway, whatever she was thinking, the suspect didn't have to raise the shotgun to fire down at her. I was at Depot Division, polishing my boots for graduation, when I heard that phrase come over the radio…"

Someone further down the table murmured: "Officer Down."

"No," Ryon shook his head. "Not in the Force. Officer Down could be an officer in any old police department. When it's one of ours, we say Member Down. Like the Masons, or the Mouseketeers.

"I heard Member Down more than once that night. Myrna's corporal and the other constable both got shot-up pretty bad, .38 revolvers against a pump-action twelve gauge and a semi-automatic hunting rifle."

Ryon suddenly started laughing and had to subdue himself with Miller before he could tell them what the joke was. "But there was a bright side to the incident—or a not-very-bright side. The suspects got away to another farmhouse and it turned into a hostage situation. The suspects demanded that the hottest criminal lawyer in the province get brought in to negotiate for them.

"The suspects—wannabe Bonnie and Clyde—had killed a bank manager in another province and took his car. Excuse me, *allegedly* killed a bank manager—that one never came to trial. Because the brilliant deal they got the lawyer to cut for them was they'd surrender peaceably, on the condition they wouldn't be charged with any offenses from other jurisdictions. So the only charge they had to face was… murdering a police officer."

Other patrons in O'Halloran's craned their heads around to see why the off-duty cops around that table were rupturing themselves with laughter. When they'd laughed themselves out, some of them logically figured the story was over and started talking to each other about their own business. Not Lieutenant Sumter. Her large, brown lips stayed firmly pressed together, and her large, brown eyes stayed staring the length of the table at Ryon. She wouldn't be any fun at all in an interrogation room.

Lieutenant Sumter said: "So why'd you go over the wall?" and the other conversations petered out.

Ryon looked back at Lieutenant Sumter like he'd already explained that. She shook her head and said: "You and your friend both knew that was the chance you were taking when you pinned on a badge. What made you take yours off and go over the wall?"

Ryon exhaled, looked down at the table and said: "Well, you start to wonder what kind of an organization you're a Member of. The funeral was…" He had to slow down his breathing. The air in O'Halloran's had suddenly become very thick and oxygen-thin. "The picture on the front page of all the newspapers across the country, and went into all the scrapbooks, was Myrna's mother breaking down at the graveside and Myrna's brother holding her up. The caption on the picture read…'Constable Melnick's Mother and an Unidentified Man.'

"You see, while me and Myrna had been getting shorter-haired and straighter, The Mystic Moron had been getting longer-haired and weirder. So it just wouldn't do, you see, for the Force to let the public get the idea that any Royal Canadian Mounted Police Officer had any connection with any strange-looking, disreputable types."

Ryon pushed his back against the chair back, blinked at the ceiling and bit out: "'…and an unidentified man…' He was her goddamned brother, for Christ's sake."

The silence that settled over the table was very different from the one when they found out Ryon wanted something from them. Someone muttered: "Fuck." Ryon didn't know whether it meant: *Fuck, we listen for twenty minutes just to find out this asshole got himself all choked-up over some stupid fucking newspaper headline.* He should've got up and left way back when they got pissed off at him.

Lieutenant Sumter held her interrogator's gaze on him a moment longer, then drifted her eyes around the bar and said: "MacKormick's got a girlfriend in Records. She can trace down anybody on the Eastern Seaboard. Hey MacKormick, get your white ass over here!" She shifted her eyes back onto Ryon. "What was the name you were looking for…?"

"Doude. D-O-U-D-E."

"Well, that'll be easier 'n Johnson."

"Initial F. Or possibly listed under A."

Lieutenant Sumter had a kind of twisted look on her face that maybe was her version of a smile. Weird that eyes that big should be so difficult to read. She cocked her head, clucked her tongue and said: "May The Force be with you, Corporal."

X

THE 7:32 FROM Paddington Station to Cambridge departed and arrived precisely on schedule, naturally. In Cambridge, Ryon stepped down from the train before it had quite come to a halt. He walked briskly out of the station without pausing to ask directions. Cambridge wasn't that large a town, and he'd spent two years there not attending university. The final straw had been the barmaid in his rooms.

But the college spires and passing taverns brought back no memories, because he didn't see them. All he could see was that at the end of one of these picturesque, snow-covered lanes was someone who could finally tell him something concrete about the wisps and ghosts that had taken possession of his life.

In a peripheral sort of way, it did strike him as bizarre that he could remember the layout of the town of Cambridge but couldn't remember where he'd got the long scar on his chest—except that he knew it had happened sometime between when he was expelled from Cambridge and when he was expelled from Britain.

The house the Doudes had chosen was on the south-east edge of town, with a view of the Gog Magog Hills to break the flat, featureless fens in all other directions. Ryon sprang up the front steps and plied the doorknocker like pounding a spike.

The door was opened by a harried-looking choregirl. Ryon presented her with one of his cards and asked to see Mrs. Doude. The girl looked at the card confusedly, then shouted over her shoulder: "Mrs. Doude!"

Audrey Doude came out of an inner room wearing a faded day dress and a knit shawl. It was impossible to say whether any middle-aging white had crept into her hair in the years since Ryon last saw her, because her hair had always been the palest ash blonde, almost as pale as her skin. She was still as sepulchrally tall and straight-spined as ever, and she still carried a kind of hovering air about her. Someone had once referred to her and Fergus as: "The elf and the specter." She would've been a perfect, statuesque model for the Pre-Raphaelites, except that her shoulders tended to tighten forward and the only color in her was the olive of her eyes.

She glanced at the card the choregirl handed her and said: "Oh, a journalist," as though she were still accustomed to the daily attentions of the literary press.

Ryon had to fight the urge to grab her by her bony shoulders and shout: *What happened to Maddie Prue?* But this was England, not the backwoods of North America, so he said: "I wondered if I might trouble you, Mrs. Doude, to answer a few queries about your work?"

"I never promise to give answers, Mr. ..." She glanced at his calling card again. "...Ryon, until I hear the questions. I was just sitting down to a cup of tea. Would you care to join me?"

"Thank you. That's very kind of you."

He followed her into the sitting room, waited until the tea was poured and the choregirl nowhere in sight, then said: "My card doesn't tell the truth, exactly. I'm not a journalist, although the card does give the real goods about where I've come from and my name." It was highly unlikely that a woman who ran a boarding house would ever be chatting with the Ryon-Chiltons or anyone of their acquaintance.

Audrey Doude smoothed her skirt and said: "You had best explain yourself, Mr. Ryon."

"I was acquainted with you and Mr. Doude years ago, back in the days of Anemone."

"That long ago? Forgive me for not remembering you, but there were so many, um..."

"So many hangers-on. No need to fear offending me. The reason I came back to England is, someone sent me this..." He drew *Windflowers Gathered by The Doudes* out of his inner pocket and handed it to her across the tea tray.

"Oh dear, speaking of years ago... But it's still in pristine condition, though, isn't it?" She glanced at the flyleaf. "Would you like me to sign it for you?"

Ryon was taken aback by the *non sequitur*, but he said: "That would be very kind of you."

She fetched a pen and ink and inscribed the title page in an elegant, flowing hand that bore no resemblance to the workmanlike printing on the package Constable Ducharme had brought him. Then she handed the book back to him with a smile which assumed that the reason he'd come three thousand miles and crossed the ocean was to get his book signed.

He said somewhat dazedly: "Thank you." Then he blurted out: *"D'ja think her fell?"*

"Pardon me?"

"There is a poem in this book, *Fools All,* which suggests to me that either you or Mr. Doude, or both of you, believed that Madeline Prue's death wasn't accidental."

She looked utterly confused, so he opened the book to the poem—by now it didn't need a bookmark—and handed it back to her. She glanced through it and said: "I remember it now, but it was so long ago I honestly can't remember whether it was one of mine or one of Mr. Doude's; we worked so closely together. As for what it was intended to convey—the poet is not always in command of the muse. Sometimes we say things without realizing.

"I certainly recall having no overt reason to believe poor Maddie's death to have been anything but a very tragic accident. But if you were at all acquainted with Maddie, you must be aware that she would fling herself toward companions and situations which other, more cautious souls would tend to avoid. More than once I tried to advise her to be more wary, but never to any avail. It was all so long ago..."

"Did you send me this book?"

"Mr. Ryon, you told me I need not fear offending you, so allow me to remind you that I have not the vaguest recollection of ever having met you, much less that you were living in Many-toe... Manny-two..."

"Manitoba. It means 'Where the voice of God whispers in the waters,' or words to that effect. Forgive me for asking blunt-headed questions, Mrs. Doude, but this business of what might've happened to Maddie Prue has become extremely important to me. Could it have been Mr. Doude who sent me the book?"

"I neither know nor care what Mr. Doude may or may not have done at any point during the past two years. I have no idea even where he's living, or if."

"Ah. Well... Do you have any idea where any of the other old members of Anemone might be living today?"

"Oh, dear. So long ago... I have an album of photographs, perhaps that will refresh my memory." She fetched out a velvet-covered, lock-clasped, fat book with cardboard pages, and beckoned Ryon to sit beside her on the settee so they could leaf through it together. She had to snug her leg against his to open the album out across both their laps.

Within the cardboard page-frames were photographs of Anemone in theatrical costumes or street clothes, although with Maddie it was sometimes hard to tell the difference. There was Anemone posed with William and Jane Morris, with Swinburne, with the American Whistler…

Ryon found it more than a bit disconcerting to see the misty figure who'd been haunting his dreams suddenly laid out on photographic paper in front of him. Even in sepia or black and white, she looked exactly as his long-stored memories portrayed her: stubby nose, high cheekbones giving contours to a wide, round face, broad hips and shoulders for her height, eyes that could look roguish or basilisk-direct. Seeing her frozen in an instant of time, instead of moving fluidly through his dreams and memories, he could see that Ned Burne-Jones had been right—her head was out of proportion with her body. Burne-Jones had also been right that it didn't matter a pinch of coonshit.

Ryon suspected it must be just his own predilection that made it seem as though everyone else in the photographs was background. Or perhaps it was simply the fact that she favored light-colored clothing while the others' were mostly dark. But no, when he looked closer there was a genuine difference that went beyond the fact that she knew which tones would stand out in a photograph. Everyone else looked at the camera; she looked through it at the people on the other side.

Audrey Doude gently skated a fingertip along Maddie Prue's photographic outline and sighed: "Poor, dear Maddie." Ryon wondered just how 'dear' Maddie had been back in the days when Audrey Doude would disappear into the wallpaper whenever Maddie Prue came through the door.

Audrey Doude pointed out a recurring figure in the photographs: a gnome-like, prematurely balding little man with wire-rimmed spectacles. She said: "The last correspondence I had with him was years ago, but I can't imagine him ever changing residence." She jotted down an address in the southwest of London. The post mark on the parcel had been London SW.

Ryon noticed another recurring figure in the photographs: an extremely tall, spidery-looking man who always seemed to be standing possessively close to Maddie Prue. Like the gnome, the elegant spider-man seemed very distantly familiar, but Ryon had never paid much attention to the individual members of Anemone except Maddie Prue and Fergus Doude.

Ryon said: "Who's that, the tall man?"

"Oh, Delaney. Jack Delaney. A good musical sense, but not a first-rate mind."

"He and Maddie Prue seem close."

"Oh, they were. Extremely close."

"They were lovers?"

"Oh dear," Audrey Doude laughed. "If you start tracing down *that* list you'll never get back to Many-toba. Some wag remarked that the crowd who filled the church at Maddie's funeral was entirely composed of her immediate family and old lovers." Her *bon mot*-sharing suddenly turned apologetic. "Oh dear, were you…?"

"I'd emigrated several years before her funeral."

"That long ago? Then how ever did you know where to find me?"

"From William Morris's address book. I told him I was a journalist."

"Hmm. How is Janey?"

"I only passed her on the staircase. She looked relatively well."

"I hope so. When one thinks of it, it's small wonder that so many of the men of that circle were smitten with Maddie. They seemed to have a fascination with women from coarse backgrounds; almost an instinctive urge for an infusion of new, more vital blood. Morris's family found it hard enough to live with the fiction that Janey's father ran a livery stable; they would've shriveled up in mortification if they'd known he was merely a groom."

She nodded to herself. "And then there was Rossetti's Lizzie Siddal. 'The Sid,' they called her. Poor Lizzie, floating for hours on end in a cold, tin bathtub so Millais could paint her as Ophelia."

Mrs. Doude turned back to her guest. "Few people are aware that it was Janey's fingers, actually, that were the foundation of The Firm—turning Morris's sketched designs into beautiful embroidery that one could hold and feel. In the early days, as she told me, she was in it up to the elbows, helping them paint stars across the ceilings… But then, once The Firm became established, it became just The Lads, and they forgot that Janey'd ever been anything but an object to capture on canvas."

"Was it like that with Anemone, that once it was a going concern, Mr. Doude and the lads—?"

"Oh dear me, no. For one thing, Maddie never would've stood for it. She either would've boxed their ears or left them cold. Hm, but then she did leave them cold, didn't she? But, for another thing, I believe in giving the devil his due, and Mr. Doude was never one to ignore the contributions of a woman. Any woman."

"Ah. Well… this Delaney, the tall man, do you know where I might find him?"

"I haven't heard a word from him or of him since Anemone disbanded But, believe me, Mr. Ryon, if you're looking to discover anything other than the business hours of the nearest tavern, there is no point hunting up Jack Delaney."

She turned the page. The next photograph was a print of Lewis Carroll's famous portrait of Rossetti looking like an over-ripe, self-satisfied mesmerist. Ryon whiffed an opportunity to make Audrey Doude more inclined to help him, given what she'd said about Jane Morris and 'The Lads'. He said: "I've often thought that what made Rossetti so devilish petulant was that his sister was a better poet than he was." It wasn't just a ploy, he *had* often thought that.

"Not many literary critics would agree with that assessment."

"Then they haven't read *Up Hill*."

Audrey Doude condescended to smile. She said: "Well, regardless of critical assessments, Christina was better rewarded than her brother."

"How so?"

"She's still alive."

Whether because of Ryon's ploy, or because Audrey Doude's memory had tripped over something, she ceased turning the pages one by one and flipped toward the back of the album. She tapped the photograph she'd turned to and said: "Here is someone who could tell you a great deal more about poor Maddie than ever I could."

Ryon leaned forward to look. It was a solo picture of a woman who hadn't been in any of the other photographs. In the days when Ryon had been haunting the salons where Anemone performed, he would've called it a picture of an old woman. Now she looked to him to be in a very healthy and robust middle age, disdaining jewelry or rouge to distract the eye from the deep laugh lines.

Audrey Doude said softly: "Celina Rushton… She led The Circle. We were mostly women, but a few men as well. Fergus—Mr. Doude—was a regular attendant. We were searching for the source, following the chain back through time…"

"Guinevere to Venus to Ishtar; The Bacchantes…"

"Why Mr. Ryon, you surprise me."

"I had a great deal of time to re-read Anemone's books on the crossing. Pretty bloodthirsty stuff here and there."

The thin, pale lips drew tighter and thinner and the olive eyes fixed him with a hooded glare. She said coldly: "Blood thirsty."

Brilliant move, cleverlad, now you've gone and turned her against you for the sake of a flip remark. "Well, um, you must have expected, Mrs. Doude, that subject matter that powerful would have a chilling effect on the reader. I've tried to absorb what Anemone was trying to say to the best of my abilities, and intend to keep on trying."

"Well, then you no doubt understand that the subject is not one for idle chit-chat. Miss Rushton is whom you should approach. She lives in seclusion now, but is not averse to visitors."

As Audrey Doude jotted down the address, the choregirl appeared in the doorway and said: "Mrs. Doude, ma'am…? Shouldn't we be starting in the kitchen soon…?"

"Of course. You see, Mr. Ryon, if one is to earn one's bread providing room and board, one must provide the board. And hiring a cook would rather defeat the purpose."

"Of course, Mrs. Doude—I shouldn't have taken so much of your time. But if I might ask one more question: who was the anonymous donor who contributed to the publication of Maddie Prue's posthumous book?"

"I can't say. Because I don't know. All I can tell you is that without his, or her, generosity, all of Maddie's bereaved friends' pooled resources would not have come close to paying the printer. We all of us made the fatal mistake, you see, of pursuing the arts without first inheriting wealth. I'll see you to the door."

"No need. I can see myself out."

"Mr. Ryon, I am only poor in money, not manners."

When they got to the door, Audrey Doude said: "Do you know why we chose the name Anemone, Mr. Ryon?"

"For the flower, I suppose. Just like the title of your book—your and Mr. Doude's book. They call anemones windflowers, don't they—for some reason or other."

"More to the point is why they call them anemones. The anemone is not just any flower. Anemone means 'the blood of Adonis'. In Asia Minor, you see, where Venus and Adonis lived—or Ishtar and Tammuz in earlier times—

there is a tiny, purple-red flower which covers the riverbanks at the same time of year when the beautiful hunter is said to have met his death. That time of year is also the rainy season, and the rains wash the carpet of flowers down into the rivers and thus into the sea. A stain of red spreads for miles out into the blue Mediterranean.

"A pleasure to have made your acquaintance, Mr. Ryon."

XI

THE U-DRIVE SARDINE CAN putted out of Cambridge onto the Massachusetts turnpike and Ryon pointed its nose back toward Manhattan. Once he'd managed to Merge without merging with any of the other eight billion vehicles, he put his eyes, hands and feet on Automatic Pilot and switched on the cassette deck.

The cut that came out was one of Audrey Doude and Maddie Prue's duets, honky-tonking *Silver Threads and Golden Needles*. Maddie had generously let Audrey take the verses and only came in on the chorus.

Listening to it this time, Ryon wondered whether Maddie was being generous or wicked. It reminded him of the "favor" Mick Jagger did Carly Simon by singing back-up on the last chorus of *You're So Vain*. Maybe Old Liver-Lips had intended it as a favor, but the end result was that Carly Simon got undercut by that buzz-saw voice made for slicing through the World's Greatest Raucous-Roll Band. Audrey Doude's voice sounded like it was firing on all cylinders, until Maddie Prue's pulled up beside it and idled.

It also seemed to Ryon that Maddie was putting a strange twist on the lyrics, leaning just a bit on: "Silver threads and golden *needles...*" And with another feather-light nudge of emphasis on a syllable, she made you wonder just exactly what was meant by: "You can't buy my love with money, for I never was that *kind*."

The next cut was an Anemone cover of an odd little Donovan song—as if they all weren't a little odd—called *Guinevere*. It put Ryon back in mind of Audrey Doude's weird talk of "The Circle." He had a ballpark notion of what The Circle's search had been about. Robert Graves had called it The White Goddess. A pile of poetical-mystical hoo-ha, nowadays grown into a pile of New Age feminist hoo-ha. The original Trinity, The Triple Goddess: mother, lover and killer; or maiden, mother and crone; or birth, life and death, or whatever way somebody wanted to define the indefinable. The White Lady.

A fragment floated up from the depths of Ryon's stagnant memory well and hooked onto him. It was a footnote he'd read, from back in the days when he used to read books with footnotes. Guinevere's name came from a phrase in one of those ancient Celtic languages: *gwynny-fer*. The White Lady.

Ryon felt a tingling at the back of his neck. He shook it off, snarled at the tape deck and snapped the radio on instead. This was getting more than ridiculous. He was just going through some sort of stupid mid-life crisis. Only instead of buying a red sports car he was running around chasing some woman who fell off a cliff sixteen years ago, and getting himself all caught up in crazy-making nonsense about old myths and moonlight.

He pushed all that stuff away and focused his attention on the highway and the music coming out of the radio. *New* music, not stuff with mold growing off it. Digging into moldy, old things wasn't going to get anybody anywhere but infected. What he should do was drive to the hotel to pick up his bag and pay his tab, drop the U-drive at the airport and take the first flight home from his middle-age-crazy wild goose chase.

The song on the radio was a female singer in front of a stripped-down electric band. Ryon didn't listen to enough new stuff to recognize the band, but it was probably one of those acts that was making magazines and trend-groupies cream their jeans about rock'n roll women being a 1990's invention. Like Hell. Maddie Prue had been doing that twenty years ago and no one had made a big deal about it—it was just Maddie Prue doing what Maddie Prue did.

Whoever the singer on the radio was, the kid had a hell of a voice. But the voice was all covered with Attitude. She couldn't just shut up and sing, she had to keep pointing to "look at how tough I am." When Maddie Prue sang tough, it was naked: just the facts, ma'am.

Ryon told himself to stop being an old fart. It was hardly fair to use an old pro like Maddie Prue as a yardstick against this kid, who would probably get better given time...

Then it hit him that the singer on all the cassette tapes he'd brought in his suitcase had been pretty much the same age as this kid.

He got a choking sensation, saw a rest stop up ahead and pulled in. He got out of the car, slammed the door and started kicking it. When he'd kicked it enough times, he propped his hands against the roof rim and breathed himself out.

Maddie Prue hadn't been given time. It wasn't right. It just wasn't fucking right.

He muttered: "Maintain The Right, Corporal," and started to climb back in. Then he realized there was applause coming from behind him. He turned to look. A family of tourists was standing around a rental car the same make as his. He waved at them and turned the key.

At the U-Drive, Ryon retrieved his flashlight from under the driver's seat and tucked it into his overnight bag. The woman behind the counter said: "Any problems, sir?"

"No. There's a few dents in the driver's door. Somebody whanged it in a parking lot." Which, strictly speaking, was exactly what had happened.

"We'll add the repairs to your Visa bill, sir."

"No you won't. I'm one of the suckers who went for the extra insurance scam."

"You didn't read the paragraph about the five hundred deductible."

Ryon sighed wearily. She obviously didn't know about the Law of Bullshit Leeway. If a citizen isn't telling you the entire truth, but is lying within the rules, you let it ride. He said: "Well, I've got my copy of the contract, you got yours. Bill me what you want and if it isn't airtight legal you'll hear about it."

Back at his hotel, he had a late supper but only ate half of it. American restaurants had a habit of piling enough on a plate to fill all the basic food groups for a family of four. Even more so in New York.

He did have to admit, though, that one thing he appreciated about the concrete anthill was being able to get whatever he wanted to eat and drink at any time of night. But there was a little place in Wahpeston, Manitoba where he could do that, too. It was called home.

He had no doubt that Lisette was taking care of the place and the critters better than he could. On impulse, he bought a postcard in the lobby and wrote on the back: "Having a time." Good bet Lisette had never got a postcard from New York City before.

It took him a while to get to sleep, wondering whether the guy whose address Audrey Doude had written down for him was the one who'd sent the tape. In his dreams, he wandered up to the front row of a packed concert hall where Anemone was playing. Elfish Fergus Doude was turning a medieval ballad into feedbacked Stratocaster riffs. The short-sighted hobbit that Ryon was going to try to hunt up tomorrow was walloping a bodhran. The Bodice-Ripper pirate Jack Delaney was prowling the stage with an electric fiddle.

And Maddie Prue was standing in front of two mikes with an acoustic twelve-string.

Ryon had noticed before that you could tell just from a snapshot whether someone knew what they were doing with an acoustic guitar, by the way they were holding it. Maddie was definitely not just some singer who could chord along.

Then her guitar was gone and she was only singing: arms out from her sides, eyes closed, sweat gluing her hair to her forehead, ribcage swelling and contracting like a bagpipe bellows. Her breasts seemed like part of her resonating chamber. As always, there were probably some experts in the audience who would write about how she was performing the song; as always, the true fact was that the song was performing her.

She stepped back from the mike and slid off the stage to flop down on the empty seat beside Ryon's. She said to him: "So, what do you think?"

"Oh! It, uh… Sounds real good, like always."

"That's not what I meant, but thank you." The audience and the band were gone. She stood up and said: "Let's go for a walk."

It was summer outside the hall. She was wearing a Chinese silk jacket and wrinkled old jeans that fit her like a surgical glove. She fingered the jacket and chuckled: "I had a Chinese lover once—an hour later I was horny again. Smile, Ryon, you great goof, that was supposed to be at least a *little* funny. Cracked 'em up at The Village Gate."

She slipped her hand in his—small and soft-palmed, but strong enough to barre chord an acoustic twelve-string all night long—and they walked over the green hills, not saying much. After a while she let go of his hand and turned to face him—smoky blue eyes and pumpkin-colored hair. She said: "Everybody else has gone. You won't give up on me…?"

He shook his head. She raised her hands to his neck, pulled his head down and kissed him. If he'd still been only as old as she got to be, he would've said her lips were experienced and mature; now they felt achingly young and tender—*apocalips*. She let go of him and stepped back. She looked squarely at him and said: "You might wish you had," as a sickle-shaped moon rose over her shoulder.

A herd of people were suddenly milling around them, elbowing each other out of the way to get where they were going. He lost her in the crowd.

In the morning Ryon set off armed with his subway map. Shreds of the night stayed with him. But he didn't get too spooked about the fact that the woman in his dreams was becoming more real to him than the people brushing past him in daylight. Because Carl Jung had a logical explanation. Crazy Carl had written that it was fairly common for the subconscious mind to fasten upon a specific human figure to incarnate the dreamer's creative side. In a male dreamer the figure tended to be female, which Carl had christened the *anima*, while women tended to dream of an *animus*. Carl had assured his readers that it was a harmless enough phenomenon—as long as you didn't get the silly idea that your anima really was that happily-married bank teller you used to date in high school.

The one flaw in that logical explanation, though, was that Ryon knew damned well he didn't have a creative side. Except when it came to creating idiot theories about hidden messages in old art-rock albums.

When Audrey Doude had written down the last known address for Anemone's token hobbit—"Philip Norman, but everybody called him Flip"—she hadn't written down a phone number. The phone book had shown no listing for a "Norman" at that address. Maybe Flip had an unlisted number. Or maybe Flip was long gone.

The address made an unlisted number not likely. It was on some street called Stuyvesant Oval, which the map placed down around Avenue A and Avenue B and all. People in Alphabet City didn't go in for extra expenses like unlisted phone numbers. Maybe the neighborhood had gone up-scale in twenty years.

It hadn't, if the walk from the subway stop was anything to go by. But then, there didn't seem to be a sidewalk in Manhattan these days that wasn't home to a few dozen of the severely fucked-over. The Armani suits and stretch limousines swam and wove around the derelicts like weaving around lumps in the pavement. The imperial city of the world's last standing empire at the end of the millennium.

The street called Stuyvesant Oval took Ryon by surprise. For one thing, it wasn't a street at all, but a kind of park with identical, low-rise apartment buildings dotted around it. For another thing, everything looked neat and clean—well, clean for New York City—and instead of drug dealers patrolling the walkways, there were private cops putting along on little scooters. But the tenants bustling in and out of the apartment blocks didn't look particularly wealthy.

Ryon found Building #32, and there on one of the mailboxes was "P. Norman". He had to press the intercom button twice before a tinny voice came out: "Yeah?"

"Flip?"

"Who are you?"

"My name's Ryon. I—"

"I don't know any Ryon," and the intercom went dead. Ryon pressed the buzzer again and got no response.

A leather-coated woman came in lugging several shopping bags, and struggled to juggle the bags and her key to unlock the security door. Ryon said: "Let me help you, ma'am," and reached to hold one of her bags. She looked him up and down before letting him take it.

She propped the door open, took her bag back and said: "Thank you." But when he tried to follow her into the lobby, she blocked the doorway and said: "Let me see your key."

He considered showing her his ID, but she'd probably be even more suspicious of some guy claiming to be a Mountie. So he said: "You know Flip Norman? Little guy with big glasses, lives in apartment C?" She didn't nod or shake her head. "I haven't been in the city in years, and he won't believe it's me until he sees me. So, I could stand in the foyer all day and hope he comes out sometime, or I could go knock on his door."

She squinted at him carefully, then smiled: "I think sometimes Flip wouldn't be sure his own mother isn't an acid flashback," and let him in.

There was no answer when Ryon knocked at apartment C. But he could hear soft, scuffing noises inside, and got the feeling he was being peered at through the fish-eye. He said to the door: "Flip? My name's Ryon, I used to hang out with Anemone in the old days," which was more than a bit of an exaggeration.

A flat voice came through the door: "I don't remember any Ryon."

"Do you remember trying to put a pick-up on a bagpipe chanter?" There was a pause, then the deadbolts clicked back and a hand beckoned Ryon inside.

It was a small, studio apartment furnished with a bed, a worktable and several dozen acoustic instruments. Flip Norman's moon face had grown more puckered since the band pictures were taken. But he still had as much hair as he'd had when he was twenty-five, which wasn't much.

As Flip stumped to the table and picked up a joint and an antique lighter, Ryon said: "Audrey Doude told me where to find you. She said it was an old address but you probably hadn't moved."

Flip seemed to forget the joint and lighter in his hands. "Move? Why would I wanna move? Best fucking apartments in New York City. One of the first housing projects, but not like what they call 'Projects' today. Built in the forties by an insurance company to house employees. Rent-controlled and security like Fort Knox. I had an aunt used to work in the rental office who scammed me in, and they pay me to do a bit of maintenance work. Good gig." He noticed the joint again, lit it, sucked in a toke and offered it to Ryon.

"No, thanks. I gave it up when I got my badge."

Flip choked and his eyes bugged out against his glasses. Then he exhaled, coughing laughter, and said: "You really had me going there. I *should* remember you. So, how's old Audrey?"

"Seems to be getting by. Seems a little strange."

"Audrey was always a little strange."

"There's something a lot stranger. I got something in the mail a while ago…" Ryon glanced at the window, but kept the corner of his eye on Flip Norman to see if he twitched, "that said Maddie Prue's death maybe wasn't an accident."

Flip just twitchlessly breathed out his latest toke and murmured: "Maddie. Huh. Old Maddie. That was a fuck of a long time ago."

"There's no statute of limitations on murder."

"Fuck, you really *are* a cop."

"Yeah, but don't worry, I'm a long way out of my jurisdiction. This is personal. Did you have any suspicions at the time about the way she died?"

"Suspicions?" Flip licked his stubby fingers and snuffed out the joint. "Man, for the longest time I thought it wasn't even her. I thought maybe she wanted to disappear, and saw her chance when somebody else slipped off that cliff. The way they found the body, it could've been anybody about her same size and hair color."

"'The way they found the body'…?"

"Oh. I guess they didn't put much details in the papers. Just lucky for her family she wasn't a big enough star for the tabloids to be interested. And in those days the fucking tabloids weren't all over everything that fucking moves."

"'The way they found the body'…?"

"Well, for one thing, the body had been in that tidal pool for a week or so. For another, there were no clothes or jewelry to identify her."

"She was naked?"

"Oh, that was nothing to think twice about. Maddie's idea of a good time was getting naked and wandering around the woods at night, dancing around a bonfire in nothing but war paint. Why do you think she packed up and bought that place in Carmel? Freeze her tits off in upstate New York."

"They must've done an autopsy, finding a naked female corpse at the bottom of a cliff…"

"Yeah, I guess they did an autopsy, for cause of death and all. But I don't know if they went to all the trouble of, like, checking dental records—or even if they could. That body bounced off a lot of rocks on the way down.

"Nobody questioned it was Maddie. Nobody but a comic-book-brained idiot like me would think it was maybe just one of Maddie's crazy friends at the bottom of that cliff, and someday I'd get a phone call with this funny Scotch accent on the other end saying: 'Guess who?' I guess it's about time I stopped expecting the phone to ring—hell, I don't even have a fucking phone—after thirteen years."

"Sixteen."

"Sixteen? Yeah, I guess you're right."

"Do you remember anyone you thought might want to kill her?" Although the odds didn't seem high on Flip Norman even remembering his date of birth.

"Hell, everybody wanted to kill her at one time or another. Maddie could sometimes be a little…"

"Self-centered?"

"You don't go picking up a microphone in front of twenty thousand people without being a little self-centered. She was a fucking genius, and they can be hard to take. She wasn't just ruthless, her and Ruth weren't ever even introduced.

"People got used to it with Maddie, or they cleared out. She had to defend herself. Everybody wanted a piece of her. Literally. It just got worse when the major labels started nosing around. Those people, man, they don't just take no prisoners, they shoot the wounded."

"Isn't that, uh, the same thing? Take no prisoners; shoot the wounded…"

Flip blinked at him. "I mean they shoot their *own* wounded, man. I thought we were better off sticking with the comfy little record company we started with; nothing flashy, but solid. But Maddie and Fergus, they said: 'If you get an offer from the big leagues, you either take it or quit playing the game.'"

"And what'd Delaney say?"

"Delaney?"

It seemed to Ryon that it wasn't Flip's memory that had gone evasive. "Jack Delaney. He was in the band as long as anybody. He must've had an opinion."

"Well, uh, I don't remember him saying anything about it. But he must've thought it was a good idea, 'cause Maddie said it was a good idea."

"You mean he always went along with her, or she went along with him?" Flip didn't appear to get the distinction, or pretended not to. "From what I can remember of the two of them," Ryon lied—he could barely remember Delaney at all, "and from the old band pictures, Jack Delaney had her sewn up pretty tight."

"Yeah, well, Spider Jack was her… security. She needed all the security she could get. Didn't have any of her own, except *in*. People catching glimpses figured she was this heavy-duty mama, but anybody that knew her knew she didn't have any self-confidence at all—except when she was singing. And then, when the song was over…" One of Flip's synapses appeared to misfire, and he said intently: "Did you ever front a band?"

"Not really, just high school stuff."

"I did a few times, with Anemone—Maddie figured we all should have our little showpiece. I sure didn't like it. Up front ain't the same as playing side. You can't think about what you're doing. Self-consciousness'll kill you, man. I mean, a little corner of your mind is keeping track of whether you're staying in time and in key, but the rest of you is just putting out.

"So you come to the end of the song and you really don't have a fucking clue what you've just done, only that you just did it in front of two thousand people. And the more power you put out, the more vulnerable you make yourself. Maddie put out power like Con Edison."

Ryon was leaning in the doorway of a green-room that'd seen too many parties. Applause was still echoing from the hall, and the kid from Canada was waiting to do his bit as part-time roadie. The members of Anemone were flopped on the tattered couch or sprawled in corners. All except Maddie Prue, who was standing in front of them screaming: "A wa-wa? A fucking wa-wa guitar in *The Wild Mountain Thyme?*"

Fergus Doude said: "Come on, Maddie, we do that all the time, mixing in instruments nobody'd figure would fit until you try it."

"Oh sure, we do that all the time—in practice or in the studio. But not on the fucking stage!" She was flailing her arms around and the split of red wine in her hand was spattering in all directions.

Fergus Doude said: "Me and the boys tried it out this afternoon and it seemed to work."

"You and the boys?" Now she was crying and roaring at the same time. "You and the sodding boys aren't the ones standing up front with your tits hanging out, trying to sing about the purple heather while some fucking monkey-ass wa-wa guitar is making Donald Duck sounds all around you!"

She fired the bottle in their general direction and ran out of the room. The bottle went through the drywall and hung there, gurgling its last drops down onto the couch. The rest of the band stayed where they were, shrugging or looking at the ceiling. Ryon waited a minute to see if anyone was going to do something, then took another split out of the case, uncorked it and carried it to her dressing room door.

He was going to knock, but he could hear her sobbing inside, so he just opened the door a crack and peeked in. She was hunkered with her feet up on the chair and her head on her knees, shivering and snorting and hissing: "Fuckers!"

He stepped in and carefully set the bottle down on the make-up table in front of her. She had one hand clamped across her eyes, so probably didn't even know he was there. He raised his hand toward her shoulder, then hesitated. His hand hung there a moment, then closed on air and lowered itself again. It was none of his business. He closed the door softly on his way out.

An Economy-Size owl was staring at him curiously. Ryon blinked, and the owl was just Flip Norman with his head cocked and his coke-bottle lenses catching the light. Ryon said: "Uh…"

Flip said: "Where'd you go, man?"

"Oh, just trying to piece things together."

"Ain't we all?"

Come on, smartboy, get back on the case. "Do you know, uh, do you know where Spider Jack is now? Maybe he knows some things you didn't know about."

"Fuck, man, you really got a bad case of Maddie, don't you?"

"Yeah, I do."

"Well, last I heard of Spider Jack he was in San Francisco. Wife and kids. Had a gig as houseband in a place with a funny name. Green... uh, yeah, Green Onions. Might be still there. These days, you got a gig you hang onto it."

"What about Fergus Doude?"

"Audrey couldn't tell you?"

"No."

"You got me, then. Last I seen Fergus was before he walked on Audrey. You could try his agent or his record company."

"They told me if I wanted to send him a fan letter they'd forward it, maybe. Um... Were you in on this 'Circle' that Audrey and Maddie and Fergus were tied up with?"

"Shit, man, is Audrey still talking about that shit? Naw, I never got into it—just enough to see that what they were trying to do was nuts. I told them: 'You can't find an explanation for this stuff, it's like trying to nail down mercury.' They said: 'You do the thinking, Butch, that's what you're good at.'"

Ryon tried to think of something else to ask. He only had about eight million questions left hanging, but it seemed he'd pumped Flip Norman dry. It also seemed pretty obvious that Flip wasn't the one who'd sent the tape. Or if he had, and his goofy innocence was just an act, it was too good an act to trip up without hard evidence. So Ryon just said: "Thanks. I appreciate you letting me pick your brains."

"Not much left to pick, is there? Wasn't much to start with, unless somebody had a cracked fretboard or the piano went out of tune. Hey, no sweat, man, I don't get much chance to shoot the shit about those days." Flip paused and then asked a question he tried to make sound casual. But to Ryon it sounded something like a plea. "Did you, uh, did you really hang out with the band?"

"No, not really. I carried a couple of amps once or twice. Audrey couldn't remember me, either."

"Huh. You really think somebody snuffed Maddie?"

"I don't know. But I do know there's something pretty fucking strange about the whole deal."

"Well, if you do find her, I mean if it wasn't her they pulled out of that tide pool... Tell her Flip says 'How's it going?'"

Ryon was reaching for the door handle when he remembered a question he should've asked Audrey Doude; the first question out of Homicide 101. He turned back into the room. "Do you know who inherited Maddie's estate? She must've left a lot of money."

Flip cackled. *"Money? Maddie?* You gotta be nuts! I'd be surprised if she left anything but debts. She was pretty slackadaisical about the business end of the music business. The first good paying gig we got, she walked home handing out hundred dollar bills to panhandlers. She was just a baby." The puckered eyes behind the glass misted over and focused on something far away from Ryon. "Crazy baby…"

Fractured fragments were floating back whether Ryon wanted them to or not. He got out of the subway and back into his hotel room as quickly as possible, locked the door, grabbed a can of Miller out of the sink, flopped onto the padded chair and held onto the arms as he reversed down memory lane.

He was walking along a sidewalk in Greenwich Village, casually ogling the hippie chicks and smoking a joint. It was the only dope he had on him, so if a cop happened to catch a whiff of it he could just swallow it. The pint of Southern Comfort in his jacket pocket wasn't going to get him in the same trouble it would back in the land where carrying an unsealed liquor bottle was as scandalous as carrying a handgun.

The Village was a disappointment. The corner of Bleecker and MacDougal—featured in so many Downtown Folk albums he'd worn the grooves off of in Junior High—was now a family steakhouse and some bland office storefront.

"Hey, man!" Ryon looked around and a blonde chick in wire-rimmed sunglasses handed him a piece of purple paper. It was a print-shop xerox folded over to pretend to be a pamphlet, advertising a concert tonight in a deconsecrated church around the corner by a band called Anemone. Two dollars at the door.

At two bucks a ticket they couldn't be much of a band. But even camped out in a rooming house and living on bacon and eggs at Chock Full o' Nuts, New York City ate up money like candy. He'd only been in New York for two weeks, lost in the crowds, which was exactly what he wanted to be. But that was long enough to learn that if he got a chance to get distracted for an evening for only two bucks, take it. He had $5,637.00 Canadian in his knapsack in a locker at the Port Authority—last year's summer wages and what he'd squirreled away from his pay at Depot Division—but no prospects of any more coming in, and the exchange banks always took a piece.

He got to the defrocked church early; the fat guy at the card table in the lobby hadn't even opened his cashbox yet. But he took Ryon's two bucks and waved him on in. The band was still setting up. Ryon took a pew at the back of the hall and wondered what he was in for.

There were four guys and a woman on stage, dressed in rags and tags of Salvation Army splendor. They were in a huddle around the bass amp, which kept putting out an unpleasant hum no matter how many nobs and dials they twiddled. Folkies trying to deal with electronics. Finally Ryon couldn't stand it anymore, and he called out: "Reverse the polarity!"

They turned and looked at him. He felt like an asshole, but now as he'd gone and opened his big mouth… He got up and walked partway down the aisle, saying: "Reverse the polarity. Unplug it, turn the plug around, plug it back in."

They did. The amp came on again with no hum. One of the band guys— with thick, long hair and slanted eyes, looking a bit like an elf out of *Lord of The Rings*—said to Ryon: "You wanna earn ten bucks, ace?"

"Sure."

"We're running late, there's still some equipment out in the van. You haul it in and help us take down, we'll pay you ten bucks when we get paid."

"Sure."

The rental van was snugged up to the back door, with a couple of small amps and odds and ends inside. Ryon ferried them onto the stage feeling a bit like a geek in his plain T-shirt and jeans and his Depot Division haircut just starting to grow out. The gypsy-dressed band members didn't ask his name or introduce themselves. Ryon wasn't surprised or put off—handshakes and "Pleased to meet you" weren't cool.

The hall started to fill up and Ryon went back to the pew where he'd left his jacket with the mickey in one pocket and his last pack of Canadian cigarettes in the other. Not *too* long after the billed start time, the houselights went out. Ryon took another slug of Southern Comfort, eyed the band stepping up to the mikes and muttered: "Well you *look* good, but can you play?"

They sure as hell could. None of them could play like The Mystic Moron, but that was like saying a jazz fiddler wasn't as good as Stephane Grappelli. So maybe they didn't know much about bass amps—there were probably a lot of damn good race car drivers who couldn't change a transmission. They were a bit raggedy around the edges, but Ryon had a feeling this was very early days for where Anemone was going.

The best parts were when the chick singer took front-and-center. Chick singer, hell, she played damn good rhythm guitar and even better piano. When her voice took hold of a melody, the rest of the band could wing off in any direction any of them felt like flying—like tap-dancing on the deck of an aircraft carrier. Just about any other singer Ryon could imagine would've been buried by the wingy electric improvs storming around her—but *this* voice; if you closed your eyes, it sounded like the singer was playing all the instruments. And that had nothing to do with showing off how many octaves she could reach, or cramming fifty-seven notes into a bar, or screeching into the mike. Just happened to be that no matter how many clothes you put on the lady, she was naked in the song, and more electric than a stack of Marshall amps.

This Anemone band would've come across as the Celtic Rock version of white kids playing the blues if it wasn't for Maddie. Ryon had picked up from the on-stage banter that the rhythm guitar player's name was Maddie and the elfish, lead guitar player's name was Fergus. She had an accent that was maybe North England or South Scotland, but definitely gritty working class, except for the occasional convent-school vowel here and there. And she knew how to play an audience—or, rather, how to *not* play an audience. If her way of talking to the audience like they were an old friend at the pub was just an act, it was a hell of an act.

At one point she started a finger picking intro, stopped dead, gave out a stoned giggle and said: "Me fingers is so bloody numb I don't think I could pick me nose." Then she ripped straight into a kick-ass ballad that had been written four hundred years before Alice Cooper or KISS were born and was beyond their worst nightmares—*Tom o' Bedlam*.

There were so many verses to *Tom o' Bedlam* that Ryon would've figured it impossible to sustain any audience's interest, except that Maddie colored it with a kaleidoscope of shadings, letting the lyrics carry her from viciously black humor to pussy willow soft to insane rage. Ryon knew the lyrics well but hadn't known they'd ever actually been set to music. Back in Junior High School he'd spent a couple of Library classes accidentally leafing through an old anthology put together by Dame Edith Sitwell, which by rights should've been titled *The Few English Language Poems I Admire But Did Not Write Myself*. The old Dame had spent most of her Introduction hedging around her theory about who had written the anonymous *Tom o' Bedlam*. She hadn't had the jam to come right out and say it, but she had gone so far as to declare that there was only one English writer ever who'd had the chops to be that dark and funny and scary and gentle all at the same time, and that the poem's usual identification as "Pre-Shakespearean" wasn't entirely accurate. The "Pre-Shakespearean" came from the fact that *Tom o' Bedlam* got referred to in *King Lear*, so it was actually only "Pre-King Lear."

If the old Dame was right about what she'd been hinting at, Ryon was certain that a certain baldheaded guy in Stratford would be grinning in his grave if he could hear what this Maddie broad was doing with his song.

When the encores were all done and nobody left except a few friends and fans hanging around the front of the stage, Ryon started hauling amps and wrapping cable, keeping his mouth shut. Maddie and Fergus disappeared down the stairs to the basement—Ryon assumed that's where the office was, and the fat guy with the money.

The van was all loaded up and still no Maddie and Fergus. Ryon sat sipping Southern comfort and waiting for his ten bucks. The remaining three members of Anemone and their friend-fans waited, too. They passed a joint around but didn't offer him a toke. Some of them looked a little nervous about toking up in front of him.

Ryon sucked the last slug out of the bottle, looked at the empty and said: "Fuck this." He got up and went down the basement stairs.

There was a basketball court in the basement, and an open door at the far end. Ryon got as far as that doorway and then thought the doorframe would be a very good thing to lean against until his eyes started focusing again. Maddie and Fergus were standing with their backs to him in front of a desk the fat guy was sitting behind. Maddie was saying: "But it was a full fookin' house, for fook's sake!"

The fat guy said: "I know, but at two bucks a head... I got expenses. You know how much it costs to heat this place? And paying off the Fire Marshall? Think of the publicity you got out of this gig. Look, I've almost made my nut for this month—maybe if you want to do another show next Saturday night, I could give you the whole gate."

"We've got another gig across town next Saturday."

"Well maybe I should book you in on Friday. Or maybe I should open up Sunday for a change."

"Or maybe," Ryon suggested from the doorway, "I should just rip your fucking head off and shove it up your ass."

Maddie and Fergus turned around to look at Ryon in the doorway. The fat guy didn't have to turn, just raise his eyes to look between the human bookends. When the fat guy's eyes met his, Ryon's lungs seemed to open up for the first time since he'd hit Smog City. He could feel the adrenalin transmuting the alcohol and oxygen into jet fuel. He didn't move from his crossed-arm lean against the doorway, but he smiled.

Before the smile reached its full growth, the fat guy was taking out his wallet and counting bills onto the desk. On the way back up the stairs, Ryon screwed up his courage to say something to Maddie. "You're not from here…"

"Neither are you."

Out at the van, Fergus handed Ryon ten bucks and said: "We're playing the Students' Center at Columbia next Saturday. Feel like lugging some more amps?"

"Sure."

"Seven o'clock. If you don't show, that's cool — see you another time, ace."

"Sure."

Two of the band guys got into the van and the rest of the peacock-colored crew headed down the sidewalk, gabbling and laughing. It seemed to Ryon that just before he started off in the other direction, Maddie turned her head to look back at him. Probably just his imagination.

A few nights after the defrocked-church concert, he was back wandering through The Village again, enjoying being invisible. He happened to glance through the storefront window of a passing laundromat and saw her, the chick singer from the band. She was way back toward the dryer section, folding clothes and making small talk with the only other person in the joint this late at night—a doughy-looking, middle-aged frump with her hair in curlers. Although the window was big, it was pretty grungy and the streetlight was much dimmer than the flourescent glare inside. Ryon figured he'd be only a shadow to anyone looking out, unless they had their face pressed to the glass. Should be safe to stop and look in for a minute.

He found it kind of cute to watch the woman who blazed from the stage now folding her two bucks' worth of laundry like a pizza waitress on her night off. What made it even cuter was to know that a few months from now, or maybe even a few weeks, the frumpy old doll she was passing the time of night with was going to open up her newspaper to the Show Biz section and see that face from the laundromat under: "Signed Long Term Contract With RCA; World Tour In Offing." Then again, this being New York City, maybe the doughy, middle aged woman in curlers was in rehearsals for her fourteenth Broadway show.

Maddie turned away from the folding table and toward the window to shake out a pair of faded jeans—a long pair of jeans, and way too thin in the hips for her. Her sea-gray eyes lifted away from the flapping denim, as though she'd caught sight of a shadow in the window. Ryon swung away and started walking again, hoping he wasn't seen. He was just about certain he wasn't seen.

XII

SHE EMPLOYED THE *fireplace tongs to lift a pebble of smouldering coal out of the kitchen stove. With the tongs clamped gingerly in one hand, and a burning scarlet candle in the other, she went out into the snow-flecked garden. It was a still night, not even enough of a breeze to ruffle the leaf of sketching paper she'd laid out on one of the flagstones. She'd fingerpainted in ochre a naked man with stag's antlers. Holding the candle high so the hot, red wax dripped over her fist, she knelt in the snow and set the glowing coal down on his heart.*

The one-horse hansom cab carrying Ryon to Waterloo Station slowed to a crawl in the congestion of a London morning. He rapped his fist against the roof and called up to the cabman: "Close enough, I can walk from here."

The reins dangling over Ryon's head tightened to halt the horse. As he climbed out and reached up to pay the fare, the cabman said: "I'd think twice about walking, guv. Man could freeze his lungs today."

Ryon had to laugh. After seventeen Manitoba winters, temperatures that made Londoners pull their hats down were open-coat weather to him. People with only theoretical acquaintance of prairie winters were wont to say: "Well it's a *dry* cold, isn't it, so not near so uncomfortable." They didn't understand that "uncomfortable" doesn't enter into: *you will freeze to death between the house and the barn.*

Ryon did have to admit, though, that people who only knew English winters were tougher than prairie people in one sense. During his long years away, he'd forgotten that the English notion of heating was one tiny coal fire for every four or five rooms. Where he needed his coat and muffler was *indoors.*

It should've been only a few minutes' walk to the station, but there wasn't enough unpopulated room on the sidewalk for Ryon to stretch his legs. Once he'd adjusted his pace to the current of bundled-up pedestrians, he tugged out his pocket watch. There was still an abundance of time to catch the 9:37 to Amesbury and the environs of Celina Rushton, the woman whom Audrey Doude had called the leader of The Circle. Whether Celina Rushton could or would tell him anything helpful was an open question. But at least he had an address for her, which was better than Philip Norman's vague recollection of a tavern somewhere around Portsmouth that Jack Delaney had once been rumored to haunt.

Under the vast, glass-vaulted roof of Waterloo Station, Ryon edged through the crowds milling along the platforms. He still hadn't quite overcome the lung-squeezing sensation from having so many people between himself and the horizon, but he had rediscovered the city-dweller's knack of bobbing and shifting around human impediments without breaking stride.

One of those impediments suddenly decided to reverse course just as he caught up with her. They almost collided, and their eyes met for an instant. She froze in place like playing "Statues," and her big, dark eyes and little, pink mouth fell open.

He swerved quickly around her without even murmuring *Pardon-me*. He heard her hesitantly call from behind him: "Harry…?" but he kept on moving. His eyes were stinging and he had to fight the urge to either break into a run or turn back. She called his name again with more conviction, but by then there were so many bustling and chattering people between them that he barely heard her voice.

She was his baby sister, Penelope. In that one brief glimpse he'd seen that she wasn't a baby anymore, and he knew she'd already borne three of her own, but she always would be the baby sister. She was the only member of the family who'd kept in contact with him; the quarterly remittance checks were mailed directly from his father's bank. Penelope had sent him a letter every Christmas for the last seventeen years, and he to her—which had necessitated some subterfuge when she'd still been living in their father's house. Before Ryon had climbed on the train from Wahpeston he'd handed Lisette a letter to post come December, telling Penelope details about his spring and summer, and generalities about the harvest and onset of winter.

He found his compartment and was relieved to see that one of the window seats was still open, so he could turn his face away from his fellow travelers. He said to himself: *Didn't think of that, did you, cleverlad? Thought the only ill that might come of bumping into one of the family was losing your precious allowance. Didn't think what it might do to them.*

He convinced himself that Penelope would convince herself that she'd only seen some stranger who looked vaguely like her Harry might look after donkey's years of mucking about the colonies. But that didn't make him feel any better.

As the train huffed out of Waterloo Station, Ryon took himself by the scruff of the neck to turn his mind elsewhere than bootless melancholia. Unfortunately, the only other place for it to turn was the squirrel-wheel labeled Maddie Prue.

Philip Norman had put a mad thought in his head, as if all his thoughts weren't mad these days. Maybe Maddie Prue *was* still alive, and it was she who'd sent the Doudes' book across the ocean. What if, all those years ago, Maddie had been deathly afraid of something, or someone—for instance, the spider-man Jack Delaney—and had seen her chance to disappear when some anonymous friend had fallen off the cliff behind her cottage during one of their moonlight rambles? What if something had happened recently that could disarm whomever or whatever she was still afraid of? But she couldn't bring it out into the open without revealing herself; she had to lure someone else into tracking it down.

But then, Ryon asked himself, why the devil would she pick on someone three thousand miles away whom she'd barely been acquainted with? He immediately answered himself with another question: who else from the days of Anemone could she trust to pursue it to the end? That laudanum-soaked, hermit gnome Philip Norman...? Fergus Doude—wherever he was—who had written of his suspicions years ago and then done nothing about it? As mad as it seemed, part of Ryon was beginning to expect that once he'd got to the bottom of this, Maddie Prue would step out of the shadows and take his hand.

He shook himself and endeavored to clear his mind. *What's the point of having a window, cleverlad, if you don't see through it? Almost twenty years since you've seen West England countryside, and you'll never get the chance again.*

The sooty, cindered snow and frozen mud of the railway embankment passing by the window brought back to mind another long-forgotten encounter with Maddie Prue...

He was in Whitechapel in East London, back before The Ripper made Whitechapel a more frightening destination than Darkest Africa. Most people found it frightening enough even then—the haunt of petty thieves, cheap whores, scavengers: the dregs who no longer much cared if you or they might have an accident with a broken bottle.

But they were a lively crew. Whenever Ryon began to feel too self-conscious in the society of arts salons, or gentlemen's clubs, or gaming houses, or—God forbid—the stultifying house in Grosvenor Square, he would put on a ragged old suit of clothes with a very few shillings in the pockets and hike into Whitechapel. Young Harry Ryon traveled in a lot of different circles, never staying in any of them long enough to get too well-known. Whitechapel just happened to be one of them.

Learning the language of Whitechapel had taught Ryon a lesson that no one who graduated from Cambridge was ever likely to know: the appalling smallness of what people would steal or scavenge. A *cabbage-nacker* went around to tailors' shops scrounging the shreds of cloth left over after a pattern was cut out. A *pure-finder* picked up dog droppings to sell to tanneries. A *clout-nap* pickpocketed cotton handkerchiefs. But the borders of London's separate neighborhoods were so efficiently patrolled that a girl born in Hammersmith could live to a ripe old age without ever suspecting that there were women just across the river who would consider it a banner week if their husbands managed to pilfer a brass watch chain.

Ryon was standing on a Whitechapel corner sharing a cigar with Blacktooth Nell, his landlady of the night before, when he spotted something decidedly out of place coming down the street: a fresh-faced, young woman in an unpatched, bright tartan cloak, her combed-out mane of Saxon Gold rippling in the breeze. She had a heavy-looking Gladstone bag in each hand and was strolling along as though the back streets of Whitechapel were a picturesque path through the Lake District.

Blacktooth Nell's youngest son left off clinging to his mother's skirt and started toward the approaching apparition. Nell grabbed him by the hair and pulled him back, hissing: "You wait 'ere or I'll box yer bum for ya. If she stops she stops, if she don't she don't—and you leave 'er alone."

Maddie Prue swerved toward them and set down her Gladstone bags as she crouched in front of the boy. She said: "What's your name, love?"

"Fred."

"I bet you're hungry, Fred. I bet you're always hungry. Here's a little something. Not much, but it's something." She opened one of her bags, took out a sandwich wrapped in butcher's paper, handed Fred the sandwich and kept the paper.

"Ta."

"Ta yourself, Fred. Stay out of trouble, if you can."

As Maddie Prue stood back up, her eyes clicked against Ryon's for an instant. He was quite sure she hadn't recognized him: he was out of context, hadn't shaved for three days and had a bit of mud across one cheek from a debate with a sporting gentleman that morning. Besides, his was only one of several hundred faces she saw when she looked out from the stage set up in Morris's country garden.

Gaping at the back of the expensive, tartan cloak wafting along through the den of thieves and desperate people, Ryon muttered: "She must be *mad*."

Nell said: "Right you are, 'Arry—that's The Mad Lady. Glad you didn't try to say anyfink to 'er. She only talks to the children. Sometimes she gives 'em sixpence, sometimes a bite to eat."

Ryon could easily understand why she only talked to the children—she could reach down to them without making them feel small, or her feel like she was playing Lady Bountiful. But that didn't make what she was doing any less insane. He said: "But… a woman alone in Whitechapel, with two bags full of food and her pockets full of coins…!"

"Oh, she's safe as 'ouses 'ere, 'Arry. Anybody raised 'is 'and to The Mad Lady'd 'ave the 'ole street down around 'is neck. She ain't one of yer Salvation Army saints what make you eat a page of the Bible with every bowl of soup, or starch-nickered prissies 'anding out charity and 'olding their noses. As soon as she opens 'er mouth you can 'ear she's one of us. Well, North Country, but still she ain't no bleedin' toff.

"Some people figure she's some toff's tart and that's where she gets 'er lolly. Some say she's likely a blackmail tout, or maybe just a fancy dressmaker, who remembers where she came from. Me, I don't know nor care—she's just The Mad Lady, and God fuckin' Bless 'er."

Not far from the railway station at Amesbury, Ryon found an ostlery to hire a saddle horse. He suspected that Miss Celina Rushton's backwoods retreat might not feature a carriage drive. A short-stirruped English saddle felt prissy and fussy after years of riding on a workingman's Western saddle, but he adjusted. After the first few miles of trotting through blowing snow, he wished he hadn't left his buffalo coat stored at the hotel in Montreal.

There was a roadside inn where he ordered a hot toddy to warm his bones, and asked directions to Rose Farm. The barmaid said: "Rose Farm? Why'd you want to go there? T'isn't really a farm at all, 'tis it?"

"I have some business to discuss with Miss Celina Rushton."

"Business? Didn't know she had any business, outside of playin' her flute in the moonlight and afrighting the owls. Oh, she's a sweet old dear in her way, but we don't see her in the village but twice a year. Well, to get to Rose Farm you follow the High Road till you get to a broke-down old mill with a cart-track running off behind it…"

Ryon followed her directions into a stark and silent forest, along a winding path carpeted with snow broken only by the tracks of birds and rabbits. At the end of the path was a thatched, stone cottage with a cowshed attached. As Ryon climbed down off his horse, two Irish wolfhounds came padding up to sniff at him. A crow perched on the roof peak did a credible imitation of a watchdog barking. A badger nosed out from under the front step to see what was going on. Ryon felt quite at home.

The door opened before he reached it. The big-boned woman from Audrey Doude's photograph album had dead-white hair now, making her weather-painted face look even ruddier and healthier. Ryon said: "Miss Rushton? My name is Henry Ryon. Audrey Doude suggested I should speak with you."

"Then I suppose you should. Come in, Mr. Ryon, don't fret your boots, you can hang your coat on the hook there. I was just staring out the window trying to stir myself to make a pot of tea." She swung the kettle in over the fire, which Ryon appreciatively noted was stoked high enough to keep the place cosy. "I spend a lot of time staring out that window."

It wasn't hard to guess which window she meant: a large one in the back wall of the cottage's one room. The window was of much more recent construction than the rest of the cottage. Rose Farm was at the back edge of the forest, so the window gave an unobstructed view far across the windswept heath of Salisbury Plain, as far as the looming ruin of Stonehenge standing black against the snow.

As she pottered cups and saucers out of the sideboard, Miss Rushton chirruped: "I suppose that being a theoretician myself I shouldn't make mock of other theoreticians. But it does amuse me the contortions some will go through to explain why Neolithic farmers went to the monumental labor of building Stonehenge—theses theorizing Druidic religious rites, or passages to the afterlife, or any manner of fanciful inventions. It seems patently simple that to Neolithic farmers with no concept of calendars, it was worth any amount of labor to have an indestructible structure which would show every year—when the solstice suns rose over the standing stones—that the summer was half over or that the sun was indeed now starting its way back north, and the spring *would* return."

"I'm a farmer."

"Ah, then you would understand."

Ryon said deliberately: "Salisbury Plain is where Mallory placed the last battle, isn't it? The *morte* d'Arthur. Or of Adonis, or Tammuz, or Dionysus, or…"

Celina Rushton put the teapot on the table and stood looking at him silently. Ryon said: "Audrey Doude told me of The Circle."

"She spoke to you of that? She must know you very well indeed."

"Hardly at all, and not since almost twenty years. She couldn't even remember my name."

She looked at him a moment longer. It was an unnerving habit, to just pause and consider, instead of trying to fill the silence. Then she said: "I'll pour some tea, shall I, and you can explain this to me."

Ryon had come hoping she would explain some things to *him*, but conceded he would have to go first. "I came back from North America because somebody in England, I don't know who, sent me a message that Maddie Prue's death wasn't accidental. I don't know whether it has anything to do with The Circle, but Audrey Doude was of the opinion that you could tell me more about Maddie Prue than anyone else could."

Celina Rushton gazed into her teacup and said softly: "Maddie… Mad Maddie…" She raised her eyes again. "What was she to you, Mr. Ryon, to bring you all this way back?"

"I knew her a little. Not well. But I don't like the idea that someone may be walking around England today who might have murdered her."

"And who might that be?"

"That's what I'm trying to find out."

Something seemed to occur to her, and she suddenly veered to: "Where in North America did you say you came back from?"

"I didn't. Manitoba. Out west, the prairies."

"And your name is Ryon…"

"What does that mean to you?"

"Oh, nothing. Merely repeating it aloud so I have it firmly fixed. You'll find,

Mister Ryon, if you live long enough, that your faculties will need all the aids and tricks you can come up with to keep them from drifting. What did Audrey tell you about The Circle?"

"Not a great deal. But when I mentioned Anemone's writings of the connection between Guinevere, Venus, Astarte, she mentioned The Circle. What is the connection?"

Celina Rushton laughed. "I've spent my life trying to answer that question, and still can't claim to fully understand. By the time the story became Arthur and Guinevere, there was only a very pale shade left of something much more ancient. She destroyed him, you see, and yet she also was the soul of Camelot. Venus and Ishtar both had their beautiful, wild hunters who had to die— Adonis and Tammuz. Am I casting any light, Ryon?"

"I'm not sure, Miss Rushton."

"Celina. Anyone who would cross an ocean for Maddie can call me by my first name."

She got up and went to the window. After a moment, she said: "You were likely too young and resilient to feel the shock, but twenty-five years ago— two years before I met Maddie—the shape of the world changed. To those of us whose personalities had already been formed by then, it had been a fact of life that all the old legends: *The Iliad*, the tales of King Arthur, were just that. Fairy tales imagined out of whole cloth to entertain the children on a winter's night. But in 1870, Heinrich Schliemann unearthed the city of Troy, exactly where Homer said it would be."

She came back toward the table, eyes dancing with light. He suspected she didn't get the opportunity to speak to many people about her enthusiasms. "You can't imagine the excitement. Suddenly myths and legends were no longer only entertaining curiosities, but clues to the foundations of the human race." She pursed her lips, tapped a farm-chore-cracked fingertip against them a few times and then opened them again. "You wonder what all this has to do with Maddie, Ryon. A great deal. A very great deal indeed.

"What we call myths—or the deepest of them—are born out of pain. They are a way of preserving that which is too painful to remember, but too precious to forget."

She splayed her large hands on the table and leaned forward, speaking intently but matter-of-factly, "There was a real Arthur—Arthnou, or Artorius. At the beginning of what we call the Dark Ages, Roman Britain was the last light of civilization north of Rome, and Rome herself was under siege. Britain was crumbling under raids and invasions from Saxons and other tribes. But the Britons were separated into numerous kingdoms, and each of the petty little kings would only fight to defend his own stretch of coastline.

"So Rome appointed a Dux Bellorum—a War Lord. He would have supreme authority in all matters pertaining to defending the country. He invented a system of armored cavalry—knights—who could assemble quickly at any place the invaders landed to plunder. And woe betide the king whose knights did not arrive on time.

"Soon the raids grew fewer and fewer. A Briton could once again walk to his cowshed without fear of his life. But then the War Lord made a terrible mistake. He so thoroughly defeated the Saxons, at the Battle of Badon Hill, that they would not come back for fifty years. The Kings who resented the War Lord no longer needed him, and he wasn't the kind of man to fold his cards and go away. So they killed him." She turned and pointed out the window at the distant monoliths. "Out there on Salisbury Plain, in the shadow of Stone Henge."

She stood there frozen for a moment, as though the window were a window of time. Then she lowered her arm and turned back to Ryon. "The people of Britain couldn't bear to forget the man who'd saved them, and couldn't bear to remember that they'd killed him. So he became King Arthur. In the process of building the legend, they wrapped their myth around a much more ancient myth of sacrifice—one that was played out in blood on the day the massed armies of the kings met the War Lord on Salisbury Plain.

"We will always weep for Adonis. The existence of the sacrifice is no great secret. The question is: why. Why does he have to die, again and again?"

Ryon wasn't sure whether that was a rhetorical question or not. But she seemed to be pausing even longer than usual, so he said: "Well, from what I could puzzle out from Anemone's writings, it seems to have been a ritual to convince the Earth goddess to let the crops grow again."

"That is logical, Ryon," she shook her head. "Logical and impersonal—the kind of construct we or our ancient ancestors come up with after the event, to explain something born out of an emotion we can't bear to remember in its raw state. But what was that emotion? What was that original event?

"That is the question The Circle was attempting to answer. The reason we gathered together was the same reason one would prefer to have company when venturing into an unexplored cave. We all of us found it both thrilling and frightening, but it was different for Maddie. Everything was different for Maddie."

Celina Rushton paused again, but this time without that unnerving serenity. It seemed to Ryon that she was struggling to put into words something she'd never had occasion to try to explain. Eventually she said: "Maddie had no borders between her heart and her mind and her soul. The rest of us might look at a new-peeled layer of the onion and nod our heads, 'That's interesting.' But I would see Maddie shuddering, feeling something that was only intellectual to us. The theater critics who wrote that Maddie 'sang like a woman possessed' didn't know the half of it."

Ryon opened his mouth to ask 'Possessed by what?' then decided that sounded too redolent of Ouija boards and dancing tables.

"Poor Audrey," Celina sighed. "She was intelligent enough to see that Maddie had something beyond her understanding. Life would've been so much easier on Audrey if she were just a little less intelligent. Not that any of the rest of us understood what it was to wear Maddie's skin. But we had sense enough to know we didn't *want* to, thank you very much.

"That wild child. I feel I'm responsible somehow, but I don't know how."

Ryon devoted his attention to his teacup for a moment, while Celina Rushton took a handkerchief out of her sleeve and dabbed at the corners of her eyes. Then he said: "Responsible for what?"

"Oh, I don't know…" Although it seemed to Ryon that she did. "Maddie was as much my daughter as I'll ever have, and she's dead."

"Are you sure?"

She shot a look at him as though he'd just spat in the sugar bowl. Then she said: "I'm afraid your tea's gone cold, Mr. Ryon," and poured a warm-up from the pot.

After a moment of silence, she said: "I don't believe I can tell you any more about The Circle without wading you through a quarter-century of accumulated notes. I do hope I've been of some help to you."

Ryon suddenly found it grossly unfair that he should be conversing with Celina Rushton in a ramshackle, isolated cottage, instead of the plush-chaired, university offices of some dotty but respected Professor Emeritus. Which is what she would have been if she hadn't made the mistake of being born female.

When he said as much, she laughed. "Oh, Ryon, who's to say I didn't get the better part of the bargain? And the seeds do get harvested regardless, which is what matters. There is a brilliant man at Cambridge I spoke with often in the 'eighties, named James Frazer."

There was a pause, as though she expected him to respond to that. When he didn't, she said: "I take it they don't do much reading out on the western prairies."

"Some do. I did my quota years ago."

"That's very sad; I have a feeling it was one of your pleasures. But, James Frazer published a book five years ago titled *The Golden Bough*. I suspect he'll spend the rest of his life revising and appending it. It can tell you a great deal about the subject The Circle was concerned with—if you can spare a month or two to read it."

"Can it tell me about Maddie Prue?"

"No. That you'll have to find out for yourself."

As Celina Rushton escorted him out to his rented horse, Ryon said: "You were the anonymous donor, weren't you?"

"Pardon me?"

"The anonymous donor who contributed to the publication of Maddie's book."

"The phrase 'anonymous donor' is one of the few cases in the English language where the adjective weighs more than the noun."

The wolfhounds started booming and snarling behind the cottage. Celina Rushton went around the corner to have a look, and Ryon fell in behind her. A gypsy caravan was rattling across Salisbury Plain, making for a grove of trees with campfire smoke rising out of it.

Celina Rushton calmed the dogs, then said to Ryon: "Do you know why we in our farms and towns are so afraid of gypsies?"

"Well, they do say there isn't a chicken safe within ten miles of a gypsy camp. True or not."

"It's a much deeper fear than that. They live the way we used to, before our distant ancestors tied themselves to planted fields. Roaming freely to the seashore when the wild geese nested, to the deep woods when the deer were fat with autumn… When the gypsies pass by, we fear that our wife or husband, or we ourselves, will feel the old call in the blood, and throw down our hoes to follow the gypsies."

It seemed like she was trying to lead him somewhere, but he wasn't sure where. She said, as though he was proving a bit thicker than she'd expected, "Did you read any Darwin, Ryon—back in the days when you were still reading?"

"Not really. I heard enough about his theory to get the general gist. I was still at Cambridge when *The Descent of Man* caused such an unholy row."

She laughed. "Unholy is a very apt choice. There were two great steps in human evolution, that made us what we are today—for better or worse. There were an infinity of tiny steps, but two giant steps that separated us from the other creatures of the Earth.

"The first step was when we began to walk on two legs—Ha, 'first step,' my turn for inadvertent aptness. But even after that first step, the animals that walked upright and used tools still remained a part of nature for hundreds of thousands of years—until the second step. The second step was what The Circle was searching for. Oh, we didn't know that when we started, but the links in the chain kept leading further back and further back…"

"Did you ever find what you were looking for?"

"I can't say with certainty that I did. I am an intellectual, and incapable of grasping what cannot be grasped entirely by the intellect. But I have a feeling that Maddie did. There was a night—we were circled around a fire, as on many nights before, and Maddie screamed and broke away. When I asked her why, and how far back she'd gone, she said: 'Not back to the beginning, but far enough to know.' I asked her many times after: 'To know what?' but she wouldn't or couldn't explain. Or maybe she tried and I couldn't understand.

"I am capable of understanding this much, though—in the life of a species, as in the life of an individual, in order to begin anything new, something old must die. No matter how treasured that something may be."

Celina Rushton suddenly shuddered, and her eyes jolted at Ryon with alarm. But although her eyes stayed fixed on him, when she spoke it was more in a tone of speaking to herself. "*Ryon. Oh, Ryon…*"

She swerved away from him and walked briskly to her cottage door. She paused on the threshold and turned to face him. She said in a low but resonant voice: "Good hunting, Ryon." Then she stepped back and closed the door.

XIII

*S*HE SLOTTED *into the cassette deck the scratchy home dub she'd made of Donovan's* Season of the Witch *years back when she'd realized the vinyl was getting to be more scratches and skips than notes. She thought of taking out her books and candles and potions and seeing if she could cast another bit of bait. Then she laughed at her typical over-tuning compulsion and shook her head: he was well and truly hooked already, and wouldn't stop till he reached the end of the line. She remembered her grandfather telling her about the unofficial motto the Allies had tacked onto Canadians in the First World War, after the Canadian Corps had taken Vimy Ridge, where the Germans had beaten back the French and British time after time. "Too Dumb To Quit". Just what the doctor ordered.*

By the time Ryon left Professor Rushton's office it was rush hour; there were no empty seats on the subway back to his hotel. So he stood gripping the overhead swivel-bar, with his feet planted wide against the pitching and jouncing. The subway car wasn't all that was pitching and jouncing, and the hand-bar wasn't all he was gripping onto. He was trying to hang onto his sanity.

He knew better than Celina Rushton did what she'd meant by Maddie "feeling" things that were only intellectual to other people. He knew because he'd done the same thing more than a few times himself, back in that lost year. And now all the bloody little birds were starting to fly out of the cages he'd locked them away in. He told himself that Celina Rushton was just another bogus Magus, but that didn't close the cage doors.

He remembered, although he sure as hell didn't want to, that he'd been fixated on The Antlered Man—the image of a naked, moonlit man with stag's antlers. He couldn't for the life of him say where he'd first come across the image, but it popped up now and again in the corners of album covers, or in paperbacks about the good old days of barbarians and wenches. For no solid reason, he'd got the idea that The Antlered Man had something to do with the Corn King, and also something to do with Pan, whose pipes lured civilized people into wild places and out of their heads.

Ryon had figured it was just one of his own wacky little fixations that didn't have anything to do with anybody else's reality. And then he'd gone and whiled away a few insomniated nights in crash-pads reading Joseph Campbell's *The Masks of God*.

He shivered on the shoehorned subway train, the same shiver as that long-gone night alone when he'd neared the bottom of a certain page. Campbell had been riffing on the odd fact that in all the cave paintings there is only one human-like figure, the earliest known depiction of a human being. Ryon had known exactly what picture he was going to see when he turned the page. The Antlered Man.

Ryon snarled and shook himself like a dog trying to shake off skunk, then remembered he was standing in a crowded subway car. Then another memory came back that told him not to worry. It was a pleasant memory for a change, with no twisted undercurrents.

It had happened on the very first day he'd ever walked the sidewalks of New York, not ten minutes out of the Port Authority bus terminal. He'd been standing on a corner waiting for a light to change—he might as well've held up a sign saying TOURIST—when a man came up beside him and stood watching for a break in traffic. The first thing Ryon had noticed was that the gentleman was a fullback-ish, steel-wool-bearded black man wearing a raggedy motorcycle jacket over a beaded, ankle-length prom gown with matching clutch purse. The second thing Ryon had noticed was that none of the other eight million passersby seemed to care. He'd said to himself right off: "There's something I like about this town."

So a middle-aged goofball barking at himself on a subway car wasn't likely to scandalize the New Yorkers packed in with him, but Ryon liked to think he hadn't lost it that much yet. But he still couldn't stop his so-called mind from playing the old tricks on him, conning him into believing there was more than theory to the notion of archetypes and the collective unconscious and all that. Celina Rushton's story of the War Lord Arthur had been replayed in the twentieth century. Well, the Brits hadn't *killed* Winston Churchill, but they'd voted him out of office the minute the war was over. Canonized and castrated. The same story, the same dance, bred in the bone, in the blood…

He missed his subway stop and had to walk a dozen blocks back to his hotel. On the way, he picked up a Nova-Scotia-and-cream-cheese and six Millers. Back in his hotel room, fueling-up on stuffed bagel and beer, he wondered what he was going to do next.

All he had so far was a bunch of weird mumbo-jumbo and a vague lead that Jack Delaney used to play in a bar on the other side of the continent. No one seemed to have any idea how to find Fergus Doude. There *was* the fact that Celina Rushton had gone a little strange at the end of their interview, like she was afraid of something. The question was: had Maddie been afraid of something, too?

Ryon put one of Maddie's later tapes on the walkman and strained to listen for any undercurrent of fear in her voice. All he could hear was whatever emotion was in the song at hand. Or emotions—one of the reasons her songs had never been AM blockbusters was that she couldn't pick one simple mood and stick with it for three verses and a hook. Not that she was into that gutless, smartass crap they called "irony" these days—all slithery and slippery and nothing to hold onto. Like the Acid Gurus back in the days when LSD was a party favor, who would play games with blitzed-out kids by going: "Oh you think I'm joking, what an uncool fool. Oh, you think I'm serious, what an uncool fool." But Maddie's songs were like prisms, always faceted: pissed-off-but-in-love, fucked-up-but-laughing-about-it... Sorta like life.

He'd listened to the tapes so many times now that he could predict her supposedly-surprising habit of jumping from a whisper to an all-out roar, but everybody had their tricks. What he needed was a fresh pair of ears.

He took the earphones off and phoned Lieutenant Sumter's precinct. When they finally put him through to her, he said: "This is Corporal Ryon, remember...?"

"Luke Skywalker, yeah."

"Do you know where I could find a good shrink?"

"I thought you'd never ask."

"Not for me. I need kind of a... postmortem psychiatrist—forensic shrink—somebody who can listen to a taped voice and maybe hear hidden emotions. It's a long shot, but I need somebody with a good head but their feet on the ground, no bullshit jargon. If shrinks come in that size."

"Yeah, I know a guy kinda fits that description. But he'll want cash in the hand for a private consultation."

"Good deal."

When Ryon dialed the number, he got a wheezy, Germanic voice saying: "You haff reached ze office of Dr. Emmanuel Kroenberg. Please leave a message at ze tone of ze beep."

"Uh, this is Corporal Henry Ryon. Lieutenant Sumter suggested I should—"

"Hallo?"

"Hello...?"

"Hallo. I don't haff an answering machine, I just use the beeper on my wristwatch to throw off cranks. What can I be doing for you?"

Ryon explained in a general way, adding that he didn't have much time to wait for an appointment.

"This is a very interesting idea you haff, Corporal. I could see you tonight at my apartment, which is my office also. Say, nine p.m."

"Good deal."

"But I must caution you, my neighborhood is not of the best. Especially after dark."

"I'll be careful."

Ryon took down the address and hung up. He unfolded his New York City map and got a strangling jolt of claustrophobia. Times when he was out walking in the concrete canyons, all he saw was the street he was on. But the map showed that he was surrounded by hundreds of square miles of city blocks crammed against each other. He reassured himself that he wasn't going to be there much longer and that the airplane would carry him over it in minutes.

The old scar on his chest was getting even more aggravating, now a burning itch. He wondered if he'd scratched it into infection. He went into the bathroom, unbuttoning his shirt, and looked at it in the mirror. The scar hadn't changed color—no infected-flush around the edges—and it hadn't changed shape: a fingernail-sized, teardrop-shaped, puckered burn with its tail growing into a six inch long cut-line slanting across his left pectoral just above the nipple, like a rack-stretched tadpole. Lisette had shown up one afternoon when he was sunning himself in the back yard, and asked him where he'd got the scar. He told her that was where they'd cut his heart out. She'd just said: "Oh, I'd wondered when that happened."

Whenever and however he'd got the scar, he did know for certain it was back in the days when his pecs stuck out further than his gut—which the mirror reminded him was no longer the case. Well, that's why God made baggy shirts.

Ryon buttoned up his shirt again and tucked a couple of Maddie's tapes in his jacket pockets, then picked up his flashlight, just in case. Years ago, when going into a dicey situation out of uniform, he'd cut the fleece lining out of the sleeves of his ancient bomber jacket. With the flashlight shoved up his right sleeve, and his hand slightly cupped under the head, he could walk along looking perfectly civilian. But all he had to do was uncup his fingers and the two-foot, steel-barreled, lead-battery-heavy flashlight slid down into his hand. It had worked out so well he'd never bothered to re-line the sleeves, just put on an extra sweater in frosty weather.

The flashlight meant he couldn't much bend his right elbow, but his left hand could handle subway tokens. He knew the old New York City survival adage: "Subway in light, cabs at night," but it wasn't quite dark yet.

He took the A Train, humming the Billy Strayhorn tune like millions of tourists before him. Two speed-boppy young men in sideways baseball caps got on with him and flopped down a few seats away. Ryon snuck a few surreptitious glances at them, because their facial structures and complexions were a great advertisement for putting black, white, Hispanic and God knew what else in a blender. It took a careful eye to notice it, though, because their clothes hid the people inside them. Ryon didn't get the sex appeal of butt-crack, baggy pants and tent-sized jackets. Low-rider jeans to show off the tops of your silk boxer shorts just seemed ridiculous. But then, bellbottoms and beads had been pretty damned ridiculous. By rights, he and the boppers should be wearing zoot suits for the A Train.

They got off at the same stop he did, and stood arguing on the platform about which exit to take. Or at least that *might've* been what they were arguing about—rap slang was Armenian to Ryon.

Out on the street, Ryon stopped to look south toward Fort Tryon Park and the stone-walled medieval fantasy of The Cloisters. Maddie had used to spend a lot of time in The Cloisters—playing her squeakless, tenor recorder in the herb gardens, or sitting silently in the room hung with the tapestries of the hunting of the unicorn.

But Ryon wasn't going south toward The Cloisters tonight, he was heading west along Dyckman Street toward the river and under the expressway. There was nothing Fantasyland about the boarded-up buildings, and kids throwing rocks at each other on construction sights, but the general ambience probably bore more resemblance to most medieval life than The Cloisters did. There were auto body shops and tire-change joints with their gates locked for the night, and very little traffic.

What with not a lot of street lamps on these sidewalks, and none at all out on the Hudson, it was actually getting dark, not the phoney Midnight Sun of Midtown. He was almost sure he could even see a few stars if he squinted hard —the three in a row that made the belt of Orion The Hunter. But maybe that was only wishful thinking for a sign there was actually a sky beyond the smog.

Ryon was just beginning to enjoy the relative peacefulness—only the white noise of the highway in the sky, and the percussion of his own footsteps— when he heard other footsteps running up behind him. Something told him to turn around fast. But before he'd got halfway around, a hand grabbed his shoulder and spun him back against the wall. Another hand shoved a gun in his face: a shiny, pocket-sized pistol.

It was the two boppers from the subway. The other one had a knife. The one with the knife yelled: "You lookin' fuh somefin', whitebread?"

The one with the gun yelled: "Gimme yo fuckin' wallet, mo fo!"

Ryon hyperventilated: "Yeah… Yeah," holding his left hand up open to show he'd do what he was told. "I got a… cast." He clunked his left hand against the flashlight inside his right sleeve, so they would understand that his struggles to get his left hand into his wallet pocket weren't meant to inconvenience them.

As Ryon squirmed to get his wallet out, the one with the knife yelled again: "You lookin' fuh somefin'?"

The one with the gun hollered into Ryon's face: "Maybe you lookin' where you should'n' be lookin'! Maybe you should stay the fuck at home!" Both pairs of eyes were lit up like pinball machines, and the one with the gun kept jerking it from side to side like he was dancing.

The one with the gun snatched the wallet out of Ryon's hand and said: "And yo jacket, fuckah. Fuckin' leather jacket."

Ryon said: "Okay, okay, but I gotta… the cast…"

"Fuckin' cripple." But they stepped back a few inches to give him room to unzip and shuck.

As Ryon exaggerated the clumsiness of his left hand fumbling with the snaps and zipper, most of his mind was screaming at him: "You can get another jacket and replace the credit cards!" But a small part was needling: "They followed you. *You lookin' for something?*"

Ryon synchronized himself to the jerking dance of the gun: on-beat pointing at the wall, off-beat in his face. He uncupped his right hand, felt the ribs of the flashlight barrel sliding through his sweaty fingers, closed his hand and flicked his wrist, with his forearm and elbow behind it for all they were worth. The flashlight came up hard against the cocked elbow of the one holding the gun. The gun went off, spraying brick dust, and spun away.

The knife was lunging at him. He swung his left arm out to block it and jerked frantically out of the way. He leaned too far. His shoulders hit the sidewalk hard, but he managed to keep his neck bent so his head didn't bounce on the concrete. He was flat on his back looking up at a speed-freak with a knife, and baggy jeans worn fashionably with the waistband halfway down the hips to look like they would fall off any second.

Ryon grabbed a handful of fabric and yanked. Denim slides smooth off silk: the pants came down around the bopper's knees, hobbling him, but the striped boxer shorts stayed up. Ryon drove the head of the flashlight straight up between the caramel-colored thighs to the place where the stripes intersected.

Before the shriek of pain and surprise was over, Ryon was back on his feet. The other bopper was scrambling to pick up the gun with numb fingers. Stupid kid should've used his left hand. Ryon slammed the flashlight down across the back of his head, scooped up the gun and his wallet and turned back to the one with the knife. The slasher still had the knife in his hand, but was doubled over and pulling his pants up with his other hand.

Ryon brought the flashlight down across the knife-wrist, kicked the suspect's legs out from under him, knelt on his chest, shoved the gun in his face and said: "You do not have the right to remain silent. Who hired you?"

"Fuckin' cocksuck fuckah!"

Ryon rapped the baseball cap with the flashlight and said: "I asked who sent you. I asked politely. Where I come from they call us The Horsemen. You don't want to meet the other three. Who put you onto me? Was it the spider-man?"

"Spiderman? You fuckin' crazy?"

"*The* spider-man. You know who I—"

"*Yo, mo fo!*" The shout came from behind Ryon. He looked over his shoulder to see a half-dozen baggy-pants coming quickly down the middle of the street. Ryon scrambled to his feet, showed them the pistol and called: "I'm leaving.

If any of you are packing, keep in mind that I've spent more hours on the firing range than you have in the sack."

They stopped to think about it. Ryon backed to the nearest corner and
stepped around it. Then he flattened himself against the wall, right arm
extended in firing position, waiting for the sound of running footsteps. All he
heard was curses and some low moans. They weren't going to come. He
started to walk again, zig-zagging blocks, slowing his heart down. His back
and shoulders hurt like a bastard. But he didn't figure it was going to turn out
any worse than a few bruises. Lucky the body of the bomber jacket was still
fleece-lined.

He had to unfold his map under a streetlight to figure out where he'd got
to in relation to Doctor Kroenberg's address. While he was at it, he took a
closer look at the pistol, wondering whether he should keep it till he crossed
the forty-ninth parallel again. When in Rome...

But when he held the gun up to the light, it turned out to be a nickel-plated
piece of tin that was just as likely to blow apart his fingers as blow a hole in a
bad guy. He decided to hold onto it till he got safely back near his hotel and
then chuck it down a sewer.

Doctor Kroenberg's apartment block hadn't been painted since about
Nineteen Twenty-Two, unless you counted the graffiti. The stairwell smelled
of old urine and young wine, and echoed with the sounds of children crying
and adults yelling. Doctor Kroenberg's apartment had a steel door with an
intercom built into it. Ryon pressed the buzzer.

"Ja?"

"Corporal Ryon."

There was a clicking of deadbolts, then the door swung open. Doctor
Kroenberg was short and bearded, wearing a striped sweater whose stripes got
wider near the bottom. He beckoned Ryon inside and closed the door again.
As he attended to the deadbolts, Doctor Kroenberg said over his shoulder:
"You're late."

"I got held up."

"Well, the meter started ticking at nine anyway." His German accent
seemed to come and go. He beckoned Ryon to follow him down a long hallway and said: "You're not American-born. English? Scotch?"

"Canadian."

"Ah."

"And you? I don't mean to be nosy, Dr. Kroenberg—"

"Make it Manny."

"But, uh, are you German, or…?"

"Oh, the kraut-speak. No, I was born a few blocks from here. But I do a lot of court work, started very young, and I found judges paid more attention to Herr Doctor Kroenberg. I got into the habit and sometimes it creeps in off-duty."

The hallway ended in a wide living room with green walls. There was a well-aged upright piano, framed paintings, a very expensive German stereo rig, and bars on all the windows.

Doctor Kroenberg noticed him noticing the bars and said: "The bars and the door are only to keep out the desperately stupid. For serious people I have much better protection. Gang leaders can be very appreciative if their court-appointed psychiatrist says they need counseling, not incarceration."

Sitting on a glass coffee table was a corked bottle of white wine in an ice bucket beside three glasses. Sitting in a corner chair was an old black guy wearing shades, a snap-brim hat and a yellow jogging suit. He didn't say anything and Dr. Kroenberg didn't say anything about him, just said to Ryon: "So, Henry, you said you had some tapes?"

"Uh, yeah. It seems like kind of a stupid idea now, but I'm clutching at straws. Are you a Jungian therapist?"

Doctor Kroenberg laughed gleefully. "You know what Carl Jung said when someone asked him what that meant? He said: 'Vell, when a patient is fixated on power, I'm an Adlerian, if they're into sex I'm a Freudian, if they're into myths and dreams I'm a Jungian, and if they're not into any of those I make something up.' If there is an afterlife, I hope Jung is taking some comfort these days with Rudyard Kipling. 'If you can bear to hear the truth you've spoken twisted by knaves to make a trap for fools…'

"But I did get an amateur-typed inquiry once that would've made him laugh. The break in the line made the question: 'Are you a Jungian the rapist?'" Dr. Kroenberg practically ruptured himself laughing at his own joke. The old black man in the corner didn't crack a smile. Doctor Kroenberg caught his breath and said: "So, you want me to put your tape in the machine for you, or…?"

"I think I can figure it out."

"Lay it on me, Henry."

"You got it, Manny."

While Ryon pushed buttons and turned dials, Dr. Kroenberg uncorked the wine. Ryon took one of the cassettes out of his pocket and slotted it in without looking at the label. He'd spent an hour or so in his hotel room second-guessing himself on what songs to put on for the shrink, and finally decided to just slap on whatever came up.

What came up was the first cut off Maddie Prue's first solo album, *The Glove of A Lewd Woman,* and it was a song that never failed to make Ryon smile. If, like a lot of people had said, Maddie Prue sang like an angel, it was an angel with teeth. The song sounded caressingly soft, until you listened to the lyrics. She was singing to a cheating lover who'd manfully confessed his fucking around, rather than undermine their precious relationship with dishonesty. Her reply to his confession was more or less: "You're not telling me for honesty's sake; you're telling me so you can feel honorable and I'll have to live with it. If you're going to screw around, the least you can do is lie like a bastard, and *you* live with it."

What made the song even tastier was that it was written at a time when "honesty" was supposed to be the prime directive, and the world was gonna be a better place if everyone went around spewing out their innermost secrets at the drop of a floppy hat. But then, Maddie Prue was never much of a sucker for the prevailing winds. The next cut was her version of *Ain't Nobody's Business If I Do,* and she didn't follow fashion on that one, either. Most people who covered that song completely missed its sense of humor, and turned it into a kind of defiant tantrum just by screwing up one word in the intro. They'd sing:

> *Ain't nothing I can do or nothing I can say,*
> *That folks won't criticize me,*
> *But I'm gonna do just what I want to anyway...*

Maddie sang it: "So I'm gonna do just what I want to anyway..." One little syllable and the whole thing changes.

Ryon sat sipping his wine and watching Manny Kroenberg listen to Maddie Prue. The good doctor had his eyes closed and his head leaned back, tapping a finger on the stem of his wineglass. Halfway through the fourth cut, he shook his head, waggled his hand and muttered: "Turn it off, turn it off..."

Ryon went to eject the tape, saying: "Sorry. Different tastes in music."

"Hm?" Doctor Kroenberg was wiping the corners of his eyes. "No, that isn't it. Not my regular thing, but relatively tuneful. But it's... too painful."

Ryon sat back down and leaned forward. "How so? Does it sound to you like she was afraid of something?"

"Afraid? She was terrified! Whistling past the graveyard. But such a whistle."

Doctor Kroenberg took another sip of wine, but didn't swallow, as though swirling the wine around in his mouth while swirling something else around in his head. Finally he swallowed. "I'm not such a fool as to make an analysis from a tape recording. Maybe it would end up being labeled manic depression, or paranoia, or who knows? But there is a sound you learn to recognize, a voice that is trying to speak as though the walls weren't changing color and the floor moving up and down. That woman is holding herself together with glue and paper clips, but still dancing. It is the bravest voice I've ever heard."

"That *woman…*" the rasped-barrel voice came out of the old black man in the corner, nudging his snap-brimmed head sideways at the speaker box nearest to him. It occurred to Ryon that the old man might be blind. "That woman… She been down to the crossroads."

The black man in the yellow suit went back to sipping his wine, as though that was all there was to say about it. Ryon said to Dr. Kroenberg: "If you think it might've been labeled paranoia, maybe she was afraid of someone in particular?"

"I can't say. Who was she?"

"Maddie Prue. She sang in a band called Anemone, then went solo, then died in a ridiculous accident. Or maybe it wasn't an accident."

Manny Kroenberg looked at Ryon silently for long enough that Ryon considered suggesting that Doctor Kroenberg and Professor Rushton buy a condo where they could pause at each other all day long. Finally Kroenberg said: "And if her death wasn't a ridiculous accident, maybe your life isn't."

"I didn't come here to get analyzed."

"Hm. Speaking of people, Henry, who are holding themselves together with glue and paper clips…"

Ryon stood up and said: "What do I owe you?"

"Oh… send me a dub of that tape when you can. If you can. I will take it medicinally. Fat chance you'll find a cab in this neighborhood at ziss time of ze night. If some of our local youths accost you on your way to the subway station, tell 'em you're a friend of mine and you'll be all right. Probably."

As Manny Kroenberg unlocked the deadbolts and burglar chains on his steel door, Ryon remembered something else to ask. "If you're a Jungian— whatever that means—maybe you know something about… There's a theory, or a kind of quest, I've heard about but don't really understand. It started with some people trying to trace down the roots of the story of King Arthur and Guinevere."

"Not exactly my area of expertise. I *do* know that parts of that story were Freudian before there was a Freud. In the earliest versions, from Cornwall and Wales, the Holy Grail isn't exactly holy, and it isn't one object. It's two objects together: a cooking-cauldron and a white spear that drips blood from its head. A lot more fun than the Christian version—like most things."

"Well, this theory I heard about was trying to draw some kind of connection back from Guinevere and Arthur through, say, Venus and Adonis, Ishtar, The Corn King, back through all those different myths about the Earth Mother and her dead lover, and sacrifices. There's a Professor Rushton—"

"Celina Rushton?"

"You know her?"

"I read some papers she wrote. Relatively interesting, for an anthropologist. She got in a bit of shit back in the 'seventies, for a highly informal program using a group of young people as guinea pigs—trying to break through to the collective unconscious with LSD and ancient chants and Gestalt ceremonies and who knows what. It did make for some interesting papers."

"Maddie Prue was one of those young people."

Dr. Kroenberg's eyes widened. "The woman on the tape? Son of a bitch! Celina Rushton should be stood up against a wall and fucking shot. Anyone trying to open up the unconscious of the woman on that tape was playing games with a nuclear bomb!"

XIV

THE RUNDOWN LITTLE INN on the Brixton Road was hosting a knees-up in the Public Room—what they would've called a kick-up back in Wahpeston—and the noise was keeping Ryon awake. He considered tugging on his boots and stomping downstairs in his nightshirt to complain to the landlord. But he had to acknowledge that it wouldn't have been an honest complaint. If there'd been no sound but his own breathing, sleep would still be hovering beyond his reach.

The old scar on his chest was itching like Billy-o. Damned odd that it should be nothing but a dormant mark for so many years and then suddenly come to life again. He supposed it must have something to do with the change in climate; the North American prairies weren't strong on humidity. But as aggravating as the itch was, that wasn't what was preventing him from sleeping.

What actually was keeping him awake was the egg he kept rolling around in his mind. From all of his nosing-about in other people's memories, all he had was an egg shell that he could feel the contours of but couldn't penetrate.

It occurred to him that the same could be said of all his traveling. After crossing half a continent and an ocean to get to London, he hadn't really entered the city proper, only pecked around the periphery. Excepting that venture to Waterloo Station, where one brief glimpse of Penelope had confirmed his reasons for avoiding the heart of London: the heart of the heart of the most powerful country on Earth at the end of its best century thus far.

He sat up and considered the possibility that the egg was more like a pearl, nothing but solid shell until one got to the grain of sand buried somewhere in the center. Perhaps he'd gone as far as he could with probing other people's memories, and it was time to jog his own. The places he used to haunt back in the days when Maddie Prue was still alive were in the center of the city that was the center of the world.

Ryon swung his legs out and put his bare feet on the icy floor. He assured himself that even with gas lamps on every corner, the streets were dark enough that a man leaned back in a hansom cab would be practically invisible. Lying in his bed debating possibilities certainly wasn't going to get him anywhere, including to sleep. He reached for his trousers.

The three tables in the tiny public room had been pushed against the walls, and an off-duty charwoman was punishing the floor to a handclapping chorus of *Knees Up, Mother Brown*. The chorus petered out when Ryon appeared in the doorway. He loathed the fact that a bowler hat and a tailored ulster made him someone they had to kowtow to—and the corollary that if he'd appeared in the doorway in his patchwork farm clothes they would've looked down their noses. A place for everyone and everyone in his place.

The waiter came forward quickly. "Anyfing I can do for you, Guv?"

"Yes, that cabstand you mentioned wasn't close to here; how would I find it?"

"Just straight norf along the road, Guv, but it's a good 'arf a mile."

"Fair enough. And I'd like a decent bottle of—" Ryon's lips formed the W for whisky, but he altered it to "wine. You'll have to uncork it for me, then bung the cork back in. And a small tumbler, if you would."

"Done in a tic, Guv."

By the time Ryon reached the cabstand, his silly, city half-boots were half-soaked with slush. There weren't many cabs still waiting around for custom at that time of night, just two hansoms and a four-wheeled growler. Ryon told the front-of-the-line hansom driver what he wanted, handed him a gold guinea and said: "Let me know when that runs out."

"It'd be a long ride before that runs out, Guv."

"It might be a long ride."

Ryon climbed into his chariot, folded the traveling rug across his legs, closed the slanted quarter-doors in front of him and rapped on the roof. As the cab jounced into motion, he took the napkin-wrapped tumbler out of his right greatcoat pocket, the bottle of red plonk out of his left and pulled the cork with his teeth.

The Brixton Road melded into Kennington Park Road. As he looked out at the passing darkness of Kennington Park, Ryon found a forgotten memory of climbing in over the fence after the park gates were closed. But the memory had nothing to do with Maddie Prue, so he pushed it aside. The cab route passed by St. Mary of Bethlehem Lunatic Hospital. Bedlam. He thought maybe he should've just told the cabby to pull in there.

By the time the cab clattered onto Waterloo Bridge, Ryon had drunk a cup or so of wine and even his toes felt relatively warm. Ahead, The Strand looked much more brightly lit than in his day, so he lowered the shutters on the side windows to half mast. As they passed by Somerset House and came out onto The Strand, the driver slowed his horse to a sightseeing pace.

Instead of turning onto The Strand, the driver carried on along Wellington Street, following Ryon's general instructions to weave through and around the area like a fisherman's net. Ryon glanced to his left at the pillared front of the Lyceum Theater. The theater crowds had long since gone off to their homes, or to restaurant suppers, but two people were coming out of a side entrance.

They made a curious couple: a large-featured, handsome woman in her forties, arm-in-arm with a reed-thin old man. Ryon knew who they were, though he had to look twice to make sure. He'd never met the woman, but he'd seen her on stage enough times to have recognized her instantly—except that in his day she'd been exclusively associated with the Haymarket Theater, not the Lyceum.

As for the frail old man, Ryon had met him in passing once or twice in younger days, in Rossetti's garden or Morris's. He was the mathematician, amateur photographer and fabulist Charles Dodgson, whom the world knew as Lewis Carroll. The couple were even curiouser and curiouser than they appeared. No one in Ryon's day had been able to explain how a man who broke into helpless stutters with any female over the age of ten could be fast friends with Ellen Terry, who could melt a playhouseful of men with one shrug of her shoulder.

Ryon found it warming to see that the oddly-matched old friends were still friends. But the sight of Lewis Carroll also brought a chill. "Beware the Jabberwock, my son…" Ryon's last few months could easily be described as The Hunting of the Snark. And at the end, "He had softly and suddenly vanished away, for the Snark was a Boojum, you see."

Ryon came out of his reverie to discover that the cabman had made a horseshoe around Covent Garden and was emerging from Southhampton Street into The Strand. The width of The Strand made it no trouble for vehicles with actual destinations to pass around the ambling hansom. Parties of fur-caped and silk-hatted pedestrians were trilling champagne laughter over the clopping of the cabhorse on the cobblestones. Strains of music were coming from a supper club.

It became immediately clear to Ryon that he'd made a mistake to think that old haunts might trigger a few old memories. They were triggered, all right— so many and so fast he couldn't tell one from another.

A pair of opera-caped gentlemen were peering into a lighted shop window. Ryon squinted and saw that they were admiring a display of photographs of the fashionable beauties of the day. Maddie had never appeared in one of those windows. She had certainly been a beauty, in her way, but never fashionable.

Ryon looked ahead. Up to his right was an opulent-looking restaurant that had been built since his time. On the sidewalk in front of it, a woman was arguing with a *maître d'* and a constable. It suddenly brought back to Ryon a brouhaha between Maddie Prue and the staff at the Café Royal, the artists' stomping grounds in Piccadilly Circus. He'd not only been in the Café Royal when it happened, he had the distinct impression that he and Maddie had been sitting at a table for two. Or maybe his imagination had got crossed with his memory.

The site of that scene might bring back more details. He leaned up to rap his knuckles on the roof and tell the driver to make for Piccadilly. But just as his wrist flicked, the window passed directly by the woman in the sidewalk dispute, and he realized he knew her. He knocked harder and called: "Stop!"

He shoved the cork back in the bottle, extricated himself from the cab and said: "Wait here," then started back toward the argumentative trio. He could see that that brief glimpse of the woman hadn't played him false: tallish and lithe, with the same black-sheep hair, dark blue eyes and pointed features he remembered. The devil of it was, although he'd known her well—not *well*, perhaps, but intimately—he couldn't for the life of him recall her name. But he did recall that she'd been close with Maddie Prue.

The argument paused as he drew up beside them. "What seems to be the trouble, constable?"

"No trouble, sir. Nothing to concern yourself with."

"No trouble to *you*," the woman snorted at the constable. Then she jabbed her finger at the *maître d'*. "This stuffed, boiled shirtfront won't let me in, even though I told him just to put it on my chit."

"'Chit,' indeed," the *maître d'* said loftily. "The Savoy is more than glad to keep a monthly accounting for preferred clientele. But when the amount in question mounts in mid-month to eleven pounds, eight shillings and thruppence—"

"I *told* you," the woman interjected. "I'll remit the entire accounting at the end of the month. But not at the door like some fish and chip shop."

The constable said to Ryon: "As you can see, sir, it's no concern of yours."

"Oh, but it is. You see, the lady is a friend of mine." She shot him a surprised glance, then covered adroitly. The cream-white skin around her eyes still hadn't begun to loosen with middle age; she'd been a good ten years younger than the members of Anemone when she'd attached herself to their circle. "How much did you say that account was?"

The *maître d'* replied: "Eleven pounds, eight shillings and thruppence."

Ryon drew out his billfold, handed the *maître d'* a ten pound note and a two pound note, then turned to the woman. "I have a cab waiting. No doubt you prefer to take your custom elsewhere." She threaded her arm through his and strode with him to the cab.

Once they were ensconced, Ryon rapped on the roof and called: "Drive on." The cabman's long-handled whip tapped his horse back to a walk. The inside of a hansom was close quarters; inevitably the woman had to rest her leg against Ryon's under the lap rug. Amazing how body warmth could transmit itself through layers of winter-weight wool and petticoats. She seemed delighted that he happened to have a bottle of wine. He filled the tumbler for her and sipped daintily from the bottle. He said: "I'm heading nowhere in particular. It would be no inconvenience to deliver you to your door."

She shrugged, "If you like," and told him an address in Chelsea. He called it up to the driver. The driver tapped the horse into a trot, made a half-circle around St. Clement Danes and headed back down The Strand.

The woman leaned her upper body away from Ryon so she could get a long, unabashed look at him. After a moment she pronounced her verdict: "You don't know me."

"I did. Somewhat. But that was twenty years ago, or thereabouts. I was a friend—an acquaintance—of Maddie Prue's." A *very slight* acquaintance would've been more accurate, but Ryon wasn't above leaving hairs unsplit at this point.

Her eyebrows knitted together and her mouth drew in upon itself. She looked away from him at the Trafalgar Square fountains passing by. He remembered wading through the fountain basin on the way back to his digs one hot July. She said: "What's your name?"

"Ryon. Henry Ryon."

She shook her head. "I never knew any Ryon."

"As I said, it was almost twenty years ago."

"What's *my* name?"

"Well that's the ridiculous part of it. I remember you perfectly clearly, I know exactly who you are—or were. But I can't put my hand on your name."

She looked skeptical. He said: "You see, I left England a year or so before Maddie died, and haven't been back since. So there's more than a few cobwebs on my memory. I never expected to set foot in London again. But, this summer, someone in London sent me a message… that Maddie's death wasn't an accident."

Suddenly her leg and hip weren't touching his anymore. Apparently there was more room in a hansom than he'd thought. She was pressed against the side wall of the cab as though she would press herself through it if she could.

Her reaction set Ryon vibrating like a frustrated hound who suddenly strikes a scent. He endeavored to keep the excitement out of his voice, using the same unalarming tone as he'd use to a skittish horse. "Whatever may have happened, it was a long time ago, and there shouldn't be any danger to anyone now. I've already spoken to a number of people about it. But all I've been able to find out for certain is that Maddie was afraid of something, and that it had something to do with The Circle, and possibly Jack Delaney."

The dark blue eyes were wide and riveted on him, the sharp chin tucked in. She thrust her hand into her handbag and said: "I carry a small revolver. Stay on your side of the cab."

Ryon looked down. The handbag was beaded and shapeless, and it didn't look to him like the hand inside it was clutching a revolver. But he wasn't about to ask her to prove it.

She said: "You don't know me. The address I gave you is false, but it's close enough that I can walk home after you and your cab have gone on."

"Believe me, I don't intend to do you any harm—"

"And you won't. What you also won't do is say another word about Maddie Prue."

Ryon opened his mouth and then closed it again. He hadn't entirely told the truth that he didn't intend her any harm. He wanted to throttle her if she didn't tell him why the mere mention of suspicions about Maddie Prue's death turned her snakebit. But that wouldn't exactly do. He turned away from her and gripped the rim of the safety gate instead of her throat.

The driver had angled down Commercial Road onto the Chelsea

Embankment. House fronts and garden walls were on their right, the wide Thames on their left. Out on the river, a fountain of sparks showed a steam launch chugging upstream. Ryon sat chewing his lips.

As the cab horse trotted them further along Cheyne Walk, they passed a darkened house Ryon remembered. He said: "I wonder who's living in Rossetti's digs now?"

The woman said dismissively: "Any guidebook could've told you that was Rossetti's house."

"I suppose. I wasn't there often. He didn't much care for company after Lizzie Siddal died, did he? 'The Sid'. He just hunkered in behind his shrouded windows, with his private zoo out back. I wonder what became of the armadillos and all? But there was one time he actually gave a party of sorts. Anemone put on a performance. You helped them—I believe you were beating on a little drum, or a tambourine. And you were wearing the same style of dress, made out of the same shimmery, green cloth as... that woman I won't say another word of."

He turned to look at her. Her eyes had grown narrower. He said: "And your name is Annathea Drummond."

She showed no response, just stared at him. The cab turned up a side lane and reined to a halt. Ryon unbolted the quarter-doors and climbed out to give her a hand down. Once her shoes were on the pavement, she turned to him and said: "Won't you come in, Mr. Ryon?"

"I would be delighted, Miss Drummond. Or are you still...?"

"Still Miss Drummond."

As Annathea Drummond turned to lead the way, Ryon turned up to the cabman and said: "I shan't ask you to wait. I can find another cab home."

The cabman said: "Yeah, I thought she didn't look like a cab moll, but the kind as prefers 'er own digs," then winked. "A long ride, Guv. Good night all 'round," and tapped his horse into motion.

Ryon followed Annathea Drummond through a gate into a postage stamp garden and what once had been a one-horse carriage house. Once through the door, she tossed her coat and handbag on a bench and went to build up the fire in the grate. Ryon looked around. Even though the inside of the carriage house had been nicely converted, it was still cramped quarters—albeit high-ceilinged. But the painting hanging on one wall was a Burne-Jones original, and the glass-doored case of leather bound books looked like first editions.

Annathea Drummond turned from the grate and seemed surprised to see him still standing by the doorway. She said: "Well, take off your coat and hat and sit by the fire. I'll fetch some glasses to finish off your bottle of wine, and then I'll open one of mine.

"But first…" She shucked her skirt-matching jacket, then tugged the tails of her shirtwaist out of her skirt, unbuttoned her blouse and discarded it as well. She stepped toward Ryon, turned her back to him and said: "Could you unbuckle me, please?"

Ryon reached his hands up to her corset. He wondered if the polite thing would be to kiss the back of her neck while he was about it, but decided she seemed a bit too matter-of-fact for that. So he just manipulated the hooks and eyes while she sucked in a deep chest-breath to give him a little slack to work with. It had been a very long time since he'd unfastened a corset, with nothing but a very thin cotton shift between a woman's skin and the backs of his fingers.

When the last hook left its eye, she dropped the buckram and whalebone contraption on top of her jacket and shirtwaist, raised her arms to bury her fingers in her black-sheep hair and breathed like someone emerging from a long swim underwater. The shift looked even thinner than it had felt. He could clearly see the contours of her breasts: pointy and hardly yet drooping at all, with ghosts of pink at both tips showing through the cloth as though she'd rouged her nipples. Maybe she had.

She fetched two wineglasses and poured, saying: "Filthy inventions, corsets. In the days when we were all Bohemians, Maddie and I could go about hanging free in loose dresses. But if one is forced to haunt the places where respectable gentlemen are wont to gather…"

Once she'd handed him a glass, she popped open a flat wooden box on the bureau and proffered it to him. It was filled with expensive-looking, black cheroots. When he demurred, she stuck one in her mouth, scratched a match alight and said: "I hope it doesn't shock you too much to see a woman smoking."

"Not at all. The woman I see the most of back home is a *métis* girl half your age, and she rarely sits down without lighting her pipe."

She squinted at him through the puffing-alight smoke, then tossed the match in the grate and said: "*Métis*…?"

"Oh. Half-breed. Part Indian. Not Calcutta Indian; Cree, or Ojibway, or…"

She cocked her head and sucked the corner of her mouth. "What do you call 'back home'?"

"The North West Territories—well, part of the Dominion of Canada now. I'm what they call a remittance man: younger sons whose families decided would be less of an embarrassment in the colonies."

She plopped down in the chair across the hearth from his. He found it a bit disconcerting to be sitting across from a woman wearing a long skirt and boots and practically naked from the waist up. He tried not to stare. But she seemed to be staring at *him*. She said: "A year or so before Maddie died…?"

"Pardon me?"

"Back in the cab, you said you left England a year or so before Maddie died."

"That's right."

Her eyes pinned him to his chair. Her face suddenly blossomed into a grin. She stood up again, her eyes still fixed on him, exhaled a puff of smoke and exhaled with it: "You're Villon!"

"Um, no—Ryon."

She shook her head. "I know you now. Villon." His utter incomprehension must've shown on his face, because she extrapolated. "François Villon. Fifteenth century French ballad-maker, cutthroat and vagabond. The flower in the gutter."

"I, um, do have some idea of who François Villon was, but I don't see what that has to do with—"

"Then you should know that our poets were all enraptured with him: Swinburne eulogizing 'our sad bad glad mad brother,' Rossetti translating *The Ballad of Dead Ladies*…

> Nay, never ask this week, fair lord,
> Where they are gone, nor yet this year,
> Save with thus much for an afterword—
> But where are the snows of yester-year?

"Mad keen on imitating Villon they all were. But *you*…" She took another puff on her cheroot and pointed it at Ryon. "You *were* Villon."

"I never wrote a ballad in my life. Or any other kind of poem."

"But you were always getting into brawls and scrapes and mad adventures. Hanging about with thieves and racing touts. Disappearing into places like Whitechapel for weeks on end, and—"

"Whitechapel? What makes you say Whitechapel? If I was 'disappeared' why would you guess it was into Whitechapel?"

"Maddie told me she'd seen you there once. I think I was the only one who knew about her forays into Whitechapel. The rest of Anemone would've gone stark, staring bonky if they knew their meal ticket was taking such chances. There was a period of time when Maddie and I told each other everything. A short period of time.

"Although you say you didn't write poetry, Villon, you were living the kind of life that Morris and the rest might romanticize, but were scared to death of. I remember the night you came to me. I've never seen a man in such a state and still able to stand up. But you made up for it in the end."

Ryon felt himself blushing. He couldn't remember many details of that night, just that it had been... energetic.

Annathea Drummond leaned against the mantle and took a thoughtful puff on her cheroot. "I knew it wasn't me you wanted to be with, but I didn't mind."

Ryon didn't quite know what to say to that, so he said nothing. Annathea Drummond said wistfully: "Maddie... Sad, bad, glad, mad Maddie. She had the prettiest little pink cunt, and the things she could do with her tongue... Of course she was just young and experimenting, as I was with men. Does that shock you?"

"Not particularly."

She laughed. He hardly heard her; he was preoccupied trying to sort out an anomaly. When she'd referred to Maddie Prue's "little pink cunt," what had immediately leaped to mind was that he wouldn't have described it as particularly little. But then, how the hell would he know? The only possible explanation was that his deep-sleep dreams must be getting more intimate than he recalled the next day, planting details of overheated imagination that his mind might mistake for memory.

Annathea Drummond handed him a fresh bottle of wine and a corkscrew. As he went to work unscrewing the cork, he said: "Miss Drummond—"

"I think you can call me Annathea. We have been introduced, even if it was a long time ago."

"Why did you—in the cab, when I said there were some suspicions about Maddie's death—you got... rather distraught."

She turned away from him, walked to the bookcase and idly ran her finger along the fretwork. He got the feeling she was studying his reflection in the glass. She said: "Wouldn't you? If you'd lost a dear friend to an accident years ago, and then suddenly some stranger bundles you into a cab and says it might not've been an accident?"

It seemed to him there was more to it than that, but she didn't seem inclined to say so. He said: "I spoke to Celina Rushton about The Circle." She raised one inky eyebrow at that, then came forward with her empty glass held out. As he poured, he said: "The Circle seems to've been mostly women, but there were a few men involved, weren't there? Fergus Doude. And Jack Delaney…?"

She laughed: "Not hardly," then lost her laughter. "There was a streak of rot through Delaney. Likely still is. I haven't seen him in fifteen years and will be just as glad if I never do. Not a tree worth felling. But Maddie was loyal to him, for some reason. I suppose because he'd been with her when times were hungry.

"We all waxed so noble about The Poor, but we all had our little inheritances—not up to Morris's, but we'd never starve. But Maddie was *of* the poor. Thirteen children in a factory tenement. It was Delaney who brought her to London."

"But she left him eventually, when she left Anemone."

"Yes, she did."

"But she never left The Circle."

The dark blue eyes focused on him. She rolled her lips in and out as though they'd gone dry, then took another quaff of wine, tossed the stub of her cheroot into the fire and lit another. She seemed disinclined to sit, either leaning against the mantle or striding about the room. She also seemed disinclined to answer his question. He said: "Or *did* she leave The Circle—leave it high and dry like she left Anemone?"

"She's still part of it, even if it hasn't convened for sixteen years." Ryon wanted to pounce on that, but he didn't want to spook her. While he was trying to think of a subtle way to leap out of his chair, she said: "I'll show you something."

She opened one of the bookcase doors and came toward him holding out a small, black-lacquered box. She stopped in front of him and raised the lid. Inside it was a ragged-edged scrap of paper, like a corner torn out of a notebook. Annathea Drummond said: "Maddie wrote that in this room—not long before she decided we would no longer be intimate friends."

Ryon took out the scrap of paper. The handwriting wasn't easily legible—as though the writer probably had decent penmanship but was more than several sheets to the wind. It was a kind of pseudo-haiku.

> *If you can't kill your love,*
> *Who can?*
> *If you can't love your killer,*
> *Who will?*

Ryon said: "What does it mean?"

"What does it *mean?* What are you, some kind of literary professor vivisectionist? It means what it bloody means!" She snatched the scrap of paper back from him, snapped it back in the box and carried the box back to the bookcase, hissing: "What does it mean?"

Gone and stepped in something again, cleverlad—wipe your shoes off and walk softly. After a decent enough interval for the wind to maybe change, Ryon said: "Did, um, did The Circle ever find the reason why The Hunter must die?"

She moved to the far side of the room, planted her back against the wall and looked at him like she was considering whether to show him the door. Eventually she said: "Are you a Christian, Villon?"

He shrugged. "Baptized C of E. That's about as far as it goes."

"Good—a dedicated Christian might take offence. Christianity, you see, pilfered a lot from earlier religions. Especially the cult of Mithras, in Asia Minor."

"Where the blood of Adonis flows into the sea."

She cocked her head at him, then nodded and smiled. "Well volleyed." He remembered now that even at seventeen she'd had a cheeky playfulness about her. She seemed to have grown into it.

Annathea came forward to have him fill her glass again, then began to prowl about the room. "The great harm that Christianity did was to freeze the sacrifice in time—to make it only one momentous death, instead of the cycle of life. Both Aphrodite and Persephone loved Adonis, so they made a compromise: he would spend half the year among the living and half the year in the underworld. So it was with Mithras: the Bull of The Sun, born again out of the blue, virgin sky at the winter solstice—December 25th in the Old Calendar. Every year, when the bull was killed, wheat would sprout out of his blood." She stopped her prowling and planted herself in front of him. "Out of his blood. After he'd been torn to pieces by the ones who loved him."

She puffed on her cheroot, took another quaff of wine and said: "Does that sound cruel? But think of it through the eyes of the sacrifice himself." She hiked her skirts and straddled his lap. He could feel her warmth through his woollen trousers, much warmer than her leg against his in the cab. "Isn't there a release—a relief—at being taken? A sweet surrender…"

She ran her fingers through his hair, then pulled his head back gently, lowered her head and kissed him, leading his lips in the dance. She rubbed her next-to-naked breasts against his chest and whispered huskily in his ear, "Don't we all wish somewhere deep inside us that someone would give us a good excuse to stop struggling? To tell us we could make the world blossom just by closing our eyes and letting it all slip away?"

Ryon could feel himself slipping, all right, into a soft darkness with an edge of vertigo. She leaned back, smiled down at him, then slapped him just hard enough to tingle. "That's a good boy. Just lie back and let me take you."

She laughed, stood up abruptly, went to poke the fire in the grate and looked back at him wryly. "Not so objectionable, is it?"

"I would've objected if you'd tried to cut my throat."

She shrugged. "A little longer and you would've had *un petit mort* at least."

Ryon was finding it difficult to breathe. He looked at the ceiling and saw Maddie Prue wearing the flowered, gauzy dress of Botticelli's painting of spring, with the same verdant background, flowered attendants, and ethereally gobsmacked expression—except there was a teardrop of blood at one corner of her smile. He said: "What's any of that got to do with Maddie's death?"

"I don't bloody know! You're the one who said her accident might not've been an accident, and you asked me about The Circle. I'd managed to bury it away and here you come dragging it out again. Maddie was the queen of us all and she's fucking dead, isn't she? Let her rest."

She started crying. Ryon muttered: "Oh, hell," went to the fireplace and put his arms around her. She had to bend her neck for him to cup her head against his shoulder.

She stopped sniffling and murmured: "Since my experimental years men aren't my inclination. But they are my profession. You seemed to be enjoying it…"

"Um, it's a little difficult to get into the spirit of things when you know the other party is acting. But you *have* brought back fond memories of a certain night I'd lost in the past. And you've given me information no one else has."

Though what the devil he was going to do with it was another question. "Would a two pound note make up for what you might've earned if I hadn't spoiled your night?" Not to mention the twelve pounds to the Savoy, but he was past keeping accounts.

"Leave it on the table, that's the usual way."

He did, and went to fetch his coat and hat. When he turned back in the doorway, she had opened a plush-skinned reticule and was taking out a hypodermic needle and rolling up her sleeve. He said: "Do you know where I might look for Fergus Doude?"

"If I'd known you were that way inclined... Just joking. I have no idea where he's disappeared to." She slid the needle in her arm and pressed the plunger. Her head lolled back, then flopped forward. Her half-lidded eyes shone at him like cobalt beacons. She said dreamily: "It's the *fin de siècle*, Villon. The hangmen want to close the books."

He closed the door and went out into the remnants of the night.

XV

WITH THE NEW YORK CITY night loudly gearing up outside his window, Ryon sat in his unlit hotel room with his eyes focused on the Drive-In screen at the back of his skull. He'd decided that if Sweet Surrender was the name of the game, he might as well lie back and stop fighting off the memories. But the fragments weren't floating back to him now, they were flying in fast and furious and he was gripping the chair arms like Captain Kirk flying The Enterprise into a nebula storm—except he didn't have The Cosmic Cowboy's faith that his mission was going to make the universe a better place to live. As Donald and Daffy would say: "Set the controls for The Heart of Duckness."

He was in the psychiatric ward at the Misericordia Hospital—The Misery— in Winnipeg. Well, not *in* the ward—there was a potted-tree garden on the roof, with Adirondack chairs and plastic jugs of lemonade. And a high, chain-link fence cemented to the top of the retaining wall around the edge. Ward legend said that a few years ago a patient had managed to climb the fence and jump. The patient's psychiatrist had been furious at the staff's carelessness—furious because the patient had landed in the shrink's parking spot, and it was just blind luck he'd been on call at another hospital or his Volvo would've been totaled.

Ryon had kicked off his Medicare-issue terrycloth slippers to get some air between his toes. Sooner or later some nurse was bound to come along and give him a lecture about hospital hygiene and bare feet, but until then… He was feeling not too sorry for himself and happily jabbering with his Visitor, his baby sister Penny. Or *trying* to jabber happily—his mouth seemed to be filled with cotton candy that wouldn't dissolve. Maybe it was the medication, or maybe he'd fucked himself up even worse than everybody said.

He was explaining to Penny that, now as he knew some people in the big-time music business back in New York City, maybe when he got out of the hospital he'd hunt up The Mystic Moron and put another band together. Penny was nodding and smiling at him with her little, pink mouth and big, dark eyes. But there was something not quite real about her smile...

He trailed off in mid-sentence. She was humoring him. He leaned back in his bolted-down Adirondack chair and looked up at the clouds, blinking his eyes. What kind of useless fucking fuckhead fucks up so bad that his baby sister thinks she has to humor him? Time to start acting like a competent human being again, maybe even get other people to believe in the act.

He was in a crowded green-room after packing up one of Anemone's shows, hunkered on his heels in a corner drinking free boiler makers and trying to keep himself innocuous. The night had to be at least eight or nine months after he'd first carried amps for Anemone, because the green-room wasn't a grotty one and Audrey Doude was there, sitting on the floor behind a coffee table telling people's Tarot.

He figured he better split soon, before they noticed how much of their liquor he was drinking. He popped another 292 and washed it down with beer. When he'd first got into the habit, he'd thought his taste for 292s and alcohol was a dead giveaway that he was a hick kid who should be hanging around behind the 7-11 sniffing glue. But a dope-smoking pharmacologist he'd bumped into in a bar had explained to him: "No, no, it's a brilliant combination. You see, there are three ways drugs effect the central nervous system. Alcohol does it one way, codeine the second way, and acetylsalicylic acid does it the third way. So what you get is a geometric progression."

Audrey Doude pointed across the room at him and said: "You're next."

"Me?"

"Yes, you." It didn't surprise him that she didn't seem to know his name. "I've done everybody else. Your turn."

Ryon reluctantly sank down cross-legged across the table from her. They went through the ritual of shuffling and cutting and passing the deck of cards back and forth, her long, pale fingers fanning around the oversized cards like it was just a poker deck. Ryon did have to admit that for all her eerie mono-chromity—bordering on albino, except for the olive eyes—there was something kind of sexy about Fergus Doude's new lady. Good bone structure goes a long way. But he did hope Fergus was well-padded around the ribs, or wore a quilted jacket to bed.

The card that came up to signify who Ryon was was the Five of Cups—a caped, male figure seen from the back, hunched over broke-heartedly in front of a spilled cup, not seeing the four full cups behind him. Audrey Doude laid out the rest of the H-shaped format of cards, looked at the layout and wrinkled her forehead. She shook her head, murmured: "I must have done something wrong," and scooped the cards back into the deck.

They went through the shuffling and cutting ritual again. The card that came up to signify Ryon was the Five of Cups again. Audrey Doude did a pretty good imitation of looking surprised and slightly freaked. Ryon just said: "Good trick," and got up and hit the road.

He was in the wings, sitting in the shadows after helping reset the stage from the opening act. Anemone was getting so big now they had opening acts—this time a blue-leathered, dark-haired singer named Mary Anne Something-or-other. In fact, Anemone was getting so big now that when they started their road trip next month they'd be playing venues a part-time roadie couldn't come within a mile of without an IATSE card and prior arrangements with the union local. Ryon was quite sure that the only reason Anemone still let him carry mike stands for their local gigs was charity.

The crowd was getting restless—a ten-minute intermission had turned into twenty. Anemone finally came out of their dressing rooms and passed by Ryon on their way to the stage. Fergus Doude had his arm around Maddie's waist and was pretty much holding her up and navigating for her, saying: "It's only one set, Maddie, and maybe a couple of encores. You can do it."

Over the last six months, as the audiences had been getting bigger and bigger, so had Maddie's intake before each show—drinking and snorting and smoking and who knew what else when her dressing room door was closed. But Ryon had never seen her anywhere near this bad. Her head was lolling and she looked like she couldn't tell one foot from the other. Mary Anne Whatsername and her manager, standing between Ryon and the stage, looked at each other and chuckled—it seemed pretty obvious which act was going to get decent press tomorrow morning.

As Maddie hit the stage lights, she pushed off from Fergus, her head straightened and she seemed to grow six inches taller. She walked straight to the up-front mike stand and shouted over it—not into the mike, just filling the hall with her naked voice—"Are you ready for some MacRock-and-fuckin'-Roll?"

The roar that came out of the crowd drowned out The Boys vamping a rolling thunder behind her on bodhran and bass and electric strings. From backstage Ryon could see what the crowd couldn't see—the back of her loose-fitting, brocade blouse become tight-fitting as her back doubled sizes when she filled her lungs. The banshee roar that came out of her drowned out the crowd with Anemone's howling version of *The Unfortunate Rake*, leapfrogging into electrification the ancient song that had got subdivided into *St. James Infirmary Blues* and *The Streets of Laredo*.

Well, she ripped the joint up, didn't she? Roaring, crooning, teasing Celtic Blues chords out of the piano, holding the rhythm together with acoustic guitar when Fergus took center stage… When it came to Encore time, the band only came off stage for long enough for Fergus to whisper to Maddie:"Just one more, I promise." There was nothing Ryon could do but just sit back in the shadows and watch it happen to her. She loved it and she hated it; it kept her heart pumping and it was killing her. Kinda like life.

Maddie blew her last kisses and headed off-stage while The Boys were still unplugging their guitars and waving good-bye to the crowd. When she got back into the wings she slumped and staggered again. Ryon was about to jump up and offer her an arm, but she caught herself and started slowly toward the dressing rooms—walking like a wrung-out dishrag if a dishrag could walk.

As she passed by Mary Anne Something-or-other, Mary Anne snorted: "How long do you think you're going to be able to get away with that?" Maddie's left hand flew up, fingers fanned-out, past the right side of Mary Anne's pretty face. Mary Anne swung her head in that direction, as anyone would instinctively—startled and wondering what the hand was going to do—leaving the left side of her neck wide open. Maddie's right fist plowed into it perfectly, where the carotid artery runs unprotected between the jaw and shoulder. It was professionally done—Maddie's right foot even came up off the floor as she put her whole body behind her fist. Mary Anne went down like a sledgehammered steer. It put Ryon in mind of a moment when he'd got a little carried-away in hand-to-hand class and the sergeant had called a halt and announced:"Don't try that at home, kids. Either somebody's born with the instincts of a bloody street-brawling maniac or they're not. You can't teach that. Good work, Ryon—but the suspect better've been armed and dangerous."

Maddie was carrying on toward her dressing room before Mary Anne Whoseherface even hit the floor. Mary Anne's manager started to move, but it looked to Ryon like he wasn't moving to help his injured property but to injure the injurer. Ryon barked: "Don't!" He didn't.

Ryon was standing at the back of a dark, SRO auditorium—some kind of upscale university venue—watching Anemone take yet another crowd on another magical mystery tour. There was no point hanging around backstage tonight—just watch the show from the back of the house, help with the take-down and head back to his rooming house. Tonight the green-room and the dressing rooms weren't going to be their usual after-show blowout and phar-macology experiment. Maddie had flown her parents in from the Midwest for the weekend and didn't want to rub their noses in it.

Maddie could afford little extravagances like return tickets from North Dakota these days. The band was getting so close to Big Time that last month *What's Happening* magazine had featured Maddie Prue of Anemone in its Twenty Questions puff piece. When they'd asked her: What's the sexiest thing on a man? she'd said: "A dishcloth."

Fergus finished his feedbacked crash-landing to bring *The Demon Lover* home, nodded at the applause and turned to Maddie moving to the piano to start the next song. She didn't. She riffled a little music-box tinkle out of the keys and let the half-chord sustain and fade. Even from the back of the house, Ryon could read the expression on The Boys as they turned toward Maddie with their instruments at half-mast. He hadn't seen it happen often, but it only took a few times to recognize that what was zotting through their minds was: *Oh shit, what's she gonna do this time?* Maddie and Fergus always worked out the set list together, and Maddie usually stuck to it religiously. But every now and then...

Maddie didn't look back at the band but out at the audience. She said into the mike: "Me Mum and Da are in the house tonight—well, me *Step*-da if you want to get picky about it, but if Arnold Prue was picky about anything he wouldn't've saddled himself with Daisy MacGregor and her three brats. When he brought us home to America he had a good job—still does—but me ma was never one to let grass grow under her feet, so she got herself an afternoon job at a bookstore. Bought an old one-speed bicycle to get back and forth on. Well, where we come from it was nothing strange to see a grown-up woman in a long dress and business make-up toodling along on an old clunker of a bicycle, but in North Dakota in Nineteen Sixty-two...

"So, I was walking home from school one day with two girls who were actually starting to be my *friends*. Well, you know, it's bad enough being twelve or thirteen, but when you also talk with a funny accent and think football is a game you play with your feet... So we were chattering and giggling and I hear this little, rattling sound behind me and I look back and 'Oh my bloody God, it's me Ma on her bleedin' bicycle...' So I just look straight ahead and keep on walking and I'm praying: 'Please God don't let her wave or call hello. And if she stops I'll just die.'

"Well she goes on by without looking at us, and I am *so* relieved. And then—I kind of choke, and I drop me books on the sidewalk and start running down the road after her shouting: 'Ma! Ma!' She stops her bicycle and looks around and when I catch up with her she says: 'Oh hello, dear, I didn't see you.' Well of course she bloody *did*, she just didn't want to embarrass me in front of me new friends. She says: 'Is there anything the matter?'... 'No, I just wanted to say hi.'... 'Hello, dear.'... And she kisses me on the cheek and says: 'I'd offer you a ride, but you're getting a bit big to fit on the handlebars. I'll see you at home,' and she pedals off."

Maddie began to coax that music-box tinkle out of the piano again, and sang in a whispery voice into the mike:

> *Daisy, daisy, give me your answer do,*
> *I'm half crazy, all for the love of you,*
> *It won't be a stylish marriage,*
> *I can't afford a carriage,*
> *But you'll look sweet upon the seat*
> *Of a bicycle built for two.*

Two seconds later, Maddie and the band were hammering the shit out of Richard Farina's demented rewrite of *Blood Red Roses*.

There was a midnight bedroom lit by a couple of dozen candles. Or maybe it wasn't a room at all, just the candles in the void. Maddie Prue and Annie Dyke-Drummond were standing naked facing each other but not touching.

Or almost not touching. They were standing just close enough that the tips of their breasts touched. It seemed they were playing a game that might be called Kissing Nipples—arms down by their sides, staring into each others' eyes, half-giggling and doing a slow-motion Locomotion from the waist up, so that the business ends of their breasts brushed against the other's like butterfly kisses. Maddie would have to be standing on something to make their breasts the same height.

The object of the game seemed to be to see whose nerves would overload first; who would give in and tackle the other one onto the nearest horizontal surface. Dyke Annie didn't seem to be winning—the nipples on her turned-up, pointy breasts were standing out stiffly like pink fireweed spikes, almost vibrating. Or maybe it was just that Maddie's breasts weren't the kind that was as obviously readable—rounder and heavier, chunky, with nipples that were more nubbly than pointy, and puckered areolae like lightly-browned strawberry skins, the halo on the right breast twice as wide as on the left...

Ryon snarled: "Fuckhead," and wrenched around in his hotel room chair. That wasn't a memory, that was some stupid *Penthouse* wet-dream. He knew now that Maddie and Annie had got it on once or twice, but he sure as hell had never sat in and watched. There were wide gaps in his memory when almost anything could have happened, but *that* never could have. No matter how stoned or horny Maddie got, she wasn't into voyeurs. She spent enough of her life being stared at on stage; off-duty she couldn't stand the feeling of somebody watching her chop vegetables for a salad.

Ryon asked himself once again how he could be so bloody sure what Maddie Prue thought or felt; he hardly knew her. The little bits of on-and-off time he'd spent hanging around Anemone had all been on the edges of the group—on the edge, like the rest of that lost year. He replied to himself that he'd just answered his own question. People on the periphery sometimes had a clearer view of the people at the center. It didn't cross his mind that that might work the other way.

But he couldn't come up with any explanation for why he was so certain that Maddie had had mismatched tits—the same size and shape, but the right areola much wider than the left. She certainly didn't go around flashing them to every Tom, Dick and Henry. Maybe one of the pictures in the boxed-set booklet had her in something extremely low-cut, and he'd noticed without noticing. He would've thought he'd memorized every page by now, but his hard drive wasn't exactly responding on command.

He took the boxed-set book out of the drawer and started leafing through it. Right off, he noticed something he'd noticed before but hadn't really thought about. In the pictures of Maddie from Anemone days, there were always other people around her, members of the band or other bands, or out on a family picnic… But in the pictures after she went solo, she was always alone. Even in shots of her on a park bench with a frisbee team tearing up the grass behind her, she looked like she was posed in front of a painted backdrop.

Well, they were all alone now: Audrey Doude, Flip Norman, Celina Rushton… Even the AWOL punk kid who used to carry Anemone's microphones.

But when he turned another page, he saw that Maddie hadn't been entirely alone. There was a snapshot of her with her arm around a very large, bearded entity who was grinning back at her—one of her Irish wolfhounds. Ryon remembered her showing up for a gig laughing so hard she had to collapse on the green-room couch before heading on to her dressing room. The rest of the band poked their noses out to see what was going on. She caught her breath enough to explain between gasps: "Murphy's got her full growth now, and she's so long that… The distance between her head and her butt is so far that… She was stretched out on the floor having a nap, and she farted in her sleep, and she jumped up and whirled around snarling like: 'Who goosed me?'"

Well, Maddie had always had a pretty twisted sense of humor. Ryon remembered a party where she'd decided she was the reincarnation of Long John Silver's parrot and refused to say anything to anybody except in character. But if you listened closely, you heard that what she was squawking wasn't "Pieces of eight," it was "Pieces of hate."

And then there was the time she showed up for a gig looking pink and pampered, after taking Fergus's Born Again Health Nut advice to go for a swim and a steam and massage. She announced to the crowded green-room: "You were absolutely right, Fergus—I feel like a new man!" It had seemed to Ryon that her eyes had picked him out at the back of the room, but it had to be just his imagination.

Looking through the pictures of the young Maddie Prue—there were never going to be pictures of the old Maddie Prue—brought back to mind the old Remembrance Day poem: *They shall not grow old as we who are left grow old…*

Forever young. Maddie's voice said in his head: "Forever young, my ass, I'm fookin' dead."

Before Ryon had flipped through half the pages, he got sidetracked off of what he'd started looking for. One of the pictures had Maddie perched on the knee of the statue of Hans Christian Andersen in Central Park, like Hans was reading her a bedtime story. There was something about the kids' sculpture garden and playground in Central Park... He remembered reading in some guidebook that they'd got the idea for kids' sculptures in the park from the statue of Peter Pan in Kensington Gardens, but that wasn't the memory that was nagging at him...

Ryon and Maddie and a couple of other Anemone-ites were lugging a shitload of instrument cases double-time past the duck pond in Central Park. A producer with a penthouse in the East Seventies had made an appointment to hear some songs, but a fender-bender in front of Bethesda Fountain had frozen traffic. Maddie had said: "Fuck this—faster to pay off the cab and hike it."

As the Alice in Wonderland statue hove into view, Ryon noticed a tall, thin guy with short, thin hair, a goofy beret and even goofier, round glasses, keeping a close eye on a slanty-eyed kid climbing around on the bronze Mad Teaparty. The people on the benches were trying not to stare. There was something impossibly familiar about the guy, like someone Ryon had known half his life.

He heard Maddie murmur up ahead of him—her short legs chugging in the lead—"Well, well, the bad-boy finally came home to *mama-san*." Then she started singing in a cartoon Liverpool accent at the top of her lungs, and her lungs were nothing to sneeze at,

> *Oh dirty Maggie Mae,*
> *They 'ave taken her away,*
> *And she'll never walk down Lime Street anymore...*

The guy in the beret swung his hawk nose toward her. She called out: "Whatsamatter, ya Scouse git, can't sing without a kotex on your head?"

"You should 'ave one for your mouth."

"They don't make 'em that big. Ta-ra, Johnny."

"Ta-ra, Maddie."

Ryon caught up to her and panted: "Kotex?" He would've been embarrassed that he was shorter of breath than she was, except that he was carrying two guitar cases and a pig-nose amp and she only had the mandolin. He'd insisted.

She laughed. "Oh, back when he was having his year-long lost weekend with Nilsson in LA, they went into the Troubadour one night and Lennon had a kotex tied to the top of his head. The band was playing, and at the Troubadour they absolutely won't seat anybody except between sets. John got shirty and said to the waitress: '*Do you know who I am?*' And she said: 'Yeah, you're the asshole with a kotex on his head, but you still can't come in.'"

Maddie laughed some more, then said: "But what's endearing about Lennon—as if he gives a flying shag what I find endearing—is if he hadn't told that story on himself, no one would ever have known."

That was as far as that memory went, leaving Maddie Prue trucking along Fifth Avenue and Ryon sitting in his hotel room on the other side of town. It occurred to him there was a blacker twist to the funny waitress story now, one that Maddie would've appreciated if she'd lived long enough to know. The last words John Lennon ever heard, from the cop cradling him in the back seat of the cruiser racing for the hospital, were: "Do you know who you are?"

Well, John Lennon and Harry Nilsson and Maddie Prue were all dead now. Maybe the waitress was still around to tell the tale.

Ryon wondered if that memory of Maddie and John Lennon in the same place might not've just come up arbitrarily, like pulling the lever on a slot machine. Maybe Memory Central was trying to tell him something. Maybe he was being an idiot by trying to trace some kind of trail of human logic to whoever might've murdered Maddie Prue. Maybe some Mark David Chapman or John Hinkley had come looking for her and found her standing on the edge of the cliff behind her house... No. That kind of sick puppy always did it in public.

Ryon was lugging an equipment bag behind Maddie Prue and two non-Anemone musicians heading for an extra-curricular gig somewhere. They were weaving their way along a crowded subway platform, so it was early days, before Maddie and Anemone graduated to cabs and then limos. There was a derelict shambling along like the platform was empty—a moldy-looking guy with dark, greasy hair and dumpster clothes that smelled like caked shit. As a train pulled in, the bum suddenly got an urge to move faster, bumped smack into Maddie and started screaming at her to get the hell out of his way. Ryon saw that the guy had a clawhammer shoved down the waistband of his pants.

Keeping his eye on the clawhammer and the flailing hands above it, Ryon carefully set down the equipment bag—making no fast moves—and slowly and deliberately moved forward. But Maddie's arm came up in front of him and she started crooning softly at the screamer:

> Moments of magic that glow in the night,
> All fears of the forest are gone...

The loony-bar looked confused for an instant, then shouted: "He's dead! I killed him! I'm John Train!" and reached for the clawhammer.

Maddie said: "John's gonna miss his train."

The crazy, still with his hand on his holstered clawhammer, looked like he was almost going to laugh, but instead he scooted onto the subway car just before the doors closed.

Usually, whenever something got between Maddie and her route to the next gig, she would just keep charging-on the instant the roadblock was got out of the way or swerved around. But this time she stayed standing in place watching the subway train carrying away the moldering zombie she'd bashed her tits against. She said: "That was Phil Ochs," and then gave out a twisted, little laugh. "Yeah, that *was* Phil Ochs."

One of the other musicians said: "Who?"

Maddie snorted: "Bloody Rock 'n' Roll illiterates. Phil Ochs. Back in the Sixties he and Bob Dylan were neck-and-neck for the Woody Guthrie crown. Phil Ochs wrote *Changes*." Her voice got softer and stranger, like she was talking to herself. "And *Crucifixion*. 'As the cycle of sacrifice unwinds...'"

Not more than a few weeks later, Ryon picked up a paper and saw that Phil Ochs had hanged himself at his sister's house in Far Rockaway, New Jersey. Or that was the coroner's verdict.

There was a crew of professional roadies Anemone's new record company provided for big gigs. Ryon picked his way between them across the stage, looking to see if there were any tail-ends of cable he hadn't coiled up. He couldn't see any, so he headed backstage to police the area, in case any of the band had left anything behind. Nowadays, with afternoon sound checks and dressing rooms with showers, Anemone showed up for a gig toting shoulder bags crammed with stage clothes, chessboards, sketch pads, make-up kits...

The dressing room doors were all standing open. He poked his head into each one as he went along the hall, but none of the empty rooms showed any difference from when the traveling circus moved in that afternoon. A little messier, maybe, but nothing he could see that anyone would regret leaving behind.

He heard voices from the end of the hall—apparently not all the traveling circus had moved on yet. The last dressing room door was standing open, too, but the room wasn't empty. Fergus Doude was packing up his gig bag while a chocolate-skinned, sweet-legged woman Ryon had never seen before was cutting lines on the make-up counter. The legs kind of stood out—she was wearing nothing but a Ravi Shankar shirt that ended about where they began.

She gasped when she caught Ryon's reflection in the mirror—a shortish-haired guy in plain T-shirt and jeans, looking like a not-very-inventive under-cover narc. She swivelled around and almost sat down on the coke, but Fergus caught her shoulder and said: "It's all right, he's cool," and kept on picking things up to put into his bag.

The next thing Fergus Doude picked up was a fat, dog-eared paperback. He started to shove it in his bag, then stopped and said to Ryon: "You read much, ace?"

"Some. When I can see straight."

"I've pretty much worn this one to rat-shit, already bought another copy. Here."

Ryon caught the tossed book and looked at the wrinkled cover. *The Golden Bough.*

"Thanks."

"No big deal, ace." But a hooded glint in the almond eyes suggested there was something resembling a big deal.

Ryon stood up out his hotel chair, letting the glossy book of Maddie Prue pics slide off his lap onto the floor, and muttered: "Good thinking, Fergus. The only way out of it is to get into it." So far the only information he'd been getting on The Circle was secondhand scraps doled out by the people who thought of it as a sacred secret. Why not go straight to the source they'd started from? Letting his memories come back didn't seem to be solving much. When one line of inquiry peters out, try another one. Parallel investigations. Parallel lines. Geometry says they never meet, but if you look down a prairie railway you can see the two tracks come together in the distance.

The bookstore Ryon had remembered being on the corner of Times Square was out of business. But it shouldn't be that hard to find a bookstore in the publishing capital of the world. He crossed in front of Father Duffy's statue and looked around. Among the blinding signage on the Virgin Records megastore was something that looked like Books. After three or four escalators down into the bowels, he found himself surrounded by everyone from John Grisham to Geoffrey Chaucer.

They did have a copy of *The Golden Bough*—in the Religion section, of all places. "A New Abridgement," which meant only 900 pages, but Ryon wasn't planning to read it all. They were also practically giving away a coffee table sized book with no pictures, called *Timetables of History*, so he snagged that, too. As he recollected, Sir James Frazer wasn't big on cluing you into whether Babylon was around before the pyramids or vice versa.

On the way back to the hotel, Ryon stopped by the deli and picked up another six of beer. Going to be dry reading. He opened the first can and sat staring at the cover of *The Golden Bough*, thinking about waking up in the Misericordia Hospital. A still, small voice said: "Are you sure you want to do this?"

"No."

He opened it to the index. Astarte, Ishtar, Isis, Venus...

It seemed that Venus didn't just go wild for Adonis, she went wild *with* him. The story went that for awhile the Queen of Love gave up her silk and marble palace to go running through the woods with the hunter and his pack of hounds. That put Ryon in mind of Celina Rushton's lecturette about gypsies, but he couldn't say exactly why.

In the temples of Astarte, they had an annual festival for the death of her hunter when the Adonis River ran red from the windflowers and mud washed down by the spring rains, and everybody had to shave their heads in mourning. But it seemed that cutting your hair off was a *really* big deal for Phoenician women. So big a deal that some of them took the only other option open to them—which was to turn themselves into temple whores for the day and let any man fuck them who gave the priests a nickel. The Hell's Angels would've called it "pulling a train." Not exactly just lighting a votive candle.

So, Venus and Adonis were later, more cleaned-up versions of Ishtar and

Tammuz, or Astarte and Tammuz. Frazer said that Ishtar and Astarte were both descended from an earlier, Sumerian story. And *that* descended from...?

Ryon switched to The Timetables of History and looked up Sumerians. It was *way* back, where the Timetables didn't list events under, say, 1749 A.D., or 42 B.C., but 3000–2501 B.C. "Sumerian poetry, lamenting the death of Tammuz..." That would make it the oldest known poetry in the history of the human race.

4000–3501 B.C. "End of Paleolithic period along the Mediterranean Coastline. Sumerians settle on the site of city of Babylon." Well, that would be Celina Rushton's "Second Giant Step in human evolution, that separated us from the other creatures of the Earth"—paleolithic hunter-gatherers becoming neolithic farmers, the first settled towns... But why that should be, as she put it, "our species-childhood trauma" was another question. Ryon got a queasy image of The Antlered Man. He shook it off and looked to see what there was before 4000 B.C. and the Sumerians.

Nothing. That was where the *Timetables of History* began. Before that there were no signposts but carbon-dating of Stone Age hunting camps, and cave paintings. So then how could The Circle search back for some source older than the oldest poetry in human history? Celina Rushton had said herself she was an intellectual who could only understand what she could read in black and white.

Well, if you're looking for something way under the surface that science and education can't help you find, you need a dowser. A divining rod. Maddie Prue.

Ryon looked down at Maddie smiling up at him from the cover of the picture booklet he'd dropped on the floor when he got up to go find a bookstore. He remembered what he'd got sidetracked from—trying to find some explanation for why he was so sure about her weird areolae. He picked the booklet up and flipped through the second half. There it was, on the second-last page.

It was a photograph that probably wouldn't have been published while she was still alive—like Flip Norman said "the fucking Tabloids weren't all over everything back then." It was a head and torso shot of Maddie in a very skimpy two-piece, sitting on a narrow stretch of sandy beach hemmed-in by jagged, black boulders at the base of a cliff—maybe the same tide-pool she was found in. She was laughing and holding up one hand as though telling the person with the camera to bugger off. Although both cups of her top were exactly the same size and shape—actually more like triangles of handkerchief than cups—the left areola was covered completely, but the right breast showed the rim of a circle of darker, softer-looking skin poking out past the cloth.

Ryon grinned at the picture and himself. *You see, smartboy? Driving yourself crazy by thinking you're going crazy again, when all the time there's a perfectly simple explanation.* Obviously he'd looked at that picture way back when, subliminally filed the fact that her right areola must've been a couple of sizes bigger than the left, and then forgot how he knew that. Pleasant tits to look at, too—creamy, North Country skin freckled by California sun...

He stopped breathing and looked at the picture closer. One of the freckles—the big one at the top of her right areola—wasn't a freckle. It was a tear-shaped burn scar, with a white cut-line running down from it to disappear under her bra.

XVI

EVEN AT THE apogee of England's world-civilizing nineteenth century, midnight London streets weren't the sanest place to go strolling alone, but Ryon wasn't feeling very sane. He'd had enough vestigial sense of self-preservation left, though—when the evening brought him the feeling it was going to take a long time to walk himself to sleep—to find a place before the shops closed to purchase a walking stick with a lead-weighted head, just in case. As for the possibility of anyone in a passing group of revelers recognizing Henry Ryon-Chilton, he was willing to take his chances. In the highly unlikely event that his trail crossed Penelope's again, he might even speak to her and damn the consequences.

At first he stuck mostly to the parks—Hyde Park and the smaller parks dotted beyond it. Even with most of the trees bare, and snow mounded by the paths, the parks felt warmer and homeier to him than streets of houses crammed with humanity—although he had to keep moving to keep warm. Wonderful how one could walk practically right through the heart of London in parkland. He blessed whatever genius had insisted that a swath of green be left in the middle of all this sooty brick and pavement.

The winter-deserted parks also meant his uncontrollable mutterings wouldn't cause embarrassment. The phrase that came out more often than any other was: "I'm growing sick of this Sysiphus,"—of the sinkhole he'd allowed himself to be lured into by the ghost of Maddie Prue. And "growing sick" was the apt term, although the proper term for the sickness was debatable. Back in the days when the family still thought there might be some vestige of hope for him, his mother had insisted he visit several of the many alienists she frequented. One of them had diagnosed his problem as melancholia, another as dementia, a third one as monomania, and the fourth had come out with some equally sonorous pseudo-Latinism Ryon couldn't recall perzackly.

Whatever the proper term for it, the only cure for the immediate symptoms was to keep on tramping until he'd exhausted his body enough to sleep. In the meanwhile, his mind kept rolling the boulder up the hill and watching it bounce back down into a tidepool of memory and ripples.

He was sitting in Rossetti's back garden on a muggy summer day, brutally hung-over, watching the armadillo nose the sleeping dormice. Through the open window behind him, he could hear Rossetti discoursing to a roomful of women about the insoluble question of why some people are blessed with artistic ability and hence cursed with demons.

There wasn't a woman alive who would dare to contradict Dante Gabriel Rossetti in full flight—at least not a woman who would be allowed into such August company. Except one, of course. Maddie Prue said: "The question isn't why some people have demons—everybody does; the question is why some people bloody dwell on it. Or in it. No offense, Rossetti—I'm one of 'em. Or two of 'em."

So it went on: shards and shadows coming at him out of the parks and streets of London, as though they were trying to tell him something he was too bloody dull-witted to grasp. But one of them had nothing to do with London or anything else on the old side of the Atlantic, and actually gave him a fleeting moment's peace…

A coyote pup—or more accurately coyote adolescent—lying frozen to the mud and frost-crisp reeds beside the pond. But still alive—puffs of mist coming out of its nostrils. Given the ripped skirt of spring ice on the edge of the slough, it looked like the silly sonofabitch had gone chasing a duck, fallen through, and by the time he'd dragged himself back out half-drowned and soaking, the sunset had dropped the temperature ten or twenty degrees.

Ryon crouched down beside the icebound animal, expelled a long breath and sighed: "What am I going to do with you?" Coyote Jr. didn't reply. Ryon knew that every farmer between Red River and the Rockies would answer his question in a second: either take a hammer to the furry head or save yourself the trouble and let the varmint freeze to death. Anything else would be criminal.

Ryon went back to the house and put the kettle on the stove. When the kettle was warm but not hot, he carried it and a blanket down to the slough. He poured the kettle out along the uphill side of the froze-to-the-ground coyote, waited a minute, then threw the blanket over him and pried him free. The coyote made a few feeble attempts to bite him as he picked it up, but couldn't get through the buffalo coat and moosehide gloves. Bloody lucky it wasn't a wolf—even a half-dead wolf would've ripped off his arms through chain mail.

He carried the coyote up to the barn, laid him down in the empty, corner stall and shredded a few flakes of straw over him for insulation. Edgar and Esther, and especially Melinda, kept the barn above freezing even in the worst of winter. The stall walls were too high for a half-dead coyote to climb over and try to eat the heating devices. But the plan was that Mr. Coyote wasn't supposed to stay half-dead for long.

Ryon went back into the house, made a pot of tea and thought about the problem. It was pitch dark outside now, which complicated matters. He lit the lantern and carried it out behind the barn. He built a small fire about five feet out from the corner of the barn and kept intermittently feeding it while he went and fetched the fence auger, a fencepost, the hammer and three-inch nails, and carried the lantern and the swede saw down to the poplar grove.

By the time he'd cut and trimmed a dozen poplar poles and hauled them back up to the barn, the fire had thawed the ground enough to wrestle the auger in and set the fencepost. Then he started building a triangular pen— nailing one end of a pole to the side of the barn and the other end to the fencepost. It was bloody frustrating—the first end of a pole had to be tacked loosely enough that it would swivel when he lifted up the far end, but not so loosely that the nail would pop out before he got back to hammer it in solidly, and sometimes he guessed wrong and had to start all over.

By the time he got the fence up there was light in the sky. The fence was only as high as his waist, no obstacle to a healthy coyote. But once the coyote was healthy enough to jump over the fence, he should and good riddance. Ryon only had a moment, though, to congratulate himself on that bit of efficacious logic before: *Charming fence, cleverlad—that was the easy part.*

He went back into the house and got a screwdriver and the chisel. With the first blow of the chisel into the barn wall, there was a surprised coyote-yelp from behind it, then Coyote went back to quiet convalescence. Ryon made two chisel holes about two feet apart in the third plank up from the ground, then unscrewed the swede saw blade, inserted it in the first hole and started sawing downward with the naked blade clasped in his gloves.

By the time he got the last piece of plank out and tossed it over the fence, he was just about all-in and then some. He stood leaning against the barn listening to the long wheezes of his breathing and feeling the cold for the first time since he'd decided the coyote wasn't going to die. Then he heard something else: a horse clopping up the frozen road, and Bell wasn't roaring "Who goes there?" That meant only one thing: it was Lisette's appointed day to come do the mucking-out, and he'd lost track of the calendar.

He couldn't quite yet work up the energy to let go of the barn and climb out of the holding pen. Lisette saw him, guided her pony behind the barn, slid off the saddle and said: "What you gone and done now?"

He more or less told her, feeling increasingly embarrassed as he looked around at the skee-whiffed, jury-rigged excuse for a fence. She bit her lower lip and said: "You did all that last night with nobody to hold things up for you— for some evil and stupid coyote?"

"Yes."

She slanted her lower limbs against the fence so she could reach up her hands to take hold of his ears, pull his head down and kiss him on both cheeks. She said: "You come inside and I make you some breakfast, then I clean away the tools and you go to sleep." He suddenly didn't feel cold anymore, or like a fool...

It seemed that while he was back in coyote-land he'd got himself turned around and back in Hyde Park again. He stopped and leaned his back against a tree and rolled a cigarette. It took a while; his hands were shaking. It seemed there was another night he'd been walking through Hyde Park, only it had been a summer night, and he'd been going somewhere in particular...

He was striding along with the spring-kneed ease of young men—too young to know how lucky he was to still have spry knees. He was heading west for South Kensington, which was about as far west as his relatives in Mayfair Society would consider still part of The Metropolis. It was a misty night, but not a chilling, pea soup, London fog—this was a warm mist, what the Irish would call "a soft night." He felt like he was turning himself into a skulking, sneaking Peeping Tom, but couldn't shake the conviction he'd been invited to where he was going.

That afternoon there'd been an Anemone performance at Morris's place— probably the last before every moneyed Londoner lit out for their country homes and left the city dead until the fall. After the show, he'd been standing in the vicinity of Fergus Doude when Maddie Prue came up and whispered to Doude: "Tonight, midnight. Turners' on Milner Street. You know where?"

Doude had just nodded and said nothing in reply. But it had seemed to Ryon that Maddie had whispered louder than was necessary, and when her eyes crossed his as she turned away she didn't look startled or surprised that he might've overheard.

The long walk to the outer reaches, instead of taking a cab to the vicinity of Milner Street, was intended to give him time to decide whether he'd been surreptitiously invited to whatever was going on at the home of whoever these Turners were, or whether it was just his imagination. He made the long walk even longer by detouring through The Children's Playground in Kensington Gardens with its "Elfin Tree" of gnomes and fairies.

But when eventually he got to Milner Street he still hadn't decided. The strongest argument on the "not invited" side of the debate was that an address hadn't been mentioned. But Milner wasn't a long street, most of the houses were already darkened for the night, and one of the few that still had lighted windows also had a brass nameplate on the gatepost: Y. TURNER.

Ryon stood staring at the nameplate and still debating with himself. He could hear a muffled sound of human voices—not from inside the house, but behind it. The house to the right of the Turners' was completely dark, and the wisps of mists added to the cover of night. Ryon snuck into the Turners' neighbors' yard, hoping they didn't keep a mastiff.

The Turners had an unusually high, brick, garden wall—twice Ryon's height. He could hear the voices coming over it—about a dozen of them, chanting in unison, like some kind of religious service or reciting an epic poem. But he couldn't make out the words.

The Turners' neighbors had a splendid oak tree in their back yard, with a children's swing hanging from it. Ryon's eyes followed the swing ropes running up into the shadows of the oak boughs. *Don't be a blasted idiot, cleverlad. Well, it's either that or make the decision to knock on the Turners' door or go home.*

He stood on the swing, took an overhead hold on one of the ropes and held himself in mid-air just long enough to twist his right foot into the slack so his left foot could press down on it and secure him. Then he started climbing. When he got up to the stout branch the swing was suspended from, he moved very slowly and carefully, fumbling in the darkness to get himself up and onto the branch without snapping twigs. He didn't look down or over the wall until he'd got himself settled solidly, sitting on the bough and holding onto the one above it. When he did look, he almost fell out of his tree.

They were standing naked in a handholding circle around a fire: Maddie Prue, Fergus and Audrey Doude, Annathea Drummond, a handsome, middle-aged woman Ryon had never seen before, and several others he probably wouldn't've recognized even with clothes on. Well, technically they weren't entirely naked. Some of them were wearing bone necklaces, or flowers in their hair, and all of them had streaks and swirls of ochre and vermillion and woad on their skins.

Now Ryon definitely felt like a peeping tom, but he couldn't drag his eyes away from Maddie Prue's firelit, mist-kissed body—the abrupt, round swell of her hips with the heart-shaped thatch of Saxon gold between…

He could hear what they were chanting now:

> Lady of barley,
> Lady of bread,
> Lady of beer,
> Lady of abundance…

Then they switched into a language Ryon couldn't follow, but it sounded ancient and it wasn't Latin or Greek. That only lasted for a moment, and then they repeated what he'd heard before, apparently alternating the same verse over and over in English and the ancient language.

Maddie Prue suddenly doubled over and fell on her knees, with a rasping shriek-sigh squeezing out of her. Ryon barely intercepted his instinct to run toward her, which would've got him two broken legs at the least. He started to swivel around to scramble back down the rope and try to get over the wall, but saw that the other people in the circle had already huddled solicitously around her. He heard a female voice hissing: "What did you see, Maddie?" then the voices sank too low to travel.

He stayed sitting on the branch a few moments longer, until Maddie had been helped back to her feet and into the house, leaving nothing in the Turners' garden but the dying fire. He still didn't know whether he'd been surreptitiously invited to the event, or what the event had actually been. But he knew he didn't want to know.

Ryon was back wandering winter London with middle-aged knees, but not smoking the cigarette he'd started rolling. Either he'd smoked it without noticing or he hadn't finished up rolling it, he wasn't sure. Eventually he found himself walking along Oxford Street, past the closed-up fronts of the most fashionable shopping district in the world. When he came to Davies Street he stopped. His feet wanted to take him south down Davies Street. That was a bucket of madness and then some. Davies Street ran right behind Grosvenor Square and the elegant, Georgian town house beyond whose wrought-iron gates Templeton Ryon-Chilton still held court. Unless one of his progeny had finally worked up the sand to take a cricket bat to the old crock's skull. Which seemed highly unlikely. None of the great man's many sons and daughters had ever even dared to raise their voices to him. Except one.

At this time of year the family would definitely be in the city, probably hosting a late supper after the opera or the latest Gilbert and Sullivan. Although the progeny were all married off by now, at least one or two with spouses in tow would be in regulated rotating residence—"Albert and Annabelle will have the blue room from December Fourth till Eleventh; then Victoria and Morton from the Twelfth till…"—and the ones who had their own town houses would be in dutiful attendance, likely to be passing along Davies Street in their carriages as soon as it felt safe to make an exit.

Ryon felt not the least urge to get a look at the house in Grosvenor Square again. Whatever memories it might bring back were only too accessible already without priming the pump, and certainly had nothing to do with Maddie Prue. But something was pulling him down Davies Street. Might's well be sheepish as laminated.

He turned up his coat collar, pulled his bowler hat down over his eyebrows, and let his boots and his new walking stick do the thinking for him. He hadn't gone far before he realized that what he was looking for was the corner of Davies and Brook Street—Claridge's Hotel. But he still didn't know why. His heart had kicked into a gallop and he no longer felt the cold. In fact, he wanted to tear off his hat and ulster and throw them into the street.

He kept his head down till he got to the corner of Brook and Davies, then came to a halt, inhaled and turned and looked across the street at Claridge's Hotel.

It was gone. What he'd expected to see was a clump of five splendid houses that had been combined and converted into London's first truly posh hotel. One of his earliest memories was his older brother pointing across the park from the nursery window and saying authoritatively: "That's Claridge's." Claridge's had always been there, like the Thames and London Bridge. But now Claridge's Hotel wasn't there. Taking up the space where the five inter-connected houses should be was one immense, red stone building with banks of windows blazing golden light.

Ryon heard footsteps and laughter behind him. He turned to see a couple of pairs of fur-collared Society striding along arm-in-arm. He practically shouted at them: "What the Hell happened to Claridge's?"

Their mouths tightened up like sphincters and they tucked their chins down into their throats. Oh dear, he'd forgotten he wasn't in raw North America, and here ejaculations to strangers were decidedly not The Done Thing. He said: "Do forgive me, I've been in the colonies for twenty years and forget my manners. You see, I was looking up old haunts and thought I'd stop by good old Claridge's Hotel, and when I got here… it's gone. Rather took me by surprise. I do beg your pardon. Sorry to trouble you."

"Not at all, old fellow. Which colonies?"

"North America."

"Ah. Much trouble with Red Indians?"

"None to speak of."

"Good show. Well, small wonder you're surprised. A lot of people coming back from their country places for The Season were surprised. You see, old Mr. Claridge passed on just this year, and the new owners of Claridge's decided to demolish the old houses and erect a proper hotel. Progress. Have to get ourselves ready for the Twentieth Century—won't wait on us."

"I suppose we must. Thank you very much for solving my confusion. Sorry to trouble you."

"Not at all. Come along, Gwendolyn."

Ryon stared across the street at the new Claridge's, closed his eyes and saw the old one. The pavement seemed to shift beneath his feet. He leaned back against a stone retaining wall with a wrought iron fence on top of it, and reached his hands out to take hold of the bars and hold him there…

He was in a room in Claridge's Hotel—the *old* Claridge's. There was a golden knife and a red candle. The golden blade was leaf-shaped—widening from the hilt and then narrowing to its point—and shimmered in the light of the candle. Something else gleamed in the candlelight—the brass barrel of a hypodermic needle…

"Can I help you, sir?"

Ryon opened his eyes. There was a policeman standing there on the corner of Brook and Davies. Ryon said: "I wish to Christ you could."

"Beg pardon, sir?"

"It's all right, constable, I'm just a little overtired. Time I found a cab home." He pushed off from the fence and started away.

The constable called from behind him: "I'd say Piccadilly Circus is your best bet for a cab at this time of night, sir."

"Any circus in a storm."

Ryon's wet boots squelched him through the blessed dark and tree-rustle of Berkeley Square, and then into the gaslight blaze of Piccadilly. He found a hansom, told the driver the address on the Brixton Road, leaned back and closed his eyes again. A gold knife and a red candle. And a naked Madeline Prue. *Fully* naked—without bone necklaces or body paint or windflowers in her hair.

XVII

I N HIS OVERHEATED Manhattan hotel room, Ryon lay shivering on the bed. It was miles early for nap-time, but he'd flopped face-down with his clothes on and pulled the bedspread around him. Sometimes his shivering segued into a sauna sweat, but he knew he'd be shivering again before he could disentangle himself from the bedspread.

He had a pretty good idea of what was happening to him. The lifestyle magazines called it a panic attack, or anxiety attack. He muttered to himself: "Now they even got a name for it." Back when, it had just been "freaked out and fucked up". He could picture a panel of psychiatrists analyzing his little relapse. Depending on which shrink had been reading which textbook, the analysis might be schizophrenia, paranoia, manic depression… Schizophrenia might almost be accurate, though—lack of input filters. Maddie Prue sang to him breezily:

> And so the diagnosis
> Was paranoid psychosis…

He hadn't been in this place for a lot of years, but he recognized every detail. He had to fight to breathe, hauling in deep gasps, as though someone was sitting on his chest. Sometimes he'd forget to breathe for a minute or two and then suddenly his body would rear up and try to suck all the air out of the room.

He wasn't exactly dreaming and not exactly hallucinating, just skimming through the images projected on the backs of his eyelids. He'd had a lot of hallucinations back in his acid days, but only three that were absolutely three dimensional—smell, touch and all—with no trace of apartment walls showing through. All three of those living holograms had had something to do with semi-imaginary animals, but he could only remember one at the moment.

It was a moment of Buddhistic peace. He was floating across some kind of alien desert. Nothing that happened in his little life or anyone else's could possibly make any difference. If he pissed away all his savings, if nobody ever knew what happened to Maddie Prue, if he overstayed his holiday leave and got busted back to constable, the world would still keep rolling on. Up ahead there was a golden lizard lying on a rock, soaking up the sun. As Ryon floated up behind him, he could see that the old boy's back was weathered and wrinkled and puckered with scars. Been around and then some. Ryon was looking forward to the moment when the wise old lizard saw him and understood that he, too, had been through enough tussles to realize that nothing was worth fighting about.

The lizard looked over his shoulder, took Ryon in at a glance and said: "You are a death force," then turned away again.

The dismissive bolt that shot out of the lizard's gray-green eyes knocked Ryon out of the desert and back onto his hotel bed. His body jerked like he'd stuck his finger in a light socket. He shifted to another position, pulling the bedspread over his head, and muttered: "Rabalajibarubbumm—gerb…" That was how you dealt with it: when you hit one of those electric walls, let some sounds come out of your throat to distract your attention. If you got sucked into going back and trying to figure out what that wall was, you were finished.

He closed his eyes again. There were a few odd colors, then he was naked in a moonlit forest, with stag's antlers growing out of his head and fur growing on his shoulders. It occurred to him that horns on a man's head also happened to be the old symbol for a cuckold: the once and not future lover. He didn't have long to ruminate on it, though, because there were torches bobbing through the trees and people shouting. He ran, trying to keep his antlers from catching in low branches. But the shouts and torches kept heading him off and closing in.

He broke out into a clearing where Maddie Prue stood naked except for golden wheat stocks twined in her hair. She opened her arms and he ran to her and laid his gasping head against her breasts. He just happened to glance up as she raised the shining sickle high over her head. He sprang away and ran— the point of the sickle just catching his back and carving a long, hot, seeping gash along his spine.

He saw another flame in the shadows ahead: stable, not a torch this time. He crouched down, snuck forward and peered through the leaves. It was

Lisette in a beaded buckskin dress, kneeling in front of smouldering embers. She was using a crow's wing fan to waft the sweetgrass smoke around her face. She was softly singing that old, old, north prairies song that Americans assumed was theirs, like everything else…

> Come and sit by my side if you love me,
> Do not hasten to bid me adieu,
> Just remember the Red River Valley
> And the halfbreed who loved you so true.

A cold hand came down on his shoulder. Another 220 volt jolt. "Basramgraww… Fft." Roll over onto your back, try to breathe slower, hold onto the pillow.

Someone was singing *Life Is Like A Mountain Railway*. Ryon knew why life was like a mountain railway. He could see it. Boxcars rattling over rickety rails in rocky passes. Boxcars filled with ping pong balls. Ping pong balls have no substance to them—they just bang together, bounce off each other and hit the next one. On and on: Get hit; hit whoever's close to hand. But if only one of those ping pong balls could just once absorb the energy of getting hit, instead of bouncing against another and keeping the chain reaction going… Looking closer, though, they weren't really ping pong balls after all. They were skulls with living eyes.

"Mungalla twak!" Roll onto your stomach, wipe the sweat off of your eyes, but keep them screwed shut.

He was walking down a hallway somewhere, with an open door ahead. Grunting and gasping was coming from the doorway. He looked into the room. Maddie Prue was bent forward across a table, arms spread wide and fingers gripping the rim, her dress hiked up around her waist. Spider Jack Delaney was standing behind her, hands gripping her hips, ramming his long cock in and out. He grinned at Ryon and said: "That's the ticket, buddy: bumfuck, cock-suck. A woman doesn't really know you own her till you've fucked her in the ass and then made her suck you off."

Ryon jack-knifed upright in bed like he'd been kicked in the stomach. He muttered: "Sick sonofabitch," at himself. That was no recovered memory, that was his own warped and twisted imagination. He still had no defining memories of Delaney, but *that* sure as hell never happened. Or was it something he'd actually heard Delaney say once, with a bunch of guys sitting around drinking Jack Daniels and trying to talk tough…?

He held onto his knees and reminded his lungs how to breathe, then threw the bedspread off, got up and walked around the room. Occam's Razor. It had been so long since he'd been fucked up this badly, he'd forgotten Occam's Razor—the only tool sharp enough to cut away the galloping mind tumors. "Phenomena must not be extrapolated beyond necessity." Or: "The least complicated explanation is always the true one," depending on who'd translated the Latin.

There was one can of beer left on the table. Ryon popped it, flopped into the lone armchair and snagged the TV wand to give him someone else's pictures so the internal cinemascope wouldn't get between him and Occam's Razor. As he clicked from channel to channel, he said to himself: "All right, all right, get something to hold on to. Review the case. Whaddayou got? She ditched the band, she ditched her old man—lot of people pissed off at her. Enough to kill her? No inheritance, no money to follow. Well, except posthumous royalties… Nah, she wasn't exactly Janis fucking Joplin…"

Yul Brynner walked in through the wall, cocked his fists on his hips and said: "Eece a puzzlement."

"Yeah, cool, Yul. Got a cigarette?"

Yul looked pissed-off and pissed off. Ryon said to the TV: "*Somebody* had to have a motive. No financial motive, so personal motive. Emotional motive. Ego motive. Delaney.

"Nah, everybody gets walked out on sooner or later, and they don't go killing people over it. Well, some nutbars do. Nah—if Delaney was that pathetic and stupid, Maddie never would've hung around with him. But—who knows how pathetic and stupid and evil anybody can be until they prove it?

"So the least complicated explanation is Delaney—good, old-fashioned 'I'd rather see you dead, little girl, than to be with another man…'

"Or… The Circle. The Circle. Will the circle be unbroken…

"Dyke Annie said Maddie was still a part of The Circle. Did she mean Maddie faked her death, or that nobody gets out of there alive? Sure as hell no shortage of blood and murder in the territory The Circle was playing with. Dancing on the killing grounds. But the victim was always male. Astarte or Ishtar or whatever you wanna call her wept and moaned about it, but she wasn't the one chopped to pieces and scattered across the cornfields. And why the hell do I keep seeing The Antlered Man? How could there possibly be any connection between the jolly old ritual of sacrificing the Corn King, and an image from Stone Age hunters who wouldn't know a wheatfield if they tripped over it?

"There *is* no bloody connection. Cute—bloody connection. Stop trying to make sense out of it, because there's no fucking sense to be made. Like trying to find a plot line in Mother Goose. The bloody Circle was just a bunch of Iron Janes going ooga-booga around a campfire."

The pictures on the TV might as well've been animated wallpaper. He was aware that his feeble excuse for a mind had become as locked-in as the bloody box: he could jump from one image to another all he liked, he would only find variations on the same theme. But he kept on clicking channels.

"So whaddayou think you're going to do, smartboy? It's dried up, no one left to pump. Think you're going to fly all the fucking way to San Francisco and try to find a spider-man in a haystack? Ask for a longer leave, and get The Superintendent wondering maybe it wasn't such a good idea to let that nut-bar Ryon back into the Force?

"It's over. Crazy woman just fell off a cliff. And some other crazy thought it'd be funny to send a tape to the boonies up north—just picked your name out of a hat like kids doing random dialing."

His fingertips were plucking at his cheeks and the corners of his eyes. Not a real good sign. He worked the channel changer harder and took his free hand away from his face to pick up his beer again. Almost empty. He was going to have to go out sooner or later, and it looked like sooner. And maybe some medication wouldn't be a bad idea. In Manhattan you can get anything you want, including Alice.

His shirt was soaked with sweat. He put on his last clean one, went into the bathroom and splashed cold water on his face and combed his hair. He considered shaving, then decided sharp objects were a bad idea.

When he reached for the door handle to go out into the corridor, a steel belt tightened around his chest. He heaved air in and out to loosen it. From way back in the past he dredged up the old mantra he'd invented for times when he had to go out in public even though acid goblins were caroming around inside his head and climbing out his eyes: "They don't know. They don't know…" He opened the door and headed down into the lobby.

The *concierge*—or whatever the hell they called them in New York—looked encouragingly well-worn. Ryon sidled up to him, showed him his room key and said: "I don't know if you can help me out—if you know a doctor who doesn't mind writing fast prescriptions. Like a damn fool I didn't pack enough valium to get me through the trip."

The *concierge* looked him up and down and said: "What room you say you was in?" Ryon took out a twenty dollar bill, wrote 1215 on it and left it on the counter.

"I think I can remember that now. You be there in an hour?"

"Good deal."

"I'll see what I can do."

Ryon went out into the street and started towards Times Square. There was still light in the sky, although you had to look straight up to see it. None of the people he passed looked twice at him. He chortled and changed his mantra to the New York version: "They don't care. They don't care…"

He went into the deli for six more cans of Miller, then decided to make it twelve. There was a handy liquor store on one of the side streets across Times Square. Ryon snagged a bottle of Jameson's—higher proof at a lower price than he could get back home, even with the exchange. When he carried it to the counter, he noticed a rack of cigarettes behind the guy at the cash register. He hadn't had a cigarette in fifteen years, but he could definitely use one now.

As the cashier put the Jameson's into the bag, he winked at Ryon, "Good *Irish* whisky." When he'd counted out Ryon's change, instead of handing it to him he dropped the coins into a can beside the cash register. Ryon looked down at the can. It had a logo on it for some kind of Irish Widows And Orphans Fund. He'd thought all those cans would've been junked years ago, when the press was filled with proof that a lot of the money was going to buy guns for the Provisional IRA.

Ryon said: "You haven't given me my change."

The cashier's eyes slitted. "Where you from?"

Ryon realized that his "accent" might sound Brit to a New Yorker. He didn't care. He said to the cashier: "You and everybody else on the fucking Eastern Seaboard knows that fund isn't for helping widows and orphans, it's for *making* widows and orphans. You don't have to live there."

"You fucking English bastard! You can shove your change up Maggie Thatcher's ass! Get out of Ireland!"

The cashier kept on yelling, but Ryon just picked up his bag and walked out of the store. He wasn't about to get into a shouting match over seventy-seven cents. Maybe he was just being a wimpy Canadian. On the other hand, where he came from, if two guys started yelling into each others' faces, there was going to be blood on the parking lot in about two minutes.

But just before Ryon got out the door, the cashier's fragging crossed the line between *walk away* and *that's more bullshit than I can eat*: "What's your name, Limey, so I can tell the lads who to kneecap? Basil Posthlewaite-Smythe? Ian Paisley The Third?"

Ryon stopped, exhaled, and bent forward to straight-arm lean against the doorway and convince himself that turning around and going back would be a very bad idea for all concerned. Without turning around, he rasped out loud enough to fill the store: "*'sh meeshe Ryon!*" It was the only Gaelic he knew—"My name is Ryon"—but apparently more than the Michael Collins wannabe did. But Ryon didn't have a clue of where he'd learned it.

As he stepped out of the liquor store door, another door started to open— a door way, way back there: a hotel room door, and behind it was a gold knife and a red candle and a throaty-laughing female voice saying: "It's easy, you can do it—*'sh meeshe* Ryon…*" Some panicked creature in his mind slammed the door, shot the bolts, nailed a couple of two-by-fours over it and told him to look around at all the interesting doors he could go through in the here-and-now.

The Virgin Records megastore signs gave Ryon an idea. He hadn't read a novel in years, but maybe a good story to lose himself in might be just the ticket to stop him chasing his tail for a while. He went back down the string of escalators again, asked the girl at the book counter what was hot these days and she pointed him to a just-issued paperback covered with raves from the *New York Times* and other experts. Worth a try.

There was so much traffic in Times Square even New Yorkers stood waiting for the light to change. The guy standing on the corner beside Ryon was a scrawny, dark-skinned kid about eighteen, twitching with the come-down from some kind of drugs that must've been either cheap or stolen, given the kid's tattered old raincoat and falling-apart sneakers. The proverbial "born in some shithole in the South Bronx," as Larry Fishburne put it before he became Laurence. Three feet past the kid there was another guy about the same age waiting for the light to change—a blonde, suntanned kid sitting in a Mercedes SL his daddy probably gave him for graduating high school.

Ryon thought of all the tons of paper and ink used up by sociologists pondering the complexities behind the wave of urban crime, when all it took was just one picture of those two kids within arms' reach of each other and ten galaxies apart. He said to the kid standing beside him: "Yeah, if I was you I'd steal his car, too, and not feel guilty for a second."

The twitching kid jolted his pink-rimmed eyes at Ryon, then turned and headed quickly down the sidewalk instead of waiting to cross the street. About two seconds later, the light changed.

With his bags in one hand and the other rubbing itself impatiently, Ryon drifted down Broadway wondering what he was going to do to keep the monkeys in their cave for another forty minutes. His stomach was grinding itself like a blown transmission and he was sweating hot and cold. Eating something might not be a bad idea. He could find a corner in the hotel restaurant and keep his mouth occupied with chewing and his so-called mind occupied with the novel.

He rounded the block and headed up Eighth Avenue. Mistake. In his day Seventh Avenue had been Hooker Alley, now apparently it was Eighth. He didn't feel like a maybe-buyer looking over the stables, he felt like a female pilot trying to get down the corridor at a Tailhook convention. Then again, if he was looking for something to distract him for a while...

Then one of the girls up ahead caught his eye and he stopped dead. It was Lisette, in a shrink-wrap leather skirt, torn spiderweb stockings with the garter clips showing, and a leather jacket opened over a bustier that left everything but her nipples hanging out in the cold. She noticed him staring at her, winked and licked her lips.

She wasn't Lisette—the coppery skin and slanted, black eyes were almost the same, but more Oriental than Cree. But just the momentary flash of seeing Lisette in that line killed any passing notions of popping a few bucks to make one of them jiggle and suck.

The hotel dining room had an empty corner table. A waiter brought Ryon a menu and asked him if he'd like a drink. Ryon checked his watch. Still thirty-five minutes. It might not be a bad idea to have a little interim tranquillizing until the tranquillizers came—*if* they came. He said: "Yeah, please. An Afterburner."

"A what?"

"Oh. Thought they would've caught on by now. A drink I invented twenty years ago." The waiter didn't look impressed. "An Afterburner is a shot of tequila with a vodka chaser."

The waiter went away shaking his head and muttering. Ryon glanced at the menu, telling himself: "Don't get too cocky, smartboy. Keep the lid on. Just read your nice novel and keep your mouth shut till you got something to put in it." Just a plain, old cheeseburger would mean he wouldn't have to worry about knives and forks shaking and rattling. He set down the menu and took his nice novel out of the bookstore bag and the Camel filters out of the liquor store bag. The crapbrained liquor store cashier had very thoughtfully tossed in a pack of matches. Ryon lit his first cigarette in fifteen years and opened his book.

"Hey, buddy!"

"Hey, what the fuck do you think you're doing?"

The shouts had come from the tables on either side of him, and seemed way too loud to be addressed to him. He looked up anyway. People were staring at him like he'd just pissed on the carpet. Maybe he had and hadn't noticed. They seemed to be particularly glaring at his cigarette.

He looked down at the table and saw no ashtray. But neither was there a No Smoking sign. He said to the glarers: "This isn't the non-smoking section…"

"The whole restaurant's the non-smoking section! Every restaurant in New York over thirty-five seats is! So put that out or get out!"

Ryon fell back in his chair laughing. It just cracked him up that people who lived in a smog soup of carbon monoxide and soot would pass a law to protect their precious lungs from a whiff of tobacco. He picked up his bags and got up, choking out: "It's all right, I'm going. Wouldn't want to poison anybody."

The waiter appeared toting a tray with two shotglasses. "Hey, you ordered a drink."

"Try it yourself, you'll like it."

Back in his room, Ryon poured himself a shot, cracked a beer and sat down with his book and his cigarette—which he was smoking more like a cigar. No fear getting hooked again when there was nothing around to smoke but Yankee cigarettes. Funny how Americans made their beer to taste like water and their cigarettes like hops. Made damn fine cheeseburgers, though. Maybe later.

Ryon opened the book, but hadn't got through the first sentence before some sick creature in his head piped up: "Delaney wasn't in The Circle… Because he didn't want to be, or because they shut him out? Because *Maddie* shut him out…?"

Ryon told the voice to go fuck itself for at least a while, and bore down on the book. If he could force himself to concentrate on it, after a few pages the story would kick in and he could get a couple hours' recess from the sick little creatures.

But after thirty pages he gave in to the fact that there wasn't going to be a story, just stream-of-self-consciousness. He tossed the book toward the wastebasket, missed and left it there. If that was what they called a novel these days, small wonder the book business was sucking air.

He realized that his free hand had been picking at his face again. There was blood on one of his fingernails. He looked at his watch. An hour and eleven minutes.

There was a knock. Ryon jumped up, then gave himself a shake and strode at an imitation unpanicked pace to the door. It wasn't the *concierge*, or an accommodating doctor. It was a clearasil-challenged bellboy who held up two prescription bottles and said: "Five mills or ten?"

"Ten."

"Forty bucks." It seemed a bit steep, but Ryon was in no position to haggle. He handed over the money; the bellhop handed him the bottle and turned to go. "What, no room service receipt?"

The bellhop looked at him like he was nuts, which suggested the kid was a good judge of character, then said: "Oh. Joke. I get it. Ha ha." Ryon closed the door.

He washed down a couple of valiums with Miller, put the Jameson's away, clicked the TV on and sat down in front of it to wait.

> *Havelock, havelock, havelock Ellis,*
> *Into the valium depths rode the sick fellas.*

After a while, breathing stopped being something he had to work at. Everything that had been chewing at him seemed distant—still there, just wrapped in layers of cotton batten. Even the crap on the TV wasn't really all that annoying.

His eyes drifted around the room. The light outside the window had changed from smog-filtered sunlight to smog-filtered electrics. In Wahpeston, they'd've had pitch darkness for hours by now, even though the clocks read an hour earlier.

He muted the TV, picked up the phone and dialed his home number. After a few rings, Lisette's voice said: "Hello?"

"RCMP, ma'am. We've had you under surveillance and—"

"Ryon! Where are you?"

"Still in New York. Did you get my postcard?"

"Postcard?"

"Oh. I guess it takes a while. So, uh… How're the horses?" Ryon's horses were three scruffy little descendants of Indian ponies that some farmer had left to fend for themselves when the bank foreclosed. They didn't cost much to feed, and Ryon could say he was the only Horseman left who knew what a horse looked like, outside of the Musical Ride.

"They're all right. It's been so cold I let 'em stay in the barn all day."

"That's cold." Usually even at thirty below they were kicking at the barn doors to get out and play.

"Yeah. Lucky for you you're down south."

"Yeah. Lucky for me." Now that he'd got her on the phone he didn't know what else to say, but he didn't want to hang up.

After a moment of dead air, she said: "When're you coming home?"

"I don't know. Maybe not for a while yet."

"You still haven't found out who killed that Maddie woman…? If anybody."

"No, I haven't found out yet. Still looking. Though I'm not sure where."

"Maybe there's nothing to find."

"Maybe."

There was another bit of dead air, then she said: "Look, this is costing you a lot of money… Thanks for calling."

"Thanks for answering."

"Glad to hear you're all right." It sounded something like a question.

"Yeah. Bye now."

"Bye."

He put the phone down and thought about home for a while, then decided the valium was wearing off and took another. After a few minutes he felt insulated enough to let himself start thinking about what Lisette had said: "Maybe there's nothing to find." Or nowhere to find it. The nice valium still left him stuck with the same decision he'd been stuck at before it arrived. Except now he was sedated enough to look his two choices in the face: either give it up and go home, or keep on making wider circles around a trail that'd gone cold. And the circling meant: "until your money runs out or the Force sends a request south to get out the butterfly nets, whichever comes first."

He'd pretty much run out of close witnesses to Maddie Prue's life. Fergus Doude wasn't touring this year—his record company had been willing to let out that much information—which meant he could be holed-up anywhere in the world or, even worse, floating from country to country whenever he felt like a change of scenery. So the only living lead left there was even the remotest chance of finding was Spider Jack Delaney—whom Flip Norman kind of thought had maybe once upon a time had a kind of houseband gig at a place somewhere around San Francisco called maybe something sort of like Green Onions or something kind of weird that sort of sounded like that.

Ryon looked at his watch. Getting late, but maybe not too late for someone who used to keep musicians' hours. There was a standard brand of side-information he hadn't pumped for when he'd had the chance, because he'd thought he'd had so many straighter leads. Maybe finding out whether that information was available would help make the decision. At the least, checking it out would let him stall making it for a while. He looked in his notebook and dialed the number in Cambridge, Massachusetts.

"Hello?"

"Ms. Doude? I hope it's not too late to call. I'm the Mountie who came around asking stupid questions about Maddie Prue…"

"Oh, Ryon."

There was something funny about the way she said it, as though there was no comma. But Ryon had a few grindier things to worry about than people's eccentric speech patterns. "I talked to Celina Rushton, and Flip Norman—"

"Ah. And Flip told you where to find Fergus…?"

"Uh, no. He doesn't know. Nobody seems to know. But Flip did have a vague idea of where to look for Jack Delaney. A *very* vague idea."

She laughed. "Vague is probably all you want. You won't get anything worth shit from Delaney."

"Maybe not, but right now he's all I've got. Maybe he can tell me where to find Fergus. Do you remember where Delaney came from? Maybe if his parents are still alive I can get directions better than vague."

She seemed to be thinking about it. He could see Audrey Doude standing holding the phone, with that semi-sexy gesture of cupping her free hand against her neck. It occurred to him that the gesture was intended to hide the fact that her neck was aging quicker than her cheekbones. When her olive-green eyes caught the light at certain angles, the pupils glinted red, making a pair of electrified cocktail olives.

She finally said: "I never talked to him about his family. The first I remember him was in Cambridge, but he didn't come from here. Everybody came to Cambridge. Everybody talks about Greenwich Village being the start of The Sixties, but it was really the Cambridge Music Scene—our older brothers' and sisters' generation. Jim Kweskin's jugband with Maria Muldaur, well, Maria d'Amato then... Taj Mahal testifying the blues. Dylan and all the others from The Village came up all the time chasing the Baez sisters, Joan and Mimi— well, Mimi *Farina* after she married Dick. When people talk about the '65 Newport Folk Festival all they remember is the near-riot when Dylan came out with an electric band—they forget Mimi and Richard Farina putting a new light into thousands of hearts with just a dulcimer and two voices. Or was that '64...?"

She sighed. "Poor Richard. The night he was killed was the publishing party for his novel—the first novel from The Hippie Generation." She laughed. "'Hippie'—what an idiot word. But...the strange part about Richard's death was... he left the party on the back of someone's motorcycle and..." The voice coming through the phone got kind of spooky. "He left the car keys with Mimi."

"What's strange about that?"

"Mimi doesn't drive."

A flashbulb popped in Ryon's head. He blurted: "Lennon, Phil Ochs, Richard Farina..."

"What?"

"They'd all been in the same places as Maddie."

"So?"

"You said there was something strange about Farina's death, like the way I think there was something strange about Maddie's. Are you trying to tell me there's some kind of connection between Maddie's death and—?"

The voice at the other end of the phone buried him in laughter, struggled to get hold of itself and eventually said: "Oh, dear. I'm sorry, I'm not laughing at you, just... No, Dick died long before Maddie showed up on the scene. Two different worlds. All I meant by mentioning the strange part about his death was that, well, not everything fits neatly into a coroner's report. It might turn out that whatever happened to Maddie—I mean if it wasn't just an accident—has sides to it that you won't see if you go around with Joe Friday's blinkers on.

"Let me see now… Jack Delaney… Like I said, you won't get anything but nasty bullshit out of him, except that he might be able to tell you where to find Fergus—not that I give a damn if Fergus is rotting in hell, but you're the one with the obsession. It seems to me somebody said Jack had settled down in San Francisco, or maybe Oakland."

It was Ryon's turn to sigh. "Yeah, that's pretty much all that Flip could tell me, and he couldn't even remember how long ago he'd heard it. Must be long gone by now."

"No, the operative phrase is 'settled down'—wife and kids and all. Delaney never had much energy, except what he leached off Maddie. If he found himself a cosy hole, he'd stay in it. Unless… Well, unless of course he hit his second adolescence and ran out on them, which is always a possibility."

The walls of Ryon's hotel room were changing color and the floor moving up and down. He choked out: "Thank you. That's at least some help to…"

"Are you all right?"

"Sure. Uh, bye."

"Good luck."

Ryon hung up quickly, flopped his head back and fought to breathe. He propped his feet up on his chair and sat shaking, hugging his knees, hugging his disease. Two 10-mill valiums shouldn't have worn off yet… It was something else. Something about "Cambridge Music Scene"… Music scene… He remembered Delaney.

It was a big room with dishwater-colored walls. The basement green-room of one of the low-rent clubs on the circuit Anemone was playing when Ryon first started picking up small change by picking up after them. Ryon was sitting backwards on a stacking chair, speed-rapping to a palomino-haired woman with the long nails of a gut-string guitar player. Or maybe it wasn't speed at all but enthusiasm—not very cool, man. Either way, he was on a roll and not aware of anything but what he was trying to say:

"Some people say Yankee kids got no business playing Celtic Rock, but it was a couple of Yankee kids—Mimi and Richard Farina—who got the whole thing going major league, by—like—putting a new twist on medievally music. And the Celtic rock thing is bigger than just the music! It's, like— there's all these whitebread kids grew up thinking all they got in their blood is all that crap we learned in High School, so if you wanted to have anything in your soul as real as Blues music, you had to pretend to be black or Indian or something. Now they find out their own ancestors had street music just as downhome as The Blues, with as much rhythm and evil sense of humor and emotion and magic and…

"I mean, it's like the artwork Anemone puts on all their covers, those Pre-Raphaelites and William Morris and all them. A hundred years ago they were showing English people that you didn't have to pretend to be a dead Italian to create beautiful things. Now, maybe the Celtic Rock thing is gonna turn out to be just a blip, like the Pre-Raphaelites, but a blip can make ripples that give other musicians a base to build on, a new, ancient place to start from."

A shadow settled across him and threw him off. He looked way up to see the pirate gypsy fiddler looking down at him. Delaney was wearing a Fu Manchu mustache and a black, riverboat gambler's hat—last month he'd been clean-shaven and into headbands. Delaney looked down his long, elegant nose at the smalltown boy blowing his cool and smirked: "Gosh-golly-gee-whiz, you sure picked up a lot of musical expertise listening to those polka bands back home."

Ryon shrugged and said: "Well, yeah I gotta admit it was pretty pitiful growing up in a pisspot prairie town. High school dances we had to settle for Neil Young and the Squires, or the bands that grew into the Guess Who. The local coffee house saddled us with Chuck Mitchell and his wife Joni passing through from Saskatoon, or this pitiful, neighborhood guitar-player named Lenny Breau."

"Lenny who?"

Ryon burst out laughing. "Lenny who? Django who? Stephane and Yehudi who? Man, it sure is lucky you got talent, 'cause if you had to operate on brains…"

An echoing laughter came in over Ryon's shoulder: a throaty, full-bellied alto enjoying the moment immensely. Ryon didn't have to turn around to know who it was. Delaney looked over Ryon's head. Delaney's long-fingered hands didn't clench into fists, and his body stayed frozen in place. But the look in his eyes was pure murder.

Corporal Ryon was a lot more familiar with that look than the AWOL Kid had been. In the years since, he'd seen that look trained on a woman more than a few times—often in circumstances he walked into a few minutes after

Dispatch had squawked out that sphincter-tightening phrase: "Domestic dispute in progress." Usually that look meant that the woman better get a restraining order fast. And once or twice it had meant a certain Mountie paying a late night visit out of uniform but still carrying his flashlight.

The valium was definitely wearing off, but Ryon didn't feel crazy and confused anymore. Still crazy, but not confused. He whispered towards the window: "Hold tight, Spider Jack—California here I come."

He dialed the front desk to book him the first available flight to San Francisco. It turned out the only seats left open on the first available were First Class, but he still had a lot of savings to go through.

The last thing he saw of Manhattan was the same thing he'd seen on the way out the last time. The cab passed under a street-wide underpass opening onto the long stretch of fenced highway and abandoned cars leading to Kennedy. The underside of the concrete arch sported a bit of timeless graffiti. Not the technicolor spraybomb swirls of today, just a plain black stencil:

GROWTH
DECAY
DECAY
DECAY
DECAY
DECAY
DECAY

Why it made Ryon laugh was that only a hundred years ago most people in the British Empire, like the American Empire today, knew it was going to last forever.

XVIII

THE RAILWAY HOTEL in Portsmouth had a plethora of sea view rooms available at this time of year. Ryon sat at his rented balcony window waiting for sundown, looking out at the gray shingle beach and the gray waves. Sometimes, when the sun broke through the clouds, the winter-gray sea turned blue for a moment—just like Maddie Prue's eyes, turning from blue to gray depending on the light.

Ryon was aware that only a few months from now, or a few months ago, the deserted shingle and dejected bandstands on the pier would be rife with straw-hatted holidayers and whirligigging children. But even the English weren't mad enough to set out beach chairs on the English Channel in December.

He was far from solitary, though. The space between his eyes and the waves was filled with dancing Maddie Prues, leering spider-men and kaleidoscope shards of memory. Lisette was singing:

> From this valley they say you are going,
> We will miss your bright eyes and sweet smile,
> For they say you are taking the sunshine,
> That has brightened our pathway a while.

The waves turned red with sunset, just like the blue Mediterranean when the rains washed the blood of Adonis down to the sea. It was the time when the night creatures came out to play; time to go. Ryon rose from the window seat, took up his coat and hat and walking stick and went down to the lobby.

He asked the desk clerk if he knew of a tavern called The Green Man, hoping that Philip Norman hadn't bungled the name up in his laudanum-soaked memory. "Can't say as I do, sir. I'm acquainted with most of the better establishments in our environs, but I can't say as I ever heard of that one. Perhaps the head porter…" The desk clerk dinged a bell, and a large, grizzled man in a long, brass-buttoned coat hove forward from behind the potted palms. "This gentleman is inquiring after the location of a local establishment entitled The Green Man."

The head porter slitted a sideways glance at said gentleman. Ryon kept his face bland and waited. It was a habit he'd gotten into over the last few days: saying as little as possible and trying to appear innocuous, while his mind was roiling with mirages and moonlight.

The head porter said: "Someone must've given you the wrong name, sir, or be pullin' your leg. There *is* a Green Man tavern, but it's a workingman's pub up to the north end of the city."

"A *shagganappi* tavern." It slipped out of Ryon's mouth as though he'd lost control of that sphincter. The desk clerk and head porter were looking at him inquiringly.

Ryon said: "Um… *Shagganappi* is a, um, Red Indian word, you see, for rawhide. It's come to mean anything rough and unpolished. But it can also mean something quite beautiful in a scruffy sort-of way, like a braided harness, or a wild pony, or…" *For God's sake, cleverlad, stop driveling!* "Um, yes, that would be the place. I was told I could find an old friend of mine there."

"Your friend must've fallen on hard times, sir."

Ryon just nodded and kept his mouth safely shut.

"There's a trolley car runs up the high street. From the end of the line it's about a mile's walk. I could draw you a little map, sir, shall I?"

"Please."

The tram car was pulled along its rails by a jaded draft horse who gave the impression that the only thing he needed the conductor for was collecting fares. The smattering of other passengers got off at various stops along the way, leaving Ryon and the conductor in sole possession. The conductor attempted to make conversation, but Ryon just shrugged and kept his eyes out the window.

Eventually the tram jangled to a halt again. The conductor stood up and said: "End of the line, sir."

Ryon nodded and got off. As he started walking north, he glanced back over his shoulder and saw that there was one other thing that the horse needed the conductor for: to unhitch him and hitch him back up at the other end of the car.

The neighborhood Ryon found himself walking through consisted of run-down tenements and boarded-up warehouses. The gaslights were few and far between. He told his legs there was no need to hurry so: every time so far he'd thought he'd been about to find an answer, he'd only found more questions. His legs didn't believe him. Without breaking stride, he tossed the walking stick up in front of him, caught it by the haft and bounced the lead-weighted head against his left palm—trying to reassure himself that if Delaney did prove to be the answer, he'd be ready for him.

The sign of the Green Man was so weather-bleached that the only reason Ryon felt sure he had the right place was it was the only pub in the alley. His ears told him that the landlord was doing a roaring business inside. His nose told him that the innkeeper also kept a stable which didn't get cleaned out as often as it should.

He stepped through the door, took a cursory look 'round to locate the bar and headed toward it. He found it extremely difficult to keep his features bland and his course straight for the bar. Because in that cursory reconnaissance he'd seen the lanky, towering, spider-man standing in a corner sawing away at a fiddle.

The barmaid—likely the landlord's wife—had arms like a stevedore and an expression that said: *Lost your way, guv?* Ryon ordered a pint of bitter and carried it to an empty table where he could sit with his back to the wall.

The place was filled with smoke, rough laughter and the dour murmuring of people whose only escape from drudgery is in a bottle of gin. A few of the drunker ones were more-or-less singing along with Jack Delaney's fiddle. On the table beside Delaney was an upturned, broad-brimmed hat that someone occasionally tossed a coin in. Not exactly the salons where Ryon had seen Anemone perform. When Maddie Prue left the group, she'd taken Jack Delaney's plush times with her.

Ryon tried to roll a cigarette, and found his fingers shaking with anticipation. But he didn't want to approach Delaney in a room filled with people, or when Delaney was preoccupied with trying to earn his meager living. He did manage to get the cigarette rolled and lit, and it served two purposes. Not only did smoking make it easier sitting alone in a place where he didn't belong, but rolling his own might give the impression that he wasn't as out of place as his clothing suggested. "Fallen on hard times."

Ryon tried not to stare at Delaney, or at anyone else, just let his gaze drift around the room and linger on the fiddle player no longer than might be expected of someone with a passing interest in the entertainment. Jack

Delaney had let his hair grow long and straggly, and there was gray in his mustache. But he still looked like some magazine illustrator's notion of an elegant pirate, even though his velvet-cuffed jacket had patches on the elbows.

Sometimes Delaney jigged a few steps as he played, flinging out his knees and elbows, to the delight of those who were paying attention to him. His long, thin arms and fingers plied the bow and strings like a dancing spider. Ryon tried not to think of those fingers on Maddie Prue's nude body, or around her throat.

The fiddle slid into an eerie, grinding tune that no one tried to sing along with, although a few rapped their fists on their tables in time. Ryon recognized it as a setting Anemone had come up with for the ancient *Tom o' Bedlam:*

> From the hag and hungry goblin
> That into rags would rend ye,
> All the spirits that stand by the naked man
> In the book of moons defend thee.
> That of your five sound senses
> You never be forsaken,
> Nor wander from your selves…

The crowd began to thin out towards midnight, until eventually the only people left in the room were Ryon, Delaney, the barmaid, and two workbooted men who grunted companionably at Delaney as he went past them to the bar.

Delaney carried a half pint back to his table in the corner and sat down to count what he found in his hat. Ryon stood up slowly, saying to himself: *Take it easy, cleverlad, don't want to spook him into bolting.* He walked over to Delaney's table and said: "Spider Jack…?"

The spider-man's lively, dark eyes went opaque. He said: "No one's called me that in donkeys' years."

Ryon presented him with one of his counterfeit calling cards and said: "I'm writing an article on Anemone."

Delaney pursed his mustache as he read the card, then said suspiciously: "You came all the bloody way from North America just to dig up those old bones?"

"I had to come to England anyway on family business. My editor is mad-keen on anything to do with the pre-Raphaelites and the Arts And Crafts Movement. Might I buy you a pint?"

Delaney shrugged, "Pale ale."

Ryon got two pints from the bar, set one in front of Delaney, sat down across from him and said: "I've already spoken with Audrey Doude, and Philip Norman—he told me where I might find you—and Celina Rushton."

"What'd you want to talk to that old bitch for?"

"Oh, Mrs. Doude had given me to understand that Miss Rushton had kept some records on Anemone."

"What kind of records?"

"As it turned out, Mrs. Doude was mistaken. So... you reside in Portsmouth now?"

"Hereabouts."

"Philip Norman told me you have a wife and children."

"So far. You try feeding five kids on what I make here, and what the missus gets for laundry. Where's your notebook?"

"Pardon me?"

"If this is an interview, where's your notebook?"

"Oh. I prefer to make my notes after. I find that people talk so much more freely when someone isn't scribbling down their words. Now, it seems to me that the focus of the story should be how it affected the other members of Anemone when Madeline Prue—" Something got caught in his throat, and he had to cough before completing his sentence. "...went off on her own."

The dark eyes hooded. "If you're getting paid for this, I shouldn't be giving you it for free. How much are you getting for this story?"

"Oh, my editor and I will sort that out when I bring back the material."

"How many columns he giving you?"

Ryon tried to guess whether a column meant a column of print, or a columnist's weekly story. "Four."

"You're no bloody journalist!" Jack Delaney's yard-long arm shot straight-elbowed across the table to drive the heel of his hand into Ryon's chest, tipping him and his chair over backwards. Ryon hit the floor, the chair rungs gouging into his back, and struggled to extricate himself. The chair arms held him like an overturned turtle, and the walking stick that was supposed to be his protection was tangling his legs. He flipped onto his side, but before he could free himself of the chair a heavy object slammed into his head from behind, popping him out of the chair arms' embrace like a champagne cork.

The chair and the walking stick were gone and two pairs of workboots were kicking and stomping him. He tried to block them with his arms, but it wasn't much good. The spider-man pushed between the stomping workmen and stooped to drive his fist repeatedly into Ryon's face. Ryon couldn't even try to block anymore; his arms had gone numb and wooden.

Then Delaney's voice barked from far away, "That's enough. Don't want to kill him."

The blows stopped, but the pounding in various parts of Ryon's body didn't. He lay slumped in a fog. One of the kicks seemed to have jarred one side of his brain loose from his skull.

Another male voice high above the fog said: "Who is he, Jack?"

"Damned if I know. Some bloody bailiff's agent or something. Whoever he is, he won't come nosing around here again."

They dragged him out into the stableyard, flung him on top of the manure pile and headed back inside, laughing. Ryon lay there for a while, trying to learn how to breathe with ribs bruised in the marrow, then rolled over and slid down the hill. He came to rest on his side, with his head pillowed on something soft. It was Maddie Prue's lap.

He squinted up at her through the long billows of Saxon Gold framing her face. She touched his head gingerly and whispered: "Oh, Ryon, I'm sorry…"

He tried to tell her it was all right, but all that came out was a grunt. He rolled up onto his knees. She stood up and he pulled himself up her body till he was on his feet. Then she was gone.

He stood where he was for a while, trying to find something resembling equilibrium, staring at the door of The Green Man Inn. Staring wasn't easy; one of his eyes was puffed to a slit and blurry.

Maddie Prue's voice came out of the air: "You can't go back in there!"

"*You* would." He stripped off his mangled collar and necktie, ran his hand through his hair to dislodge some of the moldy, manured straw and staggered across the stableyard toward the door.

By the time he pushed the door open he was walking relatively steadily, if stiffly. The two workbooted thugs were sitting at Delaney's table now, one of them with Ryon's dented derby perched on his head. The other was admiringly turning his new walking stick in his hands. Ryon only glanced at them, then continued walking straight toward a corner of the bar. He'd noticed earlier that the corners of the bar were held up by crudely-carved limestone pillars — *shagganappi* work, but solid stone.

As Ryon propped himself against the bar, a male voice from the corner of the room called out: "Ooh, Martha, the *stink* in here," and there was laughter.

The barmaid approached Ryon uncertainly. He said with some difficulty: "I'll have a whisky, please," and pointed at a bottle that had a long neck and was only a quarter full. When she brought the bottle and a glass, he pushed a ten pound note at her and said: "Leave the bottle. The rest is for the damages."

She smirked, "Only damages I see is to you."

"Move to the far end of the bar, please, and stay there for a while." She looked dubious. He flicked his good eye in the direction he wanted her to go in, and she went.

When he took a sip from the glass, he discovered that the inside of his mouth was cut in several places, and one of his teeth wasn't quite as tightly sealed in the gum as it had been. He drained the glass, sighed the heat out of his throat and poured another.

The whisky began to numb the pain, and to do something else as well. He drank again and began to hum a song that made him chuckle:

> He was his father's only son,
> His mother's pride and joy.
> And dearly did his parents love
> This Wild Colonial Boy...

Ryon took another quaff to wash the laughter and music out of his throat. Then he turned around and pointed at the two men sitting on either side of Delaney. "You two. Out. The spider-man and I are going to have a private chat."

All three of them burst out laughing. One of the workmen said: "Why the hell should we leave?"

Ryon said: "Why...?" rolling the question around in his mouth. "Why...?" He contemplatively drained his glass, then poured what was left in the bottle into the glass. "Why...?" He took the bottle by the neck and tapped its bottom against the stone pillar. It shattered nicely, leaving him holding a stout-handled glass knife with four or five long, jagged blades. "Because I'll fucking *do* yer, mate."

There was a pause, then one of them laughed, "Just like you did before?" But the laugh wasn't quite so sure of itself.

"That was before. You've had your innings and I'm still standing. Now it's my turn. You can go out that door on your feet or on your faces, or what's left of them. Makes no bloody difference to me."

They didn't move. Ryon started toward them, deciding what he was going to do with the bottle: first straight up under the bearded one's beard, then snap it free and twist it into the fat one's belly. There wasn't a thought in his head of defending himself, only of removing the two obstacles between him and Jack Delaney.

He hadn't gone three steps before the two bullyboys flung themselves into motion, leaving the door clattering behind them and a bowler hat vibrating on the floor. Delaney looked like he wanted to go with them, but Ryon was in the way.

Ryon straightened his back and unrolled his shoulders—he hadn't realized he'd hunched into a predatory crouch. He let the bottle fall out of his hand and smiled. "You're out of your weight class, Jack. I'm not a five-foot woman with red-gold hair and small hands." Then he started walking forward.

Delaney put his fists up. His longer reach would've given him the advantage, except that Ryon was in no mood for boxing, and a few punches weren't going to do him any more damage than had already been done. Ryon kept on marching forward, not trying to block or punch, just flinging his arms out in double arcs like shooing a cow, herding Delaney back into the corner.

Once Delaney was cornered, Ryon tucked his head down and moved in. He went to work driving his fists like short-stroke pistons into the sparsely-padded ribcage, shouting in his mind: "That's for Maddie! That's for Maddie! And *that's* for Maddie!" But the pistons were pumping too fast for him to shout it every time.

He could feel the spider-man's attempts to grapple or punch back growing weaker, so he took the chance of stepping back to get a straight-arm grip on the velvet lapels. He bounced Delaney back and forth against the walls on either side. For all his rangy height, Spider Jack didn't weigh much more than a length of the cordwood Ryon tossed on and off the wagon every spring.

He bounced Delaney one last time and then planted his feet back at an angle, gasping and holding the limp bonerack up against the wall. He saw that one of his punches, or one of the walls, had connected with the bridge of the elegant, arrogant nose, and there was blood coursing down into the gray-ing mustache.

And Ryon saw something else. Spider Jack Delaney wasn't an ominous, looming presence at all. He was just a not-terribly-bright fellow with a feel for the fiddle, who hadn't asked to be born looking like Lord Byron's Corsair.

Ryon peeled the spider-man off the wall, settled him gently in a chair and called to the landlady: "A pint of bitter and one of pale ale. And a bar rag, if you please, missus. Maybe two..."

XIX

…THE NEON ORANGE bucket-chair across the table from Delaney's was occupied by Ryon's battered flashlight, where he'd dropped it after convincing Delaney's two so-tough friends to stay out of it. Ryon picked up the flashlight and flopped into the chair, with the flashlight settled in his lap and his left hand propped on the table. He said to Delaney: "What happened to Maddie Prue?"

"I don't know—"

Ryon's left fist shot up off the table to clip the spider-man's mouth. "Listen to me carefully, Jack. I'm about three steps away from a rubber room, I'm up to my fucking eyeballs in hallucinations, and I got no room left in my head for anybody shitting me."

"I'm not… How could I know? She never fucking told me. I come home one day, she's gone, all her stuff is gone. Just a note on the table saying: 'Stay away from me.' Nothing else. *Stay away from me.* Just vanished."

Ryon studied on Delaney and decided he was telling the truth, or at least part of it. There were tears in the blackening eyes that weren't just the off-shoots of a broken nose. Ryon said flatly: "Why would she tell you to stay away from her?"

"I don't *know* why. Sure, I fucked around a little. A lot. So did she. We were twenty-five years old and on the road—cute college kids were climbing through our hotel windows. I never hit her. I never hit a woman in my life—except my sister and she outweighed me. 'Stay away from me.' What is that?"

Ryon couldn't tell him.

"So, anyway, a while later I hear she's got this place up in Carmel. So I drive up there. She sicced the dogs on me. Couldn't even get out of the car." Delaney dabbed at his nose with one of the wet towels the bartender had brought. "I don't know, maybe she thought I'd drove up to hassle her for support payments. I wasn't."

"Support payments?"

"She made a lot more money out of Anemone than I did, 'cause she had songwriting and arranging royalties. Her and Fergus were the only ones that really cleaned up. I had a perfect legal right to at least some of Maddie's money, but I never asked for it."

"What legal right?"

Spider Jack blinked across the table like he'd just realized he was talking to an idiot. "Because she was my wife."

"You were *married?*"

"Well, off and on, but licenced."

"Since when?"

"Since before Anemone got together. Since I stumbled across her singing in a pisspot coffee house in an Air Force town in North Dakota where her old man was posted—well, her *step* old man—and I told her with a voice like hers she should be in New York City where people could hear it. I thought you said you used to hang out with the band?"

"Just on the edges. I guess even more on the edges than I thought."

"Well, not so surprising you didn't know. It got turned into a big secret. In those days managers and agents had this superstition that kids wouldn't get the record-buying hots for you if you weren't single and available. Hell, the only reason anyone found out Dylan was married was some reporter was snooping around backstage and found Mrs. Zimmerman hiding in a closet. And he could afford to lose more fans than Anemone ever had.

"So as soon as Anemone started getting professional management and PR advice, me and Maddie moved out of The Village to way out in Brooklyn, hardly anybody even had the phone number. Same routine when the money started rolling in and we got a little place up-state. Same thing when the band split up and Maddie said we should move to L.A. Anytime we were gigging in the city, or recording—anywhere reporters might be nosing around—it was separate hotel rooms. Had its handy side."

"But... nobody made a big secret out of Fergus and Audrey getting married."

"Different. Nobody in management ever pegged Fergus as a sex symbol. He was just Mr. Weird And Interesting—the band genius. Co-genius, if any of those fuckheads in silk suits had had the brains to see she wasn't just tits and a voice."

Delaney took a tentative sip of his Coors, wincing a little as the bubbles hit the raw spots in his mouth. "So, anyway, after the day I found that note from my wife —'stay away from me'—the only time I really saw her was through the windshield, with Wolf and Hound trying to tear the car apart like I wasn't the guy that fed them puppy chow. Next time I saw Maddie, she was in a closed coffin."

"Are you sure it was her?"

"Huh?"

"Are you sure it was Maddie, in the coffin?"

Delaney looked away from him, blinking, and said hoarsely: "That was a hell of a thing to say. That was just a… really fucking shitty thing to say."

Ryon looked down at the table and said: "Yeah, I guess it was. I'm sorry." For all the snide comments people slipped in about Jack Delaney, he'd had a hell of a lot more stake in Maddie's life than any of the rest of them. Delany sighed and waved off the infraction. Ryon looked back up and said: "Shit, man, why couldn't you've just told me all that stuff in the first place, and save us both getting the shit kicked out of us?"

"Why didn't you just come right out and tell me you were a cop?"

"Oh sure, that would've really made you chatty."

The spider-man laughed and winced and dabbed at his swelling nose with the bar-towel again.

Ryon sat back. "What do you remember about this 'circle' and Celina Rushton and all?"

"Just that it was fucking crazy. I sat in once and that was enough. Mixing acid with all that oogabooga shit… Helter-fucking-skelter, man."

"Do you know where Fergus is?"

The puffing eyes slitted. "You working for Audrey? If you're working for Audrey, you can work on me all night long with your fucking flashlight, you won't get dick out of me about Fergus."

"I wouldn't bet on that. But no, I'm not working for Audrey."

The spider-man looked at him carefully for a minute, then said: "He's at Maddie's old place. The bank put it up for sale before Maddie was in the ground. Fergus snaffled it up and never told Audrey. Hell, in those days even Audrey wouldn't notice a few thousand dollars added onto equipment expenses, or studio time. Ten thousand here, ten thousand there, pretty soon you got enough to pay off a little place on the cliffs at Carmel." He hesitated. "Hey, if you ever do find out what happened with Maddie, will you let me know?"

"Yeah. Yeah, I will. If you get a postcard in crayon, you'll know they're not letting me use any sharp objects."

When he climbed back into the U-drive and plugged in the key, Ryon got a sudden wave of tears and had to grip onto the steering wheel with both hands. He remembered standing at the back of an SRO Anemone show, and Maddie was singing *Stand By Me*. It had seemed to him that the blue-gray eyes in the Eskimo Pie-face had picked him out standing under the exit light and she was directing the song at him. But that didn't necessarily have to mean anything—everyone in an Anemone audience felt like Maddie was singing just to him, or her.

Out of all the Anemone moments that might come back to him, he could think of no reason in hell why he should get all strangled-up and weepy remembering Maddie Prue singing *Stand By Me*.

A voice in his head answered: "Because you *didn't*."

That hit him so out-of-nowhere that he doubled over and banged his forehead on the steering wheel. He shouted at the voice in his head: "Shut-up, shut-up, shut-up, shut-up, shut-up! I don't have a fucking clue what you're talking about, and neither do you!"

He wiped his eyes and blew his nose, straightened his back and turned the key. He maintained Eyes Front toward the road, avoiding the rear-view, and pointed the rental car's nose south toward Carmel.

XX

THE RAILWAY CARRIAGE swayed like a boat rocked on the waves, carrying Ryon across the Cornish moors toward the sea. He'd traveled through Cornwall before, on a jaunt between school terms. But that had been in summer, when the moors were a rolling green slashed with drifts of wildflowers and heather. Now they were matte brown and gray, and the moor people were burning off the heather: featureless, voiceless figures moving between jagged lines of flame sending black smoke up to darken the mist.

It seemed days-long he'd been staring out that swaying window at swirling mists with startling breaks of sunlight. The shafts of light showed him standing stones with faded carvings, black gorges, the stone-lipped mouths of chambered tombs or prehistoric tin mines leading down into the earth...

He decided to peel his eyes off the window and look instead at the book he'd bought in Portsmouth. He'd been wondering at the reason Maddie had decided to buy a cottage in Cornwall, instead of a seaside locale much handier to London. A few months back he would've shrugged it off as one of Mad Maddie's mad whims, but he was becoming increasingly convinced that people had been vastly mistaken to think of Maddie Prue as whimsical.

The book was a traveler's guide to Devon and Cornwall, *With Essays upon History, Architecture and Local Customs*. Ryon turned the pages, letting his eyes fall where they may. It seemed that the Cornish people were "by temperament rebels and supporters of lost causes." They had a habit of backing the wrong side, hurling themselves into massacres, and coming back to do the same in the next generation. Ryon didn't know if that national trait had been a particular draw to Maddie Prue, but he should feel right at home.

The guidebook also informed him that Cornwall had always been a proudly stubborn backwater, remaining pantheistic long after the rest of Europe had turned Christian. Recent archaeological digs suggested that

Cornwall was the last place in the Old World to change from nomad hunter-gatherers to farmers and townsmen.

That piece of information caromed Ryon back to Celina Rushton's sudden panic after her explanation of why civilized people hate the gypsies: because we fear they will awaken the ancient call to go roving wherever the wind might blow us. He saw a naked man with antlers. A wave of vertigo washed through him, although he couldn't say exactly why. He closed his book and looked back out the window.

From out of the vertigo he remembered a summer's day at someone's country place—not near so grand as Morris's, but a good deal more palatial a "cottage" than Celina Rushton's. There was a crowd out in the garden and a dozen people in the kitchen being very Bohemian—actually preparing a buffet luncheon with their own hands instead of getting it catered from the nearest inn. Ryon was at the table sawing loaves of bread for sandwiches, and Maddie Prue was over at the counter washing vegetables in a basin and chopping them up for a salad. She had a cigarette in her mouth with an impossibly surviving length of ash bouncing dangerously over the cutting board. A highly intellectual gentleman with his sleeves rolled up to mix egg salad had just finished delivering an off-the-cuff extrapolation on the fact that throughout prehistory men had gone off on hunting expeditions while women gathered nuts and berries and tended the hearth—so it was indisputably logical that women had evolved to be the maintainers of life, while men were doomed to be the explorers and adventurers and inventors of new ideas.

Without interrupting her chopping, or taking the cigarette from her mouth, Maddie Prue responded: "Well that's a liberating thought—that who we are depends entirely on what's between our legs. Fit this into your indisputable logic: if it was the women did all the plant-gathering, then it had to be those stay-at-home women that invented agriculture. Well, women or *a* woman."

She suddenly stopped cold—Ryon saw her back rivet straight like she'd plunged into icy water—and whispered hoarsely: "Oh bloody Hell!" Her cigarette ash fell into the salad. But that wasn't the cause of her stricken curse, the ash fell after the fact. Ryon thought maybe she'd cut herself and started toward her. But before he could reach her she spun around with no trace of blood on her fingers, although her face looked drained of blood. She snatched up her cloak and went out the door—not the back door to the garden party, but the front door to the road.

Ryon couldn't remember whether she'd come back that day or disappeared. And he couldn't say why his memory had suddenly chosen to dredge up that moment. If he started to sift through every moment when Mad Maddie Prue acted on an impulse that seemed inexplicable to anyone but her, he'd be a long time sifting. *Look out the window, cleverlad. Look at the here and now. Your muddled mind won't take you any closer, but the train will.*

The constant hum and rattle of the train made an aural fog in which one could imagine hearing anything. He heard Lisette's voice trying to draw his eyes to a passing manor house with a planted grove of thriving evergreens, to bright-coated children playing in a farmyard, to a herd of shaggy moor ponies kicking up their heels "just like the *shagganappi* ponies back home…" But all his eyes would take in were the low, black-mossed, dry-stone remnants of an ancient village drawing a skewed chessboard on the moor; a misted churchyard with an old man scything between the headstones…

Ryon leaned his cheek against the cold glass and hummed along with Lisette singing in his ear:

> *And the dark maiden's prayer for her lover,*
> *To the spirit that rules all the world,*
> *Is that sunshine his pathway will cover,*
> *And the grief of his Red River girl…*

The lone other passenger in Ryon's compartment—a bearded gentleman in a tweed suit—picked up his hat and overcoat, pulled his Gladstone bag down from the rack, stepped out into the corridor and slid the door shut again. Ryon hadn't thought there'd be another station soon.

He looked down at the book in his lap and recalled a fact about Cornwall that wouldn't appear in guidebooks. William Morris's family money, the income that had allowed him and The Firm to establish their cushioned corner of the world, had come from mines in Cornwall. What that had to do with Maddie Prue choosing to establish herself in Cornwall Ryon couldn't say, but it seemed a strange coincidence. Then again, the world was full of strange coincidences these days, and all of them had to do with Maddie Prue.

Miles more of Bodmin Moor passed by the window before the conductor came down the aisle announcing Camelford. The town of Camelford was as close as the railway came to where Ryon was going. When he stepped down from the train, he could smell the sea through the cinder smell of the railbed, even though he knew he was still several miles inland.

The station dog cart was loitering by the loading dock, with a shaggy little pony in its traces and a shaggy little man smoking a pipe beside it. Ryon asked him if he knew of a cottage called The Oaks, outside the village of Tintagel. The driver looked at him oddly, then nodded and climbed aboard. But then, everybody seemed to be looking at him oddly these days.

Instead of climbing up beside the driver, Ryon took the rear seat, back-to-back to the driver's. The rear seat of a dog cart could be boxed in so a hunter could transport his dogs, hence the name. Ryon didn't much like traveling backwards, but it made it less likely that the driver would attempt conversation.

They traveled through a windswept heath with no trees except along the riverbeds or where they'd been planted. When the road reached the sea coast and angled, Ryon looked down and saw they were on a tableland that dropped away in jet black, jagged cliffs to the breakers below.

They passed a dark, projecting crag with the ragged remnants of ramparts growing out of the living rock. It was surrounded by the sea, except for a camelback isthmus with a narrow, twisting path. The driver said over his shoulder: "That be Tintagel Castle."

"I know."

"Where King Arthur was born."

"So they say."

"So they *know*. It be written in books."

The road wound a little ways inland again. After awhile the dog cart jounced to a halt. Ryon looked around. They were on the edge of a rare grove of oak trees, stunted and bent inland by the sea winds. A seldom-used cart trail ran through the grove toward the sea.

The driver pointed at the path and said: "But a short walk from here. I'll not take my horse on that land. A witch lived there, and died there."

"Are you so sure she died?"

The driver made the horned sign, muttered: "Numny dumny,"—the Cornish charm to chase off ghosts—and barely waited to snatch the coins out of Ryon's hand before whipping up his horse. Ryon started up the path.

The grove gave way to groundcover and lichened rock. Ryon could see up ahead a slate-roofed cottage, and beyond it a low, dry-stone wall to shelter the garden from the salt wind. From the shadow of that wall, two immense Irish wolfhounds sprang up and came bounding and roaring toward him.

Ryon stood stock-still, except for holding his traveling bag in front of him as a feeble excuse for a shield. He knew he didn't have a hope in hell of outrunning them, and prayed they were only in a warning mood. Into his mind popped the uncomforting definition of the difference between Irish wolfhounds and Russian wolfhounds: Russian wolfhounds were bred for chasing wolves; Irish for catching them.

A shrill whistle brought the wolfhounds skittering to a stop just short of him. They bounded back toward the crest of the cliff, where a baggy-robed human figure rose up and stood silhouetted against the gray racks of clouds, a staff grounded in one hand. The three of them became a tableau from the dawn of time: the human figure flanked by the pair of waist-high wolf dogs; shaggy coats and long, unbound hair making windblown, tattered pennants. It only wanted a stone spearhead on the staff.

But that wasn't what rooted Ryon where he stood. A ray of sunlight had snuck through the clouds and cast a fleck of color in the silhouetted figure's thick, flowing hair. A glint of Saxon Gold.

Ryon pried his bootsoles free of the earth and walked forward slowly. As he got closer, he saw that the figure was too tall and the tangled mass of hair was grizzled hazel. It was only that it was still damp with salt water that had made the sun ray paint a sheen of gold. The robe was rough, thick wool—just the thing for scrambling back into after sporting with the seals in December. The eyes weren't gray-blue, but the almond, elfin eyes of Fergus Doude.

As Ryon came to a halt in front of him, the almond eyes blinked at him twice, then Fergus Doude said: "I thought you'd been banished to Many-toba."

"I was. But then someone sent me this." Ryon tugged the book out of his pocket and held it up. Fergus Doude just flicked his eyes at it and said nothing.

"Where's Maddie?"

Fergus Doude angled his head and pointed his eyes down the cliff at the surf crashing against the black teeth of the rocks below.

Ryon said: "How did you know it was Manitoba I was banished to?"

"Hard not to, mate. Maddie made damned sure she knew exactly where you'd washed up."

"That won't wash. She hardly knew me."

"Oh, she knew you, mate. Back in London days, whatever you'd got up to last was her pet story of the week. 'Did you hear O'Ryon kicked a Guards officer downstairs?' 'Did you hear O'Ryon dragged Swinburne out of an opium den and sent him home, then went back in and finished off Swinburne's pipe?'"

"QED. She didn't even know my name. It isn't O'Ryon, just Ryon."

"She didn't call you O'Ryon. She called you Orion. Orion the hunter."

Ryon felt himself teetering on the lip of a vortex. Perhaps it was the nearness of the cliff-edge. He snatched onto a compass point and said abruptly: "D'ja think her fell?"

Fergus Doude blinked, then said: "I think you'd better come inside," and started for the cottage. "And if I stand out here in the wind much longer I'll do the brass monkey. I've got into the habit of getting into the water every day, unless there's ice on the path. Gives me an excuse for putting on a bit of pudge. Local people think I'm a selkie."

"They thought Maddie was a witch."

"Witch or witched, guess it's even odds."

The interior of the cottage was cosy and homy, despite unrustic facets like a purple velvet couch. Ryon got the feeling that Fergus hadn't changed the place much since Maddie's day. On one wall hung the lost portrait Burne-Jones had done of her. Sir Ned had been right: he hadn't captured her. But he'd got the blunt snub of a nose, and the determined angle of her chin, and the fact that her head was too big for her body. The eyes, though, didn't have enough life in them.

The wolfhounds had followed them in, and were lowering their heads to sniff at Ryon's hands. Fergus Doude said: "Don't know why Maddie and her cronies couldn't glom onto another breed than Irish Wolfhounds. Call 'em The Heartbreak Dog, don't you know, 'cause they look so bloody indestructible and die so bloody young. But, they seem to suit the place, so I keep replacing them." He looked around distractedly. "I'm afraid the gasogene's broke down, so we'll have to take our whisky with plain water."

"I'd best not drink whisky. I'm afraid it makes me a little... over-excited."

"That how you got the puffy lip? Getting a little old for that sort of thing, aren't you?"

"It wasn't my idea."

"I'll open a bottle of wine, then. Maddie always kept a good cellar."

As Fergus Doude busied himself with winerack and corkscrew and glasses, Ryon said again: "D'ja think her fell?"

"I remember the poem. It was one of Audrey's. Not often she wrote something all on her own and only showed it me when it was finished, but that was one of them."

"Was it about Maddie?"

"Audrey never said and I never asked her. But I'd say it didn't take footnotes to see it was about Maddie, and Audrey assumed I saw that. Audrey's way of taking out insurance."

"How so?"

Doude handed Ryon a glass, said: "Cheers," and quaffed. "Mm. Nothing like a warm burgundy on a cold day. How did you find me?"

"Jack Delaney."

"Ah. Put up a bit of a fight, did he?"

"Not much. Not once I'd convinced his friends to let us talk alone."

"Have you, um… mentioned where I am to Audrey?"

"Not yet."

"Do me a favor, mate, and don't. 'Hell hath no fury' and all that."

"What happened to Maddie?"

"What do *you* think happened?"

Ryon rubbed his eyes. It seemed every time he asked a question it got thrown back to him. "I think… Either it wasn't an accident, or it wasn't her at the bottom of that cliff. And whatever happened was somehow bound up with The Circle, and all of you who were in it."

"Hm. What do you know about The Circle?"

"You were looking for something… buried back beyond Venus and Adonis, Ishtar and Tammuz—The Hunter," that feeling of vertigo took hold again and wouldn't let go—trying to put thoughts together while perched on the lip of The Vortex. "Some kind of connection—how can there be a connection?— between The Hunter and the Corn King, and The Lady… 'The original event.' Something too painful to remember, too precious to forget—kept wrapped in myth. Back at the dawn of time, at the birth of civilization. Born in blood.

"But… Maddie seemed to've been finished with all that. In her book, the collection of what she wrote between the end of Anemone and… whatever happened to her… there's only a few traces of that sort of thing. All the rest is… real—living in the present…" He began to lose control of his voice again. "Almost contented."

Fergus Doude said gently: "She's led you a merry chase, hasn't she, mate? Almost run your lungs out." He politely shifted his gaze from Ryon to out the window overlooking the sea. "Well, she knew a hunter when she saw one…

"And you can read—fewer people can than think they can. You're right about her book, about her growing less inclined to torture herself. Oh, she could never turn into Little Miss Sweetness, not unless they cut her brain out, but after a few decades of kicking around the world we all start to get a little scuffed and comfortable. Most of us. She was like that towards the end, at certain hours of the day. But there were other hours…

"What was published in that book wasn't all she wrote, so to speak."

Fergus Doude went over to an elegant little writing desk under the sea window and unlocked a drawer. He came back bearing several sheets of foolscap and set them down in front of Ryon. Ryon glanced at the top sheet and saw that it was covered with a neat, clear, assiduous schoolgirl's penmanship.

Doude said: "That's the fair copy she made. The original's so scratched-over and margin-scrawled you'd need a magnifying glass and a codebook. Take your time, you'll be one of the three people in the world who've read that. Likely the only three who ever will."

"Along with yourself and Celina Rushton."

"Good. Very good." But the aging-elf eyes looked like there wasn't anything good left in the world. "You just might understand."

Ryon picked up the top page and an almost painful tingling transmitted itself up his arms, as though he could feel her fingers on the paper. It seemed he finally had her in his hands. He began to read…

The Blood of Adonis
by Madeline Prue

T HE TRIBE WANDERED *where and when they would along the green river valley or the hills and plains beyond. The men with their sharp stone spears hunted deer and boar and antelope; the women with their sharp stone knives skinned and carved the meat. While the men hunted, the women roamed the fringes of the camp: digging roots with their digging sticks, filling their pouches with fruit and berries, cutting stands of wild barley with wooden-jawed sickles bearing flint teeth. When the land around the camp grew lean of game and gleanings, the tribe moved on. So it had always been.*

But still there were times of hunger, when the fish failed to come up-river to the camp of the Fishing Moon, or the Sweet-Root Moon yielded nothing but rotting tendrils. In the worst of those times, the tribe always returned to the place between two rivers where stood a meadow of barley that renewed itself with every seven turnings of the moon.

It had been the woman Eeshta's mother's mother who'd had the vision of the meadow. She had said that a portion of the barley the tribe gleaned in its wanderings should be held aside, instead of cooked into soup or hung in goatskin bags of water to make beer. Then, Eeshta's mother's mother's vision had shown, the meadow where two rivers met should be burned free of grass and saplings, and the saved barley seeds scattered on the naked earth. Since before Eeshta first bled with the moon, the barley meadow had been there.

But there came a time when Eeshta looked at the magical meadow with different eyes. It seemed there were fewer barley heads than there had been the last time—that the old, dead stocks were choking out the new. And she saw signs that much of what had grown had gone to feed deer and birds.

After what barley there was had all been gathered, Eeshta beat on the drum that always hung in the center of the camp, to call the tribe together. She said to them: "It was my mother's mother who had the vision. Now I see that it must be done again. The old must die so the young can grow strong."

Together they burned the old meadow, waited for the blackened earth to cool, and scattered a portion of the seeds they had gleaned. During that passage of days, the portion sealed in goatskins of water had worked its magic. A fire was kindled near the drum-pole, and the goatskins passed around the circle. The old woman of secrets went to those she had chosen and put into their mouths the leaves that open a path to another place.

Eeshta was one of the chosen. She chewed the bitter leaves until all the juice was gone, then spat them into the fire. The drumming and dancing faded, and she went to another place. It was the same ground she was sitting on—by the barley meadow between the two rivers—but it was not the same place.

In her vision, there were many golden fields of barley, not just the one. There were huts that were more than skin tents or hastily-woven poles and rushes. The birds and deer did not steal the tribe's barley, because the tribe was always there to guard it. Any deer that did venture near the barley meadows made easy hunting.

Eeshta saw that beyond the barley meadows were other meadows covered with the green plants that grow thick, sweet roots. She saw the inside of a hut secure against all weathers, made comfortable with more reed mats and sleeping-pelts than ever she and her man and children could carry on their backs from one campsite to another. She saw the tribe's flint-carver surrounded by mounds of arrowheads, leaf-blade knives, long-blade knives, spearheads, sickle teeth…

She saw many things she could not understand—only that all of them were things that had always been, but as altered as the ripened barley from the green shoot.

When the moon reached the top of the sky, it came time for those who'd chewed the leaves to tell what they had seen. Eeshta waited until the last. One of the others had seen nothing, one had seen fat bison on the plains, one had seen a happy meeting with a tribe downstream. Then all eyes around the fire turned to Eeshta and she told them what she had seen, as much as there were words to tell.

When she'd finished the telling, there was silence and confusion. She said: "What the vision means is we must stay here."

"Stay here?"

It was her man who had spoken, Ahton the hunter, whom all the other hunters called the swiftest runner, the surest spear. He said: "The Rain Moon is coming, when the white birds nest on the cliffs up-river."

"Then some of us can go there to bring eggs back here, where the rest of us stay."

"But after the Rain Moon is the Rutting Moon, when the stags in the deep woods will come to a hunter's call. And then comes the Dry Moon, when the water holes out on the plains are thick with game."

"Go, then—to the cliffs and the deep woods and the plain. I stay here, as the vision told me. I and anyone who stays with me."

No one spoke to stay.

Ahton said to Eeshta: "But how will you live here? What will you eat?"

"There is plenty to feed me in the woods here, and in the river. Take our children with you, all but the one who still needs my milk. When the tribe comes back to this place, I will be here."

And so it was that Eeshta stood alone with her baby in her arms and watched her man and her children and her tribe walking away. Her heart was torn to follow them, but she stayed.

In the long days alone, Eeshta found plenty to tire her for the long nights. She burned the wild grasses off another meadow and scattered the last of her barley seeds across it. She covered her hut of poles and rushes with river clay that baked hard in the sun. Where grape vines grew at the edge of the forest, she cut down the saplings and thistles growing among them. She was surprised at how much she could do in one turning of the moon—now that so many of her suns were not eaten by making camp, breaking camp and traveling to another camping place.

After seven turnings of the moon, the tribe came back to the place between the two rivers. They stood amazed to see two meadows of golden barley, vines bunched with grapes plumper than anyone had ever seen, a patch of earth thick with the sweet-root plants that had always only appeared by ones or twos in forest glades, the new hut Eeshta had made with heavier poles and a deeper coating of hard clay...

Eeshta wept with happiness to put her arms around her man again. But when the moon waned, he said it was time to wander back onto the plains, where the antelopes would be calving. She ached to go with him, but said that she would stay. This time the flint-carver said that he would stay, too, and the old woman of secrets, and several others. And Eeshta's children stayed as well—all but the oldest boy, who was ready to learn hunting from his father.

When the wandering half of the tribe next came back to the place between the two rivers, they were thin and starving. Deer had been scarce in the forest, and the herds out on the plains had roamed far out of reach. Eeshta's oldest son had hollowed eyes and gourd-like knees and elbows.

The wanderers gorged themselves on the bounty of the widening fields and gardens. Those hunters who had stayed with Eeshta told Ahton that they had still lived their time as hunters—roving out into the forest or onto the plain, and bringing what they'd killed back to the huts along the riverbank.

Eeshta's heart was full when Ahton said that he would stay. All who'd gone wandering with him said that they would stay, too. If Ahton the hunter could live in one place, so could they.

But as the moon grew and died and grew again, Eeshta saw that he could not. He went off hunting several times and always came back with meat, and once with a gash on his thigh where a wild boar had gored him before his knife found its heart. But Eeshta could see that those forays were only drops of water to a man shriveling of thirst.

When he sat knotting fishnets or binding arrowheads with the other men, or when the tribe gathered around the drum-pole fire at night, Ahton told stories of the times spent roaming where the wind blew, of living by a forest stream one moon and under the wide skies of the plains the next. When he spoke of those remembered things, sighing or laughing, she could see starlight in his eyes, and see it reflected in the eyes around him. When the drums and flutes came out and the tribe danced around the fire, he would bound like a stag, wild and beautiful, set free until the drumbeats ended.

As the Rutting Moon approached, and new, green shoots of barley appeared in the fields, Eeshta saw that he would go soon and the rest of the tribe would go with him. She knew they would, because she had no certainty she would not follow him herself. What did warm huts and full bellies matter when the falcon offered his wings?

Beer was set brewing for the full of the moon. Eeshta went to the old woman of secrets and took from her a handful of the leaves that open a path to another place. Eeshta crumbled one leaf into each of the goatskins of beer.

The full of the Rutting Moon was the night of the Antlered Man, when the chosen hunter of the tribe became the spirit of the stags who would die that the tribe might live. Eeshta could hardly remember a time when that hunter had been anyone but Ahton of the long legs, long eyes and swift-striking arm.

The fire was banked to sink low before moonrise. As the drums began to beat, Eeshta kept time clattering her knife against her sickle. Others saw her doing so and did the same. The goatskins went from mouth to mouth, and eyes grew brighter than the fire.

As the full moon rose, Ahton stepped out of the shadows, naked but for stag horns on his head, sworls of red clay on his body, and a necklace of the tusks of the boars he'd killed. Tonight he was not Ahton, he was The Antlered Man.

Eeshta stood up and went to him. He looked at her with confusion—she was supposed to stay sitting and singing, while he danced around the fire and other men with headless spears pursued him. Eeshta called the rest of the tribe to stand in a circle around him. Weeping, she hung a garland of woven, golden barley in his antlers and cried out: "The stag and the barley both give us their lives, do they not?"

Faraway voices around her murmured or shouted: "Yes!"

"The Green Man is in our fields again. But if the Green Man is to live, the Golden Man must die." *She swung her sickle against the naked neck, where she could see the life-vein throbbing. She hacked at him with knife and sickle as a wolfpack of other stone teeth bit in and turned red. In her fury at the gods who had made a world where she must do this, she tore at his body with her teeth and fingers—slick-white ribs breaking off in her hands beside the still-warm heart. Blood and tears seeped between her lips onto her tongue. Both taste of salt and water, like the sea.*

They chopped him into pieces and scattered the pieces across the fields. And though the hands of the rest of the tribe were as bathed in blood as mine, I know it was I and I alone who had slain my beautiful hunter. And so I weep for Adonis. So it was. So it must always be.

XXII

THERE WAS NO SOUND left but the Carmel surf far below, and the tail-end of the tape whipping rhythmically against the dead feed reel on the museum-piece machine — top-of-the-line twenty years ago. Ryon tried to fake himself out by pointing his nose at the mechanical, peripheral details of Maddie's never-released song cycle. Just a basement demo on a two-track reel-to-reel, but it didn't sound like that. She'd set up her double-tracked harmonies and overtones so cleverly you had to listen close to hear it wasn't a full band, just an illusion, just her and her piano. Alone. Well, nobody gets to be a genius without a little sleight-of-hand.

The mechanical details couldn't manage to hold him in safe territory for long, though. He heard the echoes of the whispery coda she'd tagged on when the music was gone:

> Now my house will be a cottage
> Beside your summer dwelling,
> With a golden door and windows
> And a red roof for the eagle time,
> A red roof for the eagle time,
> When you turn to that shining house
> Just across the lane.

He remembered from some dusty book the prescription for ridding a community of a witch. After burning the witch, you had to "burne her house, even up to the roofe-tree." Red roof and then some. Ladybug, ladybug.

Fergus Doude stopped the spindle and looped the tape back through to rewind. Then he turned to Ryon and said: "It was going to be *you*, ace — if you hadn't had your little freak-out and headed back to hockey country."

"What was going to be me?"

"Don't play dumb—to me or to yourself. What you were going to be was dead meat. With bells on, and antlers. And The Lady would weep for Adonis."

"What? You mean The Circle was planning to play out for *real* the—?"

"Not The Circle. Maddie. She was miles beyond the rest of us. Always had been. And 'planning' isn't exactly the right word. But she was going to do it."

"But that doesn't... *Me?* That doesn't make any sense. I didn't mean anything to her."

"Wrong. You were Neal Cassady."

"What?"

"You know, the *On The Road* guy, and the lone wolf in The Merry Pranksters. Dean Moriarty. The Denver Kid. The Holy Goof. Kerouac and Kesey and them were writing about living wild and free; Cassady was doing it."

"I sure as hell wasn't Neal Cassady, just a fucked-up kid."

Fergus shrugged. "Semantics. Romantics is what we all were at that age, about the people around us—little bundles of insecurities who figure the guy they're toking up with must have it all together 'cause he's wearing a fringed jacket. And *you*, you couldn't even be bothered to dress cool—just the guy who carried amplifiers and scared the shit out of managers who didn't want to pay the band. We were all just middle-class kids—well, except for Maddie—and suddenly there's this guy hanging around who wouldn't blink about going for a midnight walk through the South Bronx on acid."

"Some tough guy—most of the time I was scared shitless of opening my mouth and letting you guys know what a dork I was."

"The less you said, the more we talked about you."

Ryon shook his head. "You're wrong, I was no big deal to Anemone. Flip Norman couldn't remember ever meeting me." He realized what a ridiculous piece of evidence he'd just tried to prove his case with. "Neither could Delaney."

"Spider Jack never paid much attention to anything but his next solo or the nearest mirror."

"Audrey didn't have a clue who I was, either."

Fergus poured another glass of wine, lit a cigarette and said to the ceiling: "That what she told you...?"

"Anyway, I still ain't Neal Cassady. He's dead. Raced a freight train and lost—too dumb to quit before his heart burst."

"Sounds kinda like what you been doing since you got that cassette in

the mail. Anyway, Maddie had a lot better reason to pick you than just romantic images."

"What's that?"

"Because you loved her, ace. Still do."

It took Ryon a minute to come up with some kind of reply to that, and he
had to clear his throat before saying: "A lot of guys loved Maddie."

"Wrong again. Rita Hayworth said: 'Every man I ever married thought they
were marrying Gilda, and woke up the next morning with me.' That's how it
was for Maddie, even back when we were still playing pass-the-hat coffee-
houses. Well, Maddie would've said 'Every man I ever fucked,' but still…

"But you—you knew she didn't shit ice cream, and was just as scared of
blowing her cool as the rest of us, and you loved her. She would've spotted that
if you'd been sitting in an audience of twenty thousand people.

"She was already making up excuses to dump our equipment manager so
you could come out on the road with us, when you slid over the edge and disappeared. Lucky for you that you did. If Adonis is just a pretty-looking man,
the sacrifice doesn't mean much."

Ryon rubbed his neck and then his eyes. He said: "You gotta be wrong…
We weren't… She didn't…"

"Why'd you disappear, ace? I know you and Maddie got it on—you probably still got the scars to prove it. She told me, when I asked her why she was
wearing band-aids on her right tit…"

…In front of Ryon's eyes was a pair of suede boots and the hem of a long,
green, rose-embroidered skirt. He was doubled over on a concrete floor with
the wind knocked out of him. A small hand was touching the back of his neck
and a voice like pebbled honey was saying: "You'd better come with me." He
told his body to stand up, but it wouldn't. Her other hand came down in front
of his face, cupped and open to take ahold of his. "Come on, stand by me."

The soft hand on his neck was jarred away as another, deeper voice
growled: "That's our job, leave him to—"

"Keep your fucking hands off me!" Maddie's voice yelled back at the
Security linebacker. The wind rushed back into Ryon and he was on his feet.
The leather-coated muscleman had turned into a silhouette raising a shotgun
at a female constable who was hesitating. The silhouette was dotted with red
kill-or-cripple points: throat, bridge of the nose, heart, kneecaps…

"No!" Maddie shouted at Ryon and threw her body against his, pushing him back against the cinder block wall. Her hands came up against the sides of his face and held there. "It's all right. Nobody's going to hurt me. It's all right. Ssh…"

The wind rushing through Ryon's veins gradually slowed down to the point where his brain could register that the body pressing against his was actually—it can't be—Maddie Prue's. She stepped back and looked toward the doorway to the dressing rooms, where the rest of the band was looking out to see what the commotion was. She said: "You guys take the limo, we can find a cab." A shadow passed across Delaney's face, but he kept his mustache and lower lip tight together.

The security biker said: "I can't allow that. I'm responsible till you're back at the hotel."

Maddie said: "I probably just saved your fucking *life*, you tub of meat. But you're too sodding thick to ever know it," and took Ryon by the arm to head for the door.

The hotel was The Park Plaza. As they climbed out of the cab, Maddie said: "Im-fucking-pressive, what? But every sundown you can see a herd of rats piling out of the gutter across the street in Central Park."

When they got to her room, she tossed her purse on the table, lit a match and went around to the candles set up on the coffee table and the end tables, saying: "I've had spotlights and flashbulbs in me eyes all bloody night."

Ryon was coming down and didn't feel all that competent to play with fire. But he took out his zippo and said: "You want 'em all lit?"

"Please. Then I can turn off the blasted overhead."

He lit the pair of red candles standing on the dresser. Lying between them was a strange-looking knife, with a crude, bone handle and a leaf-shaped, gold-colored blade. He said: "Is that gold?"

"No, just polished bronze. It's a copy of something very old. Don't pick it up—it's like a razor."

She plunked down on the couch and started contorting her legs to tug off her high-heeled boots. Ryon said: "Lemme give you a hand." He could feel her ankles through the suede.

Once the boots were off, he figured he should stand up instead of staying crouched right in front of her. She said: "When was the last time you et?"

Ryon sat down tentatively on the other end of the couch and said: "Uh… morning…? No, maybe, uh…"

She called room service, then pulled the cork out of a half-empty bottle of red wine sitting by the phone and poured two glasses. Ryon sat sipping and trying not to stare at the most beautiful woman in the world perched just five feet away from him in an unbleached cotton blouse and silk skirt. She said: "Well are you going to sit there like a lump all night or come and kiss me?"

It wasn't a really tough choice to make, once he'd convinced himself that's what she'd actually said. When he first put his hand on the side of her hair and his lips on hers, he had an instant of: "Holy fucking Christ, I'm kissing *Maddie Prue*," but soon it started to feel kind of sweet and tender, like sitting on a porch swing after a Saturday night dance. Whether she wanted it to go any further than that, he didn't know. And why she would want a plain-faced, uncool, spaced-out, grunt amplifier-carrier to kiss her, he sure as hell didn't know. But he wasn't asking any questions. Her hands moving across the back of his T-shirt felt like they were drawing out all the poison.

She pulled away from him gently and said: "Just let me get my pipe." They smoked a little hash and snorted a couple of lines of coke and then room service arrived.

She certainly knew the way to a prairie boy's heart—tiger shrimp and other seafood nibblies fresh off the boat, not the expensive cardboard served up in fancy restaurants back home after it had traveled two thousand miles. Ryon uncorked the bottle of white wine that came with it and he and Maddie sat down across the table from each other, dipping chunks of cold lobster into seafood sauce and licking their fingers.

They had an after-dinner cigarette with a couple of more lines, then Maddie carried the room service tray out to the hall and hung out the Do Not Disturb sign. As she came back into the room, Ryon stood up—asking himself just how brave a trained and graduated Royal Canadian Mounted Police constable was capable of being. He stepped in close to her, stooped to get his arms around her skirt just below her hips, hoisted her straight up in the air and kissed her with their mouths at the same height.

It was meant to be a long kiss, but she started giggling. She tapped him on the shoulder and said: "Ba-a-ck, Jumbo! Mahout says 'Walk back!'" He shuffled backwards, still holding her up and pressed against him, till the backs of his knees hit the bed and she came down on top of him—a Ryon sandwich between bouncing mattress and bouncing boobs. They got each others' clothes off, got under the covers and began to get acquainted.

They got acquainted frontwise, sideways, backwards, up and down and inside out and upside down. Ryon was terrified that he was so overloaded with the wonder of it all that he'd come before his lips had even finished measuring the difference between her right areola and the left one. But once he got inside her he found he didn't have to do multiplication tables in his head to keep from disappointing her. His body seemed to have got the message that whatever had possessed her to take him home tonight wasn't likely to happen again, so he'd better make it last as long as possible. Whether going fast or slow, he kept thrusting into her as deeply as he possibly could—deeply, fatally in love; losing himself between her thighs. The rhythm went through a lot of modulations; he'd never been much of a musician, but here he was jamming with Maddie Prue.

He kept his eyes wide open, except when hers were open and in line with his for so long he was afraid it was going to make her self-conscious. He wanted to see and memorize as much as he could. Depending on what position they'd segued into, he could see her back, the nape of her neck, the mole on her left shoulder, the candlelight flickering highlights and shadows across the contours of her face… Seen that close and contorted, it wasn't a particularly pretty face—just beautiful. But the best part of all the best parts was hearing that magical, mystical, meaty, earth-child voice yelping and sighing and sounding happy.

When he did come, as soon as the shock waves had worn off, he was overcome with embarrassment. That was usually the way—Superman when the music was rolling, and then after the big crescendo faded out he realized Clark Kent had been getting a little out of hand. He rolled over onto his back and pulled the sheet up over them.

Maddie snuggled up against him and murmured:"I should've brought a calculator."

"Huh?"

"Six or seven—I lost count. I'd say we fucked our brains out if that didn't imply I'd had one. Anticipation does wonders."

"Anticipation?"

"I've been waiting to get my hands on you almost a year now."

"I, uh, I never thought I had a hope in hell of ever getting my hands on you."

"*Blokes*—what's a girl to do?" She got up to get the bottle and the glasses and they lay there drinking wine and smoking cigarettes, letting the sweat soak into the sheets and telling each other stories of where they came from and how they got here.

Maddie had been the oldest of three children whose old man ran off, leaving their mother stuck with trying to find some way to scrape together a living in a fishing village near absolutely nothing except some kind of semi-secret NATO missile base. After a few years of rotating men in uniform, a USAF mechanic named Prue had actually asked Maddie's mother to marry him, and brought the family back to the States.

Maddie said: "So whatever else might be said about Arnold Prue, he fookin' rescued us. Not just by making an honest woman out of me ma, but he rescued us from the British Class System. You know Sam Cooke once did a tour of England, and when he got back to The States he said that as bad as American racism was, the British Class System was even worse."

"Yeah, well, we made a compromise—us North Americans, I mean. You see, back when we were getting to be our own countries instead of just colonies, we had a lot of trouble deciding whether to keep the Old Country's class system or not. So, like I said, we made a compromise—we decided to keep the system and lose the class."

Her loving laughter was such a reward that he would've walked on his hands with his dick hanging upside-down to hear more of it. Except that that would've meant getting out of bed. After she'd laughed for a few seconds she made it his turn by saying: "Well whatever the system, nobody wants to lose a good piece of class."

The thing Ryon found the most amazing about lying in bed beside Maddie Prue, with his arm under her neck and her cheek resting on his chest, was that it seemed so natural. She taught him how to say: "My name is Ryon" in Gaelic, laughed at his mouth-manglings and then applauded when he got it sort of right. Then she lay whispering a long string of Gaelic that she refused to translate for him. He didn't push it.

After awhile she got up and went away, but he didn't mind, as long as she stayed in the room. He was perfectly happy to lie there all night long watching Maddie walk around naked by candlelight.

She only walked as far as the dresser. She opened a drawer, took out a kind of scaled-down attache case, worked its combination lock and did something inside it that sounded like tearing paper. She said over her shoulder: "Do you shoot?"

"Not since I left my service revolver behind with the rest of my uniform." She laughed. "I meant drugs."

"Oh. For a while, back when I was about sixteen, there was a fad for shooting Ephedrine—you could still get it over the counter and it gave a good rush. I decided it was time to quit when I got too careless—either didn't grind the pills up good enough or didn't heat the spoon enough—crystalized in the needle and when I pushed the plunger the needle and the barrel spurted apart, blood all over the place."

"Well you won't have to worry about that with this." She came back towards the bed with two paper-packaged, disposable needles for Diabetics, and two tiny jars with surgical rubber sealed over their tops. "Just a little Acid Cocktail."

"Huh. Guy I knew used to say—a guy we called The Mystic Moron—he used to say: 'Doing LSD is like playing 52 Pick-up with your brains—you just have to remember to look under the couch the next morning, or you'll wind up not playing with a full deck.'"

She laughed and looped a silk scarf tight around his left biceps. He pumped up a vein, looked away and hardly felt the needle slipping in. When she loosened the scarf, the back of his head blew off.

He went away for a while. When he came back, he realized he'd forgotten Mister Manners and she hadn't had her turn yet. But one look at her plate-sized pupils told him she'd already done herself.

They sat looking at each other for a long time, sometimes giggling but mostly just staring. He liked the tattoo patterns that kept moving and changing on her face. After a time, she said: "You make me feel safe. Nobody's done that for a long, long time."

"And you me."

There was another long, comfortable silence, holding hands. Then she said like a sacrament: "I'm yours, and you're mine. Do you believe that?"

"Um…" He had to swallow and blink his eyes. "It's hard—"

"Again?"

They both laughed like maniac schoolkids and then grew quiet again. Ryon whispered: "Hard to *believe*. But if you say *you* are—well, I was from the first minute I saw you. Well, maybe the third minute, but…"

She nodded and smiled and her eyes glistened wet. She said: "Then let's prove it."

She got up and went to the dresser again. She came back carrying the bronze knife and one of the red candles, wax dripping over her hand. She sat down on the edge of the bed beside him and said: "Do you trust me?"

The response that immediately popped to mind was: *I don't trust anybody or anything anymore.* But after looking into her sea-gray eyes a while longer, he said: "Yes."

"Then don't move. No matter what I do, don't move. Promise?"

"Yes."

She curled her left arm around behind her head and furled the right side of her hair back over her ear and behind her shoulder. Then she held the point of the knife in the candle flame till it started to glow. Moving slowly and deliberately, like an underwater surgeon, she brought the knife back toward her right breast.

Ryon shouted: "Don't!" but she pressed the flat of the knife tip against her breast, just at the top of the oversized areola. Ryon wasn't sure whether the hissing sound was her sucking breath in through her teeth, or the sound of searing skin. If he broke his promise and lunged for her hand, the blade would chop into her.

She only held it there a few seconds, then her hand shot out and pressed the branding iron against his chest. He broke his promise, but only his head moved—rearing away from the pain and encountering the wall behind it.

The knife was gone, but the pain was still there. Maddie had thrust the knife into her wine glass; the wine was steaming. She pulled the knife out again, lined the edge of the blade along the side of her breast and twitched her hand about a millimeter. There was a new, thin, bright-red line running down from the pink burn.

Ryon closed his eyes and gritted his teeth as the knife came toward him. But she'd been right when she said it was sharp as a razor—he hardly felt it at all. She tossed the knife away and fiercely clamped her body and her mouth against his. The pain of the burn was much worse than the pain of the cut, but pain wasn't all that was going on. She rolled over onto her back and pulled him onto and into her. Maybe the cuts on her right breast and his left chest didn't line up exactly, but close enough for their blood to mingle. Maddie was gasping out words and phrases in a language Ryon didn't know—maybe more Gaelic. And it seemed he was also hearing wooden flutes and drums in rhythm with the pumping of their bodies and the stabs of pain.

He didn't try to slow himself down this time. When they were done, they both lay on their backs breathing themselves out and waiting for the cuts to coagulate and stop weeping blood. Ryon figured it shouldn't take long, even without a styptic pencil. Let It Bleed. Maddie held up a red-spattered sheet corner and laughed, "They'll think I was a bloody virgin!"

And then things started getting weird.

It started casually enough, with a joke or maybe a riddle. Without turning her head to look at him, she said: "You know, Ryon..." There was a funny, little hiccup in the middle that made it sound like 'You know-oh, Ryon.'"I always assume I done wrong and I'm usually right." Then she laughed, but it was only the ghost of a laugh, with a rattle of chains inside it.

As the laugh evaporated, Maddie's breathing beside him turned into grunts from the pit of her stomach. She suddenly rocketed out of bed and started pacing around the room like a zoo bear, barking out syllables that Ryon was sure didn't come from any human language—he recognized the sounds you bark when your mind keeps grabbing hold of a 220 volt wire and you want it to stop doing that but you don't want to know what that wire's connected to.

She stopped beside the divider between the bedroom and the bathroom and started banging the side of her head against the wall and chanting:"Stop it! Stop it! Stop it! Stop it!"

Ryon jumped up and went to her. Before he'd quite got there, she yelled: "Why can't you leave me alone?"

"Okay, okay... I'm sorry. I'll—"

"No, I don't mean you, love," she muttered distractedly, then roared at the ceiling:"Son-of-a-fucking-bitch!"

Ryon managed to get an arm around her shoulders and guide her back to the bed. They perched on the edge with his arm around her shuddering shoulders and her head down like she didn't want anybody to look at her. She said against his chest:"I'm sorry, I'm sorry. Why does it have to fookin' come at me again *now?* It's just that, all my fookin' life, you see—not just the music, but long before and everywhere else—I'm always stepping out of line. And the way it goes is, you step out of line and you happen to hit the right square dead-on and everybody goes 'That's my girl!'. But you don't hit perfect and it's 'How dare you! What unseemly behavior!'

"Even if nothing gets said, you can see the fookin' sniping and kneecapping if you mis-step. But you can't know if you're going to hit the square or not until you step. I'm not complaining, I'm just explaining."

"That was a good song." The semi-rhyme was the chorus from one of her songs.

"Thank you. But I can't seem to stop bloody doing it, you see—stepping out of line. And everybody keeps bloody encouraging me to do it—so long as I don't mis-step. And I can't seem to stop doing *this*—now—of all the nights that wouldn't matter—carrying on like some fookin' diva that lured you in here so I could play out some bloody melodrama bullshit."

She clamped both hands to the sides of her head and hissed: "Stop it, stop it, stop it!" Then she jerked her head up and swivelled away from him to squat cross-legged on the bed. With her arms crossed tightly under her breasts, and tears and mucus streaming down her face, she began to rock back and forth and softly croon that gospelly, shattered, Charlie Rich song:

> Lord I feel like going home,
> I tried and I failed and I'm tired and I'm weary,
> Everything I ever done was wrong,
> And I feel like going home…

She sang all three verses and then started from the top again, like she might do that all night long. Ryon stroked her hair and said: "It's all right—we can get you home easy. We can rent a car and you can give me directions up-state. Or I could get you a limo—the record company'll cover it…" Then he realized that Charlie Rich hadn't meant anything that simple by "Going Home," and neither did Maddie Prue.

He held onto Maddie until her rocking slowed down and her voice sunk to a whisper and then to just wrung-out breathing. He coaxed her into lying down, pulled the covers up over her, and knelt beside the bed stroking her hair and her quivering back until she finally fell asleep.

He got up and sat naked on the couch shaking, smoking cigarettes, drinking the last of the wine, and muttering things like: "Oh, shit. Oh, fuck. Oh, Christ. Oh, Hell. Oh, fuck…" Every now and then he would trail off and let his eyes drift from the dancing wall in front of him to the bedspread curved up by hip and shoulder, and the firestorm of spun red gold spread across the pillows—her hair across the pillow like a sleepy golden storm. Then his eyes would snatch themselves back to the wall and he would start up his mantra again.

Even in her sleep she was still barking and twitching now and then. He had a pretty good notion of what was happening in her dreams: narrowing down, narrowing down, spiraling down to... *what?*

Most of the candles had guttered out. There was dawn light seeping through the curtains. He got up and put his clothes back on and left—for the Port Authority bus terminal...

...The Carmel surf was back again. Ryon blinked at Fergus Doude across the room pouring himself another glass of wine. But Fergus had just filled that glass two seconds ago.

"Where'd you go, ace?"

"Back to Canada."

"I know *that*—I don't mean then, I meant just now. You been gone a while."

"I, uh, remembered. Thought I'd buried it, but I guess I buried it alive. Maddie... I..." There was a king-sized bench vice squeezing the air out of his lungs and tears out of his eyes. *No statute of limitations, smartboy—no matter how many years you ran.* "I killed her."

"You were a thousand miles away when it happened." Then Fergus seemed to have second thoughts and sounded less certain, even a little nervous. "Weren't you?"

"Did you know how strung-out crazy she was?"

"Strung-out? Not Maddie. I mean, she shot up from time to time, like we all did, even tried out a bit of smack. But never the same drug consistent enough to get strung-out."

"That's not what I meant. Did you know how crazy she was? I don't mean just wild and wacky, I mean crazy. Like, when someone pulls the basement floor out of their soul, where they gonna go?"

"Well, I... Uh..." Fergus Doude rubbed his forehead and his voice got constricted. "You know how loopy everything was in those days. I just figured, you know, everybody freaks out from time to time—or they did back then. You just wait to come down and sleep it off and clean up the mess the next morning. So, uh, even with all the time I spent with Maddie—and I'm supposed to be kind of a sensitive, intelligent guy, um..." He wiped his mouth and croaked: "No, I didn't know. Until it was too late."

"Delaney must've known. He lived with her."

"Oh, they spent as much time not living together as living together. And you know Spider Jack—he'd just figure she was starting her period early. And

Maddie was pretty good at keeping things hidden, liked to hold onto at least a little dignity. So... Nobody knew."

"What about Celina Rushton?" Ryon was desperately groping for some other straw that maybe would bear at least a little of the responsibility. "She's supposed to be some kind of damned... expert or something, and she sure as hell spent enough time picking Maddie's brains. Professor Rushton must've known."

"Celina loved Maddie the way a research chemist loves his cyclotron. Except a cyclotron can't say 'I've had it' and walk out. Maddie did."

Ryon gripped the arms of his chair and rasped out: "So did I."

"You did what?"

The words wouldn't come out of Ryon's mouth. Tears were squeezing out of his eyes but his jaw was locked. He cracked it open. "Kout! Walk out! I did!"

"Hang on a second, ace." Fergus Doude got up and went quickly through a side door. Ryon pressed his hands against his eyes and pushed his head back against the back of his chair. He heard water running. A minute later he heard footsteps approaching. He brought his hands down and opened his eyes to a blurred image of Fergus Doude holding out a dripping towel.

Ryon wiped his face with the cold, wet towel and then draped it across the back of his neck. That felt a little better. "Thanks." *Well you went looking for it, smartboy, and now you found it. Face up to it.* "What it is, you see, is... You say nobody knew... about Maddie... That makes it even worse."

"Makes what even worse?"

"I knew. I could see it because the same thing was starting to happen to me, but with her it wasn't just starting. Maybe been there all her life. It's like being on acid all the time—no filters. Everything coming at you all at once. You got no idea how much you filter out just walking down the street, until the filters break down."

The words seemed to be dragging themselves out of Ryon's throat like fish-hooks. "I knew she was in deep shit and I... I ran out on her. I was afraid."

Fergus Doude said: "You had damn good reason to be."

"No, I don't mean I was afraid of—sickles in the moonlight and that. I didn't know about that, didn't know how far into it she was—or how far into her it was. But I did know she was... like a Pound dog, something broken inside, broken open."

"Nothing you could've done about it, ace."

"Nothing by smarts, or expertise, or... But sometimes with a Pound dog, all it takes is them being around someone they can trust isn't ever going to really hurt them, or dump them in the next county. Somewhere safe. That dog'll probably never be normal—who wants normal?—but they get less crazy.

"But what I did was... It's like two people are drowning in the middle of a lake. You don't know if you can make it to shore, but you know damn well if you try to help the other one you'll both go down. So... You leave her there."

That hung in the air with nothing to cover it. It seemed to Ryon that a long time passed with no sound but his breathing in rhythm with the surf. Then Fergus Doude said gently: "But you would've come back from Canada if she'd called."

"Yeah."

"Would've been Last Call for you."

Ryon was beginning to get a pretty good idea of how Maddie Prue came to be lying in a tide pool of salt water and blood. Salt water, salt blood, salt tears. He said hoarsely: "If not me, who?"

"Who what?"

"Who was going to be The Hunter?"

"Me." Fergus Doude shrugged his shoulders. "Not much of a stand-in, but any port in a storm."

"So you would've been dead meat if something hadn't happened to Maddie."

"I guess it could kinda look that way."

"And Audrey figured that out, after Maddie went down."

"Audrey was never as intelligent as she wanted to be, but always clever."

Ryon looked at his hands and said: "You, me—it still would've ended the same."

"Hard to say. Maddie got a little older."

"Not much." Ryon got up and went to the window looking out at the waves rolling in toward the rocks a hundred feet below. They were dancing in the garden: Maddie, Celina Rushton, Spider Jack, Annie Drummond, the Doudes... One by one they drifted away like autumn leaves, until Maddie was left standing alone. She stood on the lip of the cliff, looking back at Ryon in the window. He seemed to pass through the glass and was pulled closer and closer. The whole horizon was her eyes, ever-changing from blue to gray. He felt himself sinking into her eyes, into the sea. He whispered: "The Savage Goddess."

From far behind him, Fergus Doude said rawly: "You got it, ace."

Ryon turned back to Fergus Doude and said: "I think I lied to Spider Jack."

"How's that?"

"He asked me if I was working for Audrey. I told him I wasn't."

XXIII

RYON STARTED UP Audrey Doude's front walk, then saw he wouldn't have to go knock on her door after all. She was pruning dead branches in her snowy garden, wearing a ragged, old coat and sprung-seamed gloves. Her long, pale hair was coiled up under a broad-brimmed hat. She lowered her shears as he came up to her. She pretended to say: "Oh, Ryon," but this time he knew she was saying 'Orion'—in case he needed another little whiff to keep him following the trail.

He said: "I know it was you who sent me the package, and I know why."

"You found Fergus? Where is he?"

Ryon shook his head. "I won't tell you that."

"But you'll see he gets what's coming to him!"

"There's nothing coming to him."

"*What?*" She screwed up her eyes against tears that Ryon suspected would burn his fingers if he touched one. "You're not going to try and tell me it was an accident!"

"No. It was no accident."

"Then *get* him!" She jabbed her shears forward spasmodically. He figured she was probably only jabbing at the air, but after the last few weeks he wasn't taking any chances. He leaned forward to grab her wrists and twisted outwards.

The shears fell to the ground. She didn't seem to mind, or even notice, but he kept hold of her wrists just in case. She shrieked into his face: "He killed her to save himself! He knew she couldn't break the chain!"

"So did she." Ryon's eyes started burning and his heart constricted. He had to blink and swallow before he could say: "That's why she jumped."

The olive eyes goggled and popped. "*What?*"

He repeated slowly, like to a child, drawing out each throat-searing word, "That's... why... she... *jumped.*"

The olive eyes went loose and confused. She started to slump. He held her wrists until her knees touched the ground, then let go and turned away. As he walked back to the road, he scooped up a handful of snow and wiped it across his eyes.

"How do you know?" Audrey Doude called after him. It was almost a scream—clutching at last straws.

Ryon stopped and looked back at Audrey Doude on her knees in the snow. He said: "Because I knew her."

On Ryon's last night before starting home to Manitoba, for the first night in six months, Maddie Prue didn't enter his dreams. But a certain black-haired, windblown, shagganappi girl did, singing another verse of that old, old song:

> Many nights by the fire I lay waiting
> For the words that you never would say.
> Now it seems that my fond hopes are vanished,
> For they tell me you're going away.

As Ryon packed his bag in the morning, he murmured: "Just try and wait a little longer, ma'am. The Lady set me free."